Berkley Prime Crime titles by E. J. Copperman

NIGHT OF THE LIVING DEED
AN UNINVITED GHOST

continued . . .

An Uninvited Ghost

E. J. COPPERMAN

BERKLEY PRIME CRIME, NEW YORK

THE BERKLEY PUBLISHING GROUP
Published by the Penguin Group
Penguin Group (USA) Inc.
375 Hudson Street, New York, New York 10014, USA
Penguin Group (Canada), 90 Eglinton Avenue East, Suite 700, Toronto, Ontario M4P 2Y3, Canada
(a division of Pearson Penguin Canada Inc.)
Penguin Books Ltd., 80 Strand, London WC2R 0RL, England
Penguin Group Ireland, 25 St. Stephen's Green, Dublin 2, Ireland (a division of Penguin Books Ltd.)
Penguin Group (Australia), 250 Camberwell Road, Camberwell, Victoria 3124, Australia
(a division of Pearson Australia Group Pty. Ltd.)
Penguin Books India Pvt. Ltd., 11 Community Centre, Panchsheel Park, New Delhi—110 017, India
Penguin Group (NZ), 67 Apollo Drive, Rosedale, Auckland 0632, New Zealand
(a division of Pearson New Zealand Ltd.)
Penguin Books (South Africa) (Pty.) Ltd., 24 Sturdee Avenue, Rosebank, Johannesburg 2196,
South Africa

Penguin Books Ltd., Registered Offices: 80 Strand, London WC2R 0RL, England

This is a work of fiction. Names, characters, places, and incidents either are the product of the author's imagination or are used fictitiously, and any resemblance to actual persons, living or dead, business establishments, events, or locales is entirely coincidental. The publisher does not have any control over and does not assume any responsibility for author or third-party websites or their content.

AN UNINVITED GHOST

A Berkley Prime Crime Book / published by arrangement with the author

PRINTING HISTORY
Berkley Prime Crime mass-market edition / April 2011

Copyright © 2011 by Jeffrey Cohen.
Cover illustration by Dominick Finelle.
Cover design by Judith Lagerman.
Interior text design by Kristin del Rosario.

ISBN: 978-0-425-24058-8

BERKLEY® PRIME CRIME
Berkley Prime Crime Books are published by The Berkley Publishing Group,
a division of Penguin Group (USA) Inc.,
375 Hudson Street, New York, New York 10014.
BERKLEY® PRIME CRIME and the PRIME CRIME logo are trademarks of Penguin Group (USA) Inc.

PRINTED IN THE UNITED STATES OF AMERICA

10 9 8 7 6 5 4 3 2 1

To Eve, Josh and Copper. You figure it out.

AUTHOR'S NOTE

Writing books about ghosts, I have found, is a liberating experience. You can make up pretty much any rules you want that best serve the story. Some of those rules you may later regret, but they're yours, and you have to live with them or figure out a plausible way to break them. I have no complaints.

I do, however, have a great deal of gratitude, because there's no such thing a one-person show in publishing. Yeah, the author starts from scratch and creates something, but it would be a pretty sorry something if it were left alone from that point.

So thank you, as ever, to Shannon Jamieson Vazquez, the invaluable, compassionate, constantly right editor of the Haunted Guesthouse and other series. And a special shout-out to Faith Black, who took on this book and about six trillion others in addition to her own work when Shannon had the temerity to give birth to an adorable son. I shudder to think what this book would have been like without both of you.

Also, thanks to Christina Hogrebe of the Jane Rotrosen Agency and Josh Getzler of Russell and Volkening, both of whom tirelessly championed my work throughout this process.

For helping me realize how to shout above the noise of the crowd, thanks to Lorraine Bartlett, Lorna Barrett, L.I. Bartlett (all of whom are a wonderful person), Leann Sweeney, Wendy Watson, MJ Maffini, anyone I'm forgetting at CozyPromo, the incandescent Rosemary Harris, Chris Grabenstein, Julia Spencer-Fleming, Kate Carlisle, Claudia Bishop,

Juliet Blackwell and all the terrific authors I'm leaving out because I have an awful memory.

Special thanks to Linda Ellerbee for letting me use her real name. At 'em, Linda Jane!

But mostly, thanks to Jessica, Josh, Evie and the rest of my family, for not blinking once when I mention having to get back to the thousand words a day.

No cats were harmed in the writing or publication of this book.

Prologue

Five minutes into this ridiculous escapade, and already Scott McFarlane thought it was a bad idea. Waiting around in an almost completely empty room for someone he'd never met seemed a waste of time, but the second part, the thing for which he'd been "hired," was considerably more idiotic.

He hadn't been in this house before today and didn't have his bearings, so it was probably a stroke of good luck that he wasn't required to move around a lot. Still, he wasn't comfortable without a strong sense of the geography of the place, and there was little he could do unaccompanied to improve that situation.

Not to mention that just standing around here was a bore.

Scott had limited his contact with people for a very long time; he was distrustful of most and had very few friends on whom he could still rely. His acceptance of this "job" today was a way to try to reconnect with humanity, in a typically backhanded and halfhearted fashion.

The idea that he was planning to do so by scaring the hell out of an old lady brought him only minimal amusement.

He had no way of telling what time it was; the sunlight coming through the windows to his right was insufficient to gauge. He didn't even know in which direction the window was facing.

Scott had touched virtually every object left in the room, but there wasn't much. The chair on which he was supposed to be discovered when the door opened was an ancient rocker, splintered in some places and unvarnished in others. There was a wooden mantel over a fireplace, but it was bare and cared for equally badly.

Maybe it would be better to simply forget the whole thing. The bargain he'd struck was at best questionable and at worst ridiculous. He'd be amazed if his contact could actually deliver on the payment they'd agreed upon, and the odd manner of communication was enough to scream "charlatan" about its user.

But if there really was a chance . . .

Too late to back out now, anyway. Scott heard the scrape of the front door—a huge one—in the entrance hall, the next room over. The sound lasted a long time, indicating the door was being opened slowly, like the creaky door that had opened during each episode of *Lights Out* on the radio in the nineteen forties. He remembered hearing that program back when he was in his own house. At first, it had sounded so real he'd been terrified, but after he'd gotten used to it, he'd realized how completely phony the acting and the dialogue had been. It had become laughable.

"Hello?" A woman's voice, probably the old woman he'd been told about, called from the front hallway. "Is anyone here?"

"There's no one here, Arlice," another voice, lower (possibly male) and barely audible, answered. "Let's go."

Time to go to work, Scott figured. He wasn't interested in sitting on the rocker, so he walked to it and moved it, very slowly, back and forth. The resulting sound was ominous enough, and loud enough, to be heard in the next room.

"Hello?"

Scott knew well enough not to answer; even if the old woman could hear him, it would spoil the gag. But he did want to simulate the sound of boots stomping on the floor and chains rattling, so he did as he'd rehearsed and slid two five-pound ankle weights across the floor, lifting them a little, dragging and then dropping them. For the chain sound, he found the bag of coins he'd been left and shook it rhythmically.

It had the desired effect: Scott heard the old woman's footsteps, slow and labored, heading toward the door of the room in which he was waiting. There were no footsteps from whomever that other voice belonged to, so he assumed only she would enter the room. He readied his props and ran through the motions again in his head.

Grab the drapes to make them billow, then reach for the handle directly above your right thigh, pull it out, wave the fake sword over your head a few times, step on the floor pad to create the noise, and then one swipe with the plastic sword and you're done, out the window and back home.

He was situated only a few feet from the window, so reaching the drapes when the library door opened was going to be easy. And sure enough, the door did open slowly, and the old woman's voice, unusually robust and excited, called out.

"Is anyone there?" she asked again. "It's so dark, I can't see a thing." She sounded about as threatening as a butterfly, but a job was a job.

Scott pulled on the drapes and moved them back and forth with his hand. The woman seemed less frightened than fascinated. She called out, "There's someone there, isn't there? Can you speak to me?"

Scott reached for the handle of the toy sword, which had

been tied to his waist with a sash made out of an old scarf. It felt a little heavier than when he'd practiced before, and the handle was colder. It didn't feel like plastic, but then the toys these days were so realistic, it could have been anything.

The old woman still didn't scream. Maybe he didn't seem fierce enough. So he stepped on the pad, which he knew was wired to a sound system concealed somewhere in the walls. A weird, echo-driven cry of utter despair filled the room.

But the old woman still seemed less frightened than concerned. "Oh, my," she said. "Is something wrong? Where are you?"

This plan certainly wasn't going to work; Scott wasn't going to receive his compensation, and the whole thing had been for naught. But, he thought, there was no point in going this far without giving her the whole show.

He swung the sword over his head three times, marveling at how real it felt and sounded. If he hadn't known better, he'd have sworn there was a real metal blade on the thing.

"Now stop that," the old woman scolded. "You could hurt someone."

Time for the last move, and then Scott could leave. He pointed the tip of the sword, as best as he could tell, in the old woman's direction.

"Me?" she asked. "What about me?"

Then all Scott had to do was pretend to threaten her with the sword. He'd aim for what should have been her throat, the plastic sword would make a *thud* when it struck, the old woman would be frightened—or not—and then he could leave. Might as well play it for what it was worth.

He put extra effort into the swing toward the old woman, knowing the rubberized plastic of the blade couldn't hurt her no matter how hard he swung. And he let loose with a whoop and let the blade fly.

Then, the oddest thing.

The old woman stopped talking, and he heard a body—no doubt hers—hit the floor.

Scott didn't stop to find out what had gone wrong. He headed straight through the outside wall and flew away as quickly as he could.

One

"Ghosts!" My daughter, Melissa, just turned ten, came running down the stairs from her bedroom. "There are ghosts in the house!" she screamed. She ran through the front room and into the kitchen, where she hit the back door and tore into the enormous backyard.

Behind her, objects—a wax apple, a real banana, an old hat, a lace handkerchief, and a picture frame (hey—that was *mine*!)—flew around in the space behind her, held up by unseen hands, manipulated in ways that betrayed intelligent thought (except that picture frame, which I wanted back) rather than some wind-based phenomenon.

Eerie laughter (admittedly attributable to hidden speakers and recordings Melissa and I had made one night) filled the front room of my guesthouse in the New Jersey Shore town of Harbor Haven. Guests, almost all of them senior citizens, stood and watched amazed as the objects flew in a perfect circle, then began to juggle, then flew all the way up the stairs and into Melissa's bedroom, where the door slammed shut.

I checked my watch. Four o'clock already?

The guests stood transfixed, watching the spectacle. When it was over, they applauded mightily.

Perhaps I should explain.

After I divorced Melissa's father, to whom we will refer as The Swine, I bought this huge Victorian in the town where I grew up. Upon moving in (and after a series of circumstances that left me with a concussion), I discovered two ghosts who were, as they put it, "trapped" in the house and on its grounds, since they had died here.

It's a long story (told elsewhere), but two things happened when it was over:

1. A man named Edmund Rance, who represented a company offering "unique" vacation experiences to a senior clientele, offered me steady bookings throughout the Jersey Shore season (roughly April 1 to October 31), but *only* if ghosts made themselves evident at least twice a day.

2. Paul Harrison, the budding private investigator who had been working a case for the house's previous owner, Maxie Malone, when they'd both become . . . well, ghosts, asked me to get a private detective's license, so we could work on the occasional case together.

These two events meshed nicely, since I needed Paul and Maxie's cooperation to fulfill Rance's requirements and to make my guesthouse work, and Paul needed me to participate in the odd detective case. Neither Paul nor Maxie is able to leave my property, so Paul requires eyes and ears out "in the world," as he puts it, and that's where I come in.

I don't know how much persuasion it took on Paul's part, but after a few days, Maxie agreed to the plan. Part of the agreement, however, was that we not let the guests know every time Paul and Maxie were around—Maxie was especially adamant about "not wanting strangers bothering me all the time"—so I would be discreet about communicating with them other than during "performances."

I'd spent the ensuing five months placing ads (to fill the rooms Rance was not booking), making brochures and generally going through the guesthouse making sure everything was perfect.

And everything had seemed perfect the day the first guests arrived, three days ago. Melissa and I had stood outside the house on that lovely sunny morning, watching our first customers exit a navy blue minivan with the logo "Senior Plus Tours" on its side. Rance had indeed delivered on his promise: I had five available bedrooms, and there were six lovely seniors plus a tour guide who had all put down deposits and agreed to come spend varying amounts of time with me, my daughter, and two undead creatures who would haunt them vigorously a minimum of twice a day, as dictated by the terms of my contract.

Everybody has a dream vacation. Who am I to argue?

"These people know about Paul and Maxie, but what about someone who comes here and *doesn't* know about the ghosts?" Melissa had asked as we waved at our new guests.

"We'll make sure the Senior Plus tour guests know not to say anything, and we'll be discreet with the others," I answered.

"What's discreet?" she asked.

"Sneaky," I said.

Maxie had then appeared at my side out of the blue— she does that with some regularity, because she enjoys the startling effect it has—rolling her eyes and clucking her tongue at the sight of our visitors.

"You sure these old people can handle it?" she said. "I'm not interested in giving anybody a heart attack. Unless it's intentional." She was hovering a few feet above the ground, wearing a tight pair of jeans and a black T-shirt bearing the legend "Wouldn't You Like to Know?" But who knew how long that ensemble would last? Maxie's clothes tended to change—I couldn't tell whether it was intentional or not—based on her mood.

Maxie, who was only twenty-eight when she died, had not taken the transition to her new state of being easily. In fact, while she often referred to herself and Paul as dead—something Paul never did—she seemed to think the whole thing would all blow over eventually. Her main purpose these days seemed to be giving me decorating tips, when all I wanted to do was keep the plumbing working and the heat on long enough to make my guests happy.

"They'll be fine," I told her, with absolutely no certainty whatsoever. "They came here because they *want* to see you, not in spite of it, like me. Now remember, you're not to do anything . . . *obvious*, except at ten in the morning and four in the afternoon, every day."

"I can't believe you talked me into this," Maxie said out of the corner of her mouth.

"I didn't talk you into this. Paul did."

"That's who I was talking to."

Sure enough, Paul had materialized at my daughter's side just as a fiftysomething woman approached me and put out her hand. He was muscular and a bit wan (in the parts that weren't transparent), and was already stroking his goatee. It wasn't a good sign.

"Linda Jane Smith," the woman said. "I'm the designated liaison between the tour guests and the site—that's you. I'm also a registered nurse, in case there are any medical problems with our Senior Plus guests."

I shook Linda Jane's hand and introduced Melissa and myself. I didn't feel it necessary to introduce Paul and Maxie. "Nice to meet you in person," I said. "Now, I've assigned the rooms as you specified. But I hope you don't mind—I had to double you up with Dolores Santiago."

Linda Jane checked her list. "Yes, she signed on to the trip so late. But she's making her own way here, apparently; she wasn't on the van. Have you met her yet?"

"No. She e-mailed that she'll be here in an hour or so. Do you mind sharing the room?"

She shook her head. "It's fine." She looked up at the house. "It's a lovely place. And it's so big."

The house has seven bedrooms. Subtracting one each for Melissa and myself, that left five that I could rent out at a time. To keep the costs down for each guest, but to assure that I wouldn't lose money on the deal, Senior Plus Tours had offered a lower rate for those willing to share a room, and most of the guests—including Linda Jane—had jumped on the deal. That left me with only one vacant room. I was glad we weren't operating at full capacity for my first week, though on the other hand, more guests would have meant more money.

"You're sure Mr. and Mrs. Jones have a double bed, and not two singles?" Linda Jane continued. "I don't know what they're planning, but Mr. Jones was absolutely adamant about it."

I smiled my best proprietor smile. "They have the second bedroom on the second floor," I said, nodding. "It has a queen-size bed. Now, let's get inside, and . . ." The sooner I could get them inside, and away from the ghosts (mostly Maxie) until it was time for the afternoon "performance," the better. Maxie was nervous with strangers around, and tended to compensate by being, let's say, *unpredictable*.

"Actually," Linda Jane answered, "I'll just have the van driver carry all the luggage up to the appointed rooms, if that's all right."

Paul came over to me, taking care to walk around Linda Jane, which I thought was a gallant gesture on his part, since he could have walked through her. But he knew that made me a little queasy.

"We need to talk," he whispered in my ear. "I've had an offer."

An offer? What, he was going to leave for a better house to haunt? No, wait—Paul and Maxie were apparently incapable of traveling off the property. They didn't know why; Paul said some other ghosts he'd had contact with could move about freely, but there seemed to be no rhyme or reason to the process. He reminded me that, unlike in the movies, when he and Maxie had died almost a year and a half earlier they hadn't been given an "instruction manual." He was hoping that they would develop more skills as time passed. Maybe even eventually move on to another level of post-life existence.

So what could this offer be about?

Oh no.

It had to be the other half of the bargain we'd made— that if he and Maxie would "entertain" the guests at my house, I'd help Paul with the occasional investigation. But the timing couldn't be worse for that; my first guests were literally just then walking up the path to the house.

"Okay?" Linda Jane repeated. "The driver can bring the luggage up?"

"Sure," I said, moving toward the oncoming guests, who were arriving at what could charitably be called a leisurely pace. Paul moved with me as I advanced, giving me just enough time to say, "Not now. Please. No detecting now."

"Detecting?" Melissa had heard me. "Are you going to be doing some detecting?" She seemed to think this would be a great idea.

I think I whipped my head toward her a little too quickly. *"No,"* I said. Melissa's eyes registered a little surprise and a little concern that her mother had flipped out.

Paul had noted my demeanor as well, and nodded. "Fine," he said. "We'll talk about it later." And he vanished.

A lovely little woman wearing harlequin glasses and a blue suit and—I swear—a straw hat, reached out for my hand. "Hello," I'd said, taking hers, "I'm Alison Kerby, your host."

"Are there stairs everywhere in the house?" the woman demanded in a harsh tone. "And it's *hostess*, by the way."

"There are stairs—it was in the information you were given—but if you have difficulty, I'm sure we can accommodate . . ."

"Don't patronize me, Tootsie. I'm paying top dollar to stay here, and I expect to see something for my money. So. Are there ghosts here?"

I was already biting my lower lip, but I managed to smile in what I hoped was a friendly manner. "Well, you'll just have to find out, won't you?"

"I'd better," she'd snapped, and kept walking toward the front door.

Behind her, Linda Jane shook her head and smiled. "Don't mind Mrs. Antwerp," she said. "I get the impression Bernice hasn't been satisfied with anything since Eisenhower was president."

"I'm glad to hear it's not just me," I told her.

"Oh, trust me, it's not just you."

Almost all the new guests had entered the house by then, so Melissa and I started toward the door, and Linda Jane followed. "Lovely place you have here," she said.

I thanked her for the compliment. "It took a lot of work," I said.

"Everything worthwhile does," she answered.

I had to agree, although Melissa had piped up with her opinion that homework was pointless, which has been the complaint of every fourth-grader in history. "If they teach me the stuff in class, why do I have to learn it myself at home?" she asked.

Linda Jane laughed as we reached the front door and entered the house. "We're going to get along just fine," she said.

Maxie, walking in through the wall with her lip curled, rolled her eyes. "I liked the nasty one better," she said.

"You would," I said.

Three days later, the whole thing had already become pleasantly routine, except that I now got up every morning at five-thirty, which was the least pleasant part. But it gave me the chance to do whatever straightening up of the common rooms was necessary, greet the especially early risers among our guests, answer the incredulous questions about our lack of available breakfast—although to be totally honest, I do keep a coffee urn going in the morning for those who want, and I have hot water for tea—direct the more adamant to the Harbor Haven Café (where I'd made an agreement with Janice Bacon—no, really—the owner, to give my guests a 10 percent discount) and check for ghosts, although Paul and Maxie were rarely around first thing in the morning. I didn't know where they went when they vanished, but they usually answered when I shouted for them. Not that I can remember ever having shouted for Maxie. Not happily, anyway.

Then I'd get Melissa ready for school, which was usually pretty easy. If there were no footsteps upstairs or the sound of the shower after her alarm went off at seven, I'd go up to roust her out of bed. But she's a very self-sufficient ten-year-old.

After driving her to school—they *still* didn't have a school bus route in Harbor Haven—I'd get ready for the ten a.m. spook show. Sometimes I'd have to remind Maxie, but Paul gamely appeared every morning promptly at nine-fifty-five.

Except today. He showed up at nine-twenty, when I was in the library (thankfully alone) reshelving books that had been left strewn about the room.

"Wake up early?" I asked, although I didn't know if he and Maxie actually slept. I'm not sure *they* knew.

"It's time we discussed that . . . matter from the other morning," he said, his Canadian/British accent making it sound more like *mawning*.

"What matter?" There was a memoir by a politician shelved on the fiction wall, and I was considering whether to leave it there out of sheer irony.

"The offer I received a few days ago," Paul said. "About us looking into a certain situation . . ."

Suddenly, I felt very tired. "Oh, come on, Paul," I said. "You didn't really expect me to go into the gumshoe business, did you?"

"You did sit for the examination and get a private investigator license," he pointed out.

"Yeah, but that was only because I thought I'd never have to use it, and you'd leave me alone." One paperback was placed, spine splayed open, on the side table. I don't like to abuse books like that, but on the other hand, one of my guests was probably reading it and wanted to mark the place. I picked up a bookmark from a stack I keep on the table (which was right next to the paperback) and placed it in the book on the appropriate page, then closed the volume to try to save what was left of its binding.

"Well, I took it seriously," Paul sniffed. "You know how I feel about this. I was a good private detective when I was alive. . . ."

"You were a brand new private detective when you were alive, and you've told me you want to keep going to see how you'd do," I countered.

"I don't want to spend eternity putting on invisible music-hall dramas for your tourists," he came back. "We had a deal, you remember. And one word from me to Maxie can end the twice-a-day vaudeville act for good."

I pivoted and stared at him. "You wouldn't."

He tilted his head and curled his lip. "No, probably not. But you agreed to something, and I think you should at least *try* to live up to it."

I sighed. It's not something I do often, but I'm trying to perfect it. "You're right. But remember the ground rules—I won't get involved in *anything* that's going to place me or Melissa in any kind of danger."

Paul nodded earnestly. "This doesn't involve any danger, Alison. I promise you. We're just confirming an event, that's all."

"Who's the client?" The books were shelved, and now I was dusting the furniture, can of Pledge in hand.

"A man named Scott McFarlane. We haven't met, but we've . . . communicated." Paul has the ability to "speak," more or less, with other spirits, sort of telepathically. He doesn't really understand how it works, but he and I call it the Ghosternet.

"So it's a ghost, right?" Figured. I wouldn't even get paid.

"Yes," Paul admitted. "I don't talk to that many living people." As far as we knew, Paul and Maxie could only be seen by Melissa, my mother, and me. My mother says it's a "gift." I have other words I could use for it.

It was hardly worth polishing the furniture; the seniors staying in my house were tidier than I was. I put on the look Melissa calls "grumpy" and faced Paul. "I'll listen to the story," I told him, "but I'm making no promises, understand?"

"Absolutely." Paul smiled and looked away, trying but failing not to seem like a child who'd just gotten his mother to agree to a theme park vacation. "I'll have Scott here this evening after the guests are asleep."

"That's not too late," I mused. "Most of them are in bed before nine. Hey, is this Scott guy cute?" I liked to tease Paul, and he should have known I had no interest in a dead guy, but he sputtered.

"Scott is a hundred and forty years old," Paul said, and then he started to laugh. And eventually, he literally dissolved in laughter. Okay, so sometimes the teasing thing backfires on me.

When I turned toward the door, Linda Jane was standing there watching. "Was there just someone else in the room, or were you talking that way to yourself?" she asked.

I nodded. "Yes," I said.

After a quick sweep through the house to make sure everything was in order, I headed up to the attic.

I'd been giving some thought to converting the attic—essentially a large, empty space on the third floor—into a loft apartment to entice higher-end vacationers who might want more spacious, and by extension, more expensive, accommodations.

But before I could approach my contractor/mentor/friend Tony Mandorisi with any plans about such a conversion, I'd have to measure—twice, to go along with the home improvement credo "measure twice, cut once"—and come up with some plans for Tony to look at and explain why they would never work.

It also occurred to me that if I were going to create living space in the attic, it would have to be for a somewhat younger group of tourists. I loved the seniors I had now, but my legs were already starting to bark as I reached the second floor, and I'm only in my thirties.

I pulled down the staircase to the attic, flipped on the light switch, put on my tool belt (complete with flashlight, just in case; you don't want to be caught without one, if the power goes out or the bulb simply burns out), measuring tape, hammer and screwdriver. I had renovated most of the house when I bought it, drawing on my previous career working at a home improvement superstore and, more important, on advice from my dad, who had died a few years before. I could hear him now: "Never do anything the least bit like home repair without a hammer and a screwdriver handy, Alison. You might never use them, but if you want one, you don't want to have to walk down three flights of stairs to get it."

It was silent in the attic, which was quite large but completely unfinished. I had to be careful about where I stepped. No floor had ever been put down, and I was walking on bare beams, sixteen inches apart. If I stepped the wrong way, I could certainly put my foot through the second story ceiling. Probably into the room the Joneses were using. They hadn't emerged all weekend; I was convinced I'd have to burn all the bedding and buy a new mattress once they left.

The single bulb hanging from the center crossbeam didn't really do all that much in terms of illumination, so I got out my flashlight and turned it on. I made my way to the far corner facing west, and took the measuring tape from my tool belt.

And that's when I heard a sound from somewhere in the attic.

I am not a fan of rodents, so the possibility of rats in the room with me was not terribly appealing. Then it occurred to me that I was in an attic, and the squatters in this area might very well be bats, and I started thinking not especially rationally. The only thing that works with bats is a tennis racket, and what do you know, I'd forgotten to bring mine.

Slowly, surely, I got control of my breathing and scanned the flashlight around the room to find the source of the noise, which had sounded just a little like a squeak, but might have been a sob. A wounded bat? Do bats cry? Is this a question anyone's ever asked before?

Instead, my beam of light found Maxie, huddled in a corner, knees to her chest. She didn't actually have moisture on her cheeks, as far as I could tell—I'm not sure she can—but her expression was one of desperate sadness. Until she saw me. Then it became one of extreme annoyance.

"What are you doing up here?" she demanded.

"Isn't that supposed to be my line?" I asked. I walked toward her, forgetting I was dragging the measuring tape until it snapped behind me and rolled itself back up into the metal house in which it coiled.

"All those people in the house," she said. "This is the only place I can think straight."

"Were you crying?" I asked. "Is something wrong?"

"I wasn't *crying*," she said. "I don't *cry*."

"My mistake." If she was going to be like that, I could just go back to what I was doing. I got the tape measure out and started working from the far corner to the near.

"What are you doing?" Maxie asked. "Why do you need to know how big the attic is?"

Sometimes I asked Maxie's advice—just to keep her happy, of course—on home design issues. She had aspired to be an interior designer before she was killed, and she second-guessed every single decision I made about what she insists on calling "our house." Still, I figured that if something was bothering her, talking to her about design might pull her out of this mood. "I'm thinking of turning this into a loft space," I said. "Maybe put in a little suite that people can rent if they're especially interested in privacy, or want a larger area all to themselves."

Maxie did not take the bait. In fact, her eyes widened and her clothes changed from orange overalls (what can I tell you?) to all black, and her hair sprung spikes. She looked like a punk bandleader from nineteen eighty-two.

"You can't do that!" she hollered. "You can't make a room up here!"

"Why not?"

"Because you can't!" And she vanished directly into the ceiling. I got the impression she was going to sit on the roof, where she knew for a fact I could not create rental space.

It took me a few good minutes to overcome that image, but eventually I got back to making measurements and wrote my findings down on a pad I also carried in the tool belt. I looked for Maxie out the window when I was ready to climb back down, thinking perhaps I could find out what her problem was, but she was nowhere to be seen.

I spent the rest of the afternoon drawing up plans for an attic suite, seeing to the needs of my guests, picking up Melissa from school and looking for Maxie. But Maxie was not to be found.

My mother appeared (not like Paul or Maxie—she actually drove up and rang the doorbell) before dinner that evening and, despite my best efforts, stayed with us. One of the upsides of not serving food was that dinnertimes were quiet; the guests all went out to eat. One downside was that the seniors tended to eat at about five in the afternoon, so they were back before we were even sitting down to dinner in the kitchen.

Since I almost never cook anyway, my mother had taken Melissa out to get strombolis at a take-out place, and the three of us sat at the kitchen table eating off paper plates and drinking water from plastic bottles or, in my case, a beer.

Classy, no?

Maxie, seemingly unfazed by our encounter in the attic, showed up while we were eating and was hovering around the kitchen cabinets, which were mounted on the wall not nearly as high as she'd had them when she owned the house before me.

"You know, feeding a kid take-out food every night can't be good for her," she said. I rolled my eyes heavenward just a bit, but my mother, as usual, got there ahead of me.

"Don't you start, Maxine," she scolded. "Alison knows what's best for Melissa."

Melissa wedged her way in. "I'm here in the room, you know."

"They know, Liss," I told her. "This isn't actually about you. It's a turf war."

"Alison!" my mother had the nerve to exclaim.

I didn't get the chance to respond, which was probably a good thing, because Paul materialized near the back door. There was an odd moment when my mother, Maxie and Melissa all stopped talking, and seemed to be looking at the space next to Paul, but not at Paul himself.

There must have been someone there with him.

"Excuse me." Paul was never anything but polite; I'm not sure if it was his British birth or his Canadian upbringing. "Alison, I'd like you to meet Scott McFarlane."

Mom and Melissa nodded hello, and Maxie seemed to be sizing up the newcomer, and finding him amusing in some way. But to me, the space they were staring at was completely empty.

"Paul," I said, "this is going to be difficult."

Two

I could not see the visiting ghost, who had arrived at least two hours earlier than I'd expected. While that wasn't a complete surprise—the only ghosts I had ever been able to see were Paul and Maxie—it wasn't anticipated.

Luckily (depending on how you look at it), Melissa and Mom *could* see Scott McFarlane, so both they and the two resident ghosts could relay his expressions to me. But there was something strange about carrying on a conversation with someone who, to all your senses, was not there. Like talking to a ghost. Or something.

Scott, who had a slight burr to his speech, said he was troubled by something that had happened recently, and he wanted Paul (and by extension, me—in fact, mostly me) to investigate.

"Right now, the guests know I'm having dinner, and besides, they don't need much out of me in the evenings," I said. "So we can start, but if I'm called away, I'm called away. Is that all right?"

Everyone in the room looked in the direction to Paul's

left, and then nodded, which I took to mean Scott agreed with my plan.

I asked Mom for a general physical description of McFarlane, and she said he was "an older gentleman, I'd say in his sixties—oh, really? He says he was seventy-two when he passed away."

"I can hear him, Mom," I reminded her. "I just can't see him."

"You look much younger, Mr. McFarlane," she went on, ignoring my rudeness. Scott thanked her. "You're welcome. Anyway, he's not a very tall man, but he looks fit. He's wearing dark slacks and a white shirt with long sleeves and no collar. He also has on a knit cap and black boots."

"He sounds like a pirate," I thought out loud.

"Alison," my mother admonished. "Mind your manners."

I exhaled. "Look, it's making me crazy talking to someone I can't see who's in the same room with me," I said. "Can you hold something, or wear something, so I can at least locate you?" I asked the air.

"Like what?" Scott asked.

"There's that old jacket of Daddy's that's in the upstairs closet," Melissa said. "Can we put that around his shoulders?"

The last thing I needed was to have this spirit remind me of The Swine. "How about a bandana?" I asked, pulling a cloth napkin out of one of the kitchen counters. "Would that work?"

The napkin, a red one with the standard bandana pattern around its edges, liberated itself from my hand, tied itself into a scarf shape, and started floating just north of the refrigerator, to Paul's left.

"I guess so," I said.

"I want you to feel comfortable with me," something slightly higher than the bandana said.

"Of course, and I want the same of you," I said in Scott's direction. "Please, tell me your story."

"Shouldn't the child leave?" Scott said. "I'm afraid my story will frighten her."

"I've seen *A Nightmare on Elm Street*," Melissa said. "I didn't get scared at all."

"No, but you did have to sleep in my bed for a week after you saw *Pinocchio*," I reminded her. "You kept having whale nightmares."

"I was three. And I'm not leaving."

"Go ahead, Scott," I said. "Don't worry about Melissa."

"All right, then, but don't say I didn't warn you," Scott said. "I've been staying in a house a few towns over, in Avon. The place was abandoned ten years ago, and they were supposed to tear it down and put up a hotel, I think, but then the money went away. So I do what I do there. I don't need much, being dead and all."

"So I take it that you are an experienced, um, spirit?" I asked. Maxie and Paul were still adjusting to their existence after their murders. "May I ask how and when you . . . passed away?"

"It was entirely of natural causes, I can assure you," Scott told me. "Cirrhosis, I think they called it. I drank a bit when I was alive. And that was just about eighty years ago."

"So, you said you want us to verify that something happened. What is that?" It was time to get to business. Whatever business this was.

The scarf untied itself and was rearranged more like headwear. I assumed Scott had taken it from around his neck and retied it into a do-rag. "About two months ago, I was contacted by someone who wanted me to help them with something. They said it was harmless, just a prank, but that they would pay handsomely for my services."

That raised about seventy-five questions in my head. "How could someone pay you handsomely?" I asked Scott. "No offense, but what does a ghost need with money?"

"Not money," Scott replied. "The reward was that I

would be able to leave this form of existence and move on to the next level."

No one in the room spoke for quite some time. Finally, I managed to squeak out, "How were they going to achieve that?"

"They didn't say."

This guy, however dead he might be, was starting to sound like an idiot. "So you were going to perform whatever service was requested, and you had no guarantee at all that the person who contacted you could deliver on what they promised. How did this person get in touch with you? How did they know you were there?"

The answer was a long time in coming. Finally, Scott said, "I can't say how they knew I was living in the old house, but they contacted me through an old child's toy that had been left there. A set of alphabet letters—magnetized, I think—that they used to spell words out on the floor. I kicked the first one, and couldn't put the message back together, but it was back the next day when I looked for it. I would find them there at odd times, and answer the same way. I never heard the person's voice."

I didn't like the way this story was going, but there was an unmistakable sadness that pervaded Scott's voice. Even the red napkin seemed to be bowed, as if Scott was staring at the floor. I looked at Mom. I wasn't actually appealing for help, but that must have been the way she interpreted my expression.

"Mr. McFarlane," Mom asked, "who did you think this person was? No one can grant you . . . the kind of thing you were promised. How could you agree to this prank on such thin evidence?"

There was silence for quite some time, then Paul said, "Scott, are you all right?"

And I confess, my first thought was, *Of course he's not all right—he's dead!*

"I'm embarrassed," Scott's voice said finally. "I don't want to say what I thought."

"If it can help the investigation, Scott, I think you pretty much have to say who you thought was sending you the messages," I said in his general direction. "Who do you think was sending you these messages on a preschool alphabet set?"

"God," he said. "I thought it was a sign from God."

"Ah," I said.

The rest of Scott McFarlane's story was less bizarre, but not much. For weeks, he had been finding messages spelled out on the floor in what he called his "main room." It started with simple messages: "HELLO," "HOW ARE YOU" and "I SEE YOU." Then, Scott found more letters in longer messages, which became more elaborate. An easel showed up one day that the magnetized letters would stick to, and he could "read" them without bending down, or occasionally kicking the words apart accidentally, as had happened a few more times. And Scott began to ask questions, most of which he said were never answered.

"They wouldn't say how they knew I was there or why they wanted to talk to me," he said. "They never explained why we couldn't just talk in person. And pretty soon, the messages were all about how they thought they could help me, if I would just do them this one favor."

The favor, apparently, hinged on a prank the unseen visitor wanted to play on an elderly woman, whose name Scott was never told. (This part started to erode his belief that a divine presence was behind the messages, he said.) And when he would show any reluctance to comply with the requests, the messages would stop for days.

"It gets damn lonely in that house sometimes," Scott said. "I finally said yes just to keep the contact."

"Couldn't you have come here and talked to Maxie and Paul?" Melissa asked. A ten-year-old girl truly values a good playdate.

"I don't always know where other people like me are

located," Scott told her. "And it's hard for me to find my way around." Melissa nodded.

"So you agreed to play this prank," I said to get Scott back on topic. "What was it you had to do?"

"It took four days of messages to tell me the whole thing," he answered. "I was supposed to go to an abandoned hotel here in Harbor Haven."

"Probably the Ocean Wharf," Maxie said. She had done considerable research into the area before buying the house I now owned. And Scott's story must have truly captured her attention, because she was even forgetting to be detached and snide.

"On the day I was summoned, I would arrive in the ballroom of the hotel, and I'd find some . . . they called them 'props,' for me to use. A long coat, a hat, an eye patch and a sash with a sheath for a plastic sword."

I put my hand over my mouth to avoid laughing. "So they *did* want you to play pirate?" I asked. The red bandana nodded, and it occurred to me it would have been helpful in the role.

"Apparently," Scott replied. "And I'd wait there until a certain time, when the woman who was, I guess, the target would show up, and I'd rattle the sword and do some ghost stuff. Billow the drapes, throw things around. I'm guessing they figured she couldn't see me, but she could see the props, so that would be enough to scare her."

"Why did they want to scare an old lady?" Melissa asked.

"I have no idea," Scott said. "It was just supposed to be a joke. Just a joke." His voice sounded sorrowful.

"What happened?" I asked.

"The big finale, the thing that was supposed to put a capper on the gag, was that I'd pull out this plastic sword and wave it around, then act like I was going to cut her head off. But something was wrong."

"What?" Mom asked.

"The sword felt too heavy. The handle was cheap, and it might have been wooden—it wasn't metal, but it wasn't plastic. And when I swung it . . ." His voice trailed off. Then Scott continued. "When I swung it, it felt like I hit something. And I heard—damn it—I heard something hit the floor. It sounded like a body."

There was silence in the room, but I was confused. "Well, why didn't you just look to see what you'd done?" I asked. "Was it so dark in the room that . . ."

Then I noticed the horrified looks of the others in the room. "Alison . . ." Mom began.

"Mr. McFarlane is blind," Melissa told me.

"Oh," I said.

Three

After that, the conversation sort of deteriorated. I was doing my best to turn down Scott McFarlane's request, but it's hard to say no to a blind dead man. I mean, what else could go wrong for the guy?

Scott explained that he had been blinded by an accident with acid while working at a printing press in the early part of the twentieth century and had lived the last thirty years of his life without sight. When he died, he'd assumed that his sight would be restored, but was disappointed to find out that was not the case.

"Instead, I was in a run-down house on the New Jersey shore, blind as a bat and completely out of my element," he went on to say. "It's taken me a while to get used to it, but you never really stop hoping that something will change."

I looked at Maxie, who had been depressed after we'd discovered her killer, because she'd assumed that solving her murder meant she would be moving on to another level of existence. She puffed out her lips a little, not realizing

I was watching, and sighed quietly. Paul suddenly looked even more impassioned than before.

"I just need to know if I killed that poor old woman," Scott said. "I heard someone say the name Arlice, so that's something to go on. You have no idea how difficult it is living with myself like this." I declined to challenge him on the term *living*.

"Have you heard from the person who contacted you since then?"

"No," Scott answered finally. "The next day, the letters were gone. I don't know how they got in without me hearing them, but they were simply gone. And they've been gone since."

If there's one thing you learn as a parent, especially a single parent, it's how to be the bad guy and still be able to look yourself in the mirror. "Let me think about it," I told Scott. "I understand how you feel, but I can't tell you right now that I'll be happy to do what you ask."

Scott said that he understood, but Paul, Maxie, Mom and Melissa didn't look like they concurred. After a minute or so, Paul informed me that Scott had left. I already knew that, because the red bandana had vanished, too. I'd seen Paul and Maxie stuff things into their pockets, and the physical object had disappeared. Once Scott left, everyone in the room, living and not-so-much, let out a sigh of relief. The man's sadness had been palpable.

One by one, they got up and left without a word, until just Paul and I were still in the kitchen. And he looked at me with those puppy dog eyes and stroked his goatee, which I guessed no longer required daily maintenance.

"Don't start," I said.

"You did make a promise," Paul said, completely ignoring my plea.

"And it was not to get involved in dangerous pursuits," I reminded him. "If this woman was set up to be murdered, the people who did it would, by definition, be dangerous. I'm not getting myself into a situation like that again."

Paul nodded. "That's right, you're not. Because if this woman was killed, if Scott really did do her some inadvertent harm, he's not asking us to find out who was responsible. He's not asking us to solve the crime. He just wants to know if it was his fault, so he can look himself in the mirror."

"He's blind." I looked at Paul. "And anyway, *can* you guys see yourselves in the mirror?"

"That's not the point. He wants to be able to live . . . *exist* inside his own mind. Is that too much to ask? You do a little legwork, ask a few questions, find out if the crime occurred. Whether or not it did, that's as far as our investigation goes. There is no danger. The man already can't see. Do you also want him to be alone in a dark place with guilty thoughts?"

"He said he would be paid back with a promotion to the next level of existence," I reminded Paul. "How does that work? How do you know there *is* a next level?"

Paul leaned his head to the right. "There's no way to know," he said. "Some people believe if we perform the right kind of acts in this state, we are moved on to something better, something higher. Some people think this is all there is. Scott obviously believes that he needs to redeem himself to reach the next stage."

"What do *you* believe?" I asked him.

"Until seventeen months ago, I didn't even believe in ghosts," Paul sighed. "I'm not the guy to ask. But some people get so frustrated being . . . like me, that they end their existence entirely."

"That's possible? You're already dead."

Paul nodded. "I haven't seen it, but I've heard about it from other people like me," he said. "Apparently, the frustration can get so unbearable for some of us that they actually *will* themselves into a nonexistence. I'm told they just sort of dissolve into nothing."

"Ghost suicide," I said, shaking my head. "Go figure."

"That's what Scott is up against," Paul said, pushing it a little too hard for my taste.

I stood up. The guests hadn't seen me for a while now, and that was bad business. I started for the door into the den. "You're not playing fair," I told Paul. "You're trying to make me feel guilty."

"It's not a pleasant feeling, is it?" he countered.

At the door, I stopped and faced him, but he had traveled to the entrance, and was now only inches from my face. "Suppose we find out that Scott did kill that woman with a sword," I said. "Would our telling him that make him feel better?"

Paul frowned. "Now who's not playing fair?" he asked.

I walked through the swinging door and into the den, mostly because I didn't have an answer for that. The house, for a place with ten living people and two ghosts inside, was remarkably quiet. I was emphasizing peace and quiet in the advertising, and privately acknowledging the ghosts only to Rance's group, which seemed fascinated by the subject. We kept television out of the common areas, which annoyed Melissa, but she had relented when I'd gotten a flat-screen HDTV and mounted it on the wall of her bedroom.

Single moms aren't *always* the bad guys.

Tomorrow night, as had been agreed to in my contract with Senior Plus Tours, we would hold a "séance," during which I would relay Paul and Maxie's responses to questions posed by curious guests gathered for the evening. But tonight had no special event scheduled, so I toured the house to see that all the guests were getting what they wanted out of their stay.

It was early in the season, and Senior Plus had blocked out a few rooms for the next four weeks, but Rance had been explicit in his instructions that this first group was a "trial tour," and that negative reviews could jeopardize future bookings. He would personally read every evaluation form filled out by the guests at the end of their stays with me.

In short, I had to make sure everyone had a rollicking good time. Linda Jane so far had seemed quite pleased with the level of service I offered her charges (and I'd seen her at a distance talking with Dolores Santiago, who'd arrived only a half hour later than she'd predicted), though I was fairly certain she'd most likely hear from Bernice Antwerp, the perpetually grumpy woman from the group. Most of the other guests were lovely (although Mr. and Mrs. Jones rarely—if ever—left their bedroom), but Bernice could find fault in world peace if she put her mind to it.

Tonight, I found her in the library, walking from shelf to shelf (we had over two thousand books stacked), shaking her head. "Anything I can help you with, Mrs. Antwerp?" I asked, careful not to call her by her first name, a breach of propriety that had earned me a scolding her first day here. "Having trouble choosing a book?"

"There aren't any good books here," she griped, shaking her head and snarling a bit. "I can't imagine who chose all these books; they're awful." I hadn't actually chosen the books myself; I'd bought most of them in bulk from collections and estate sales, but still, she couldn't find one thing to read among two thousand books?

I was determined, though, to break through. "Well, if you let me know what kind of books you enjoy reading, I can certainly see to it that they're stocked here," I said.

"*Good* books," Bernice reiterated. Of course; why hadn't I thought of that?

"I'll do what I can," I assured her. She made a *hmmph* sound as I left the library.

Newly determined by my encounter with the unpleasable Bernice, I checked out the game room, which in reality had only a pool table in it. Two older gentlemen, Warren Balachik and Jim Bridges, were drinking beer and playing pool. They looked up when I appeared in the doorway.

"Alison!" Jim grinned. He was a friendly, gregarious man who had seemed tickled by everything that had gone on since he'd arrived. "Checking up on us?"

"I just wanted to see who was winning," I told him. "Thought I might take on the winner myself."

"Do you play?" Warren, a smaller, slighter man with a permanent bend in his neck (which was actually something of an advantage at pool) asked.

"No. So it's easy to beat me," I answered.

They laughed, and Jim said, "I think I'll beat Warren, and then just beat him again."

"Your choice," I reminded him. Good to see the guys were enjoying themselves.

I'd barely made it out of the game room when I found myself face-to-neck with Dolores Santiago, the last-minute addition. Dolores, who appeared to be in her sixties, had inch-thick glasses and wore her long gray hair tied in a mammoth ponytail in the back. She stood about six feet tall and had not once so much as cracked a smile in my presence, but she had been very, *very* interested in everything ghost-related that went on in the house. Dolores was definite in wanting to observe what she called an "ongoing paranormal incident" going on in my guesthouse. She'd signed on to the tour only two days before the group arrived, and her payment had been directly deposited into my business account only the day before.

"Mrs. Kerby," she said, although I have never used *Mrs.* in my name and *Kerby* is the name I was born with, "I'm wondering if you might direct me toward the paranormal presences in your home. I would like the opportunity to commune with them outside of the group. Other people only complicate my impressions."

I had thought of getting a Dolores-to-English dictionary, since she seemed to talk like this all the time, but instead, knowing how hard it was to convince Maxie to do even the few appearances she made during each day, I told Dolores once again about the séance planned for the following night, during which she'd be free to ask the two "paranormal presences" anything she'd like.

"It's not verbal communication I'm discussing," she said. "I have a few devices in my room that can measure the vibratory presences in your home, and their efficiency is hindered by other living beings."

Devices that could measure vibratory presences, hmm? I bet. But best not to comment on that, especially since Paul chose that moment to materialize right behind Dolores. Even though Dolores was quite tall, I was baffled by how short Paul appeared until I realized that he was about calf-deep in floor, and therefore a bit less imposing than normal.

"What is she talking about?" he asked, but I ignored the question. If Dolores saw me talking to him now, Paul—or more significantly, I—would get not a moment of peace until Dolores was safely on the way back to wherever it was she had come from.

"I don't really have that much control over the ghosts," I told her instead. "They come and go as they please. Feel free to talk to them if you believe you feel a presence nearby, however."

"There's nothing you can arrange?" she said. Uh-oh. The customer is always right, Alison.

"I can't promise anything, but I'll see what I can do," I told her.

Dolores actually curled her lips in a somewhat upward direction. It wasn't exactly a smile, but it turned her perpetual frown into something resembling a straight horizontal line. "Thank you," she said. "I will look forward to it." I considered asking what it was exactly she was looking forward to, but decided not to press my luck. I walked down the hallway, saw Dolores head into the game room of all places, and maneuvered into a corner where I could quietly talk to Paul.

"It's a lot harder to talk now that we have guests," I more or less hissed at him. "You can't just pop up and expect to have a conversation."

"I don't see why not, since the fact that Maxie and I are here is the reason you've been able to rent the rooms out." So he wanted to play hardball, eh?

"If you're trying to persuade me of something, your salesmanship skills are coming up way short," I told Paul.

Paul retreated. "You're right; that was a cheap shot." He really is a softie behind all the transparent muscles and the private-detective attitude. Canadians don't like it when it's implied they're being rude. "It's very frustrating wanting to do something, and being unable to because you're . . . like me."

So now he was playing the dead card. "I'm not heartless," I told him. "I'm cautious. I don't see this Scott thing turning out well for anybody. And I have no idea, even with my extensive investigator training, how to find out if somebody died when I don't even know who that somebody might be."

"Your extensive investigator training consisted of me telling you how to pass the exam," Paul reminded me, oblivious to the sarcastic edge in my voice, I guess. "And I think if someone died from a sword injury in an abandoned hotel, that might narrow the field of possible victims somewhat."

"Fine. I'll ask around a little tomorrow. But I have to be around for the séance tomorrow night, and so do you. And I'm still wondering exactly how we're going to break it to your new best friend if we find out that he did in fact kill a little old lady."

Paul bit his lips. "We'll have to decide that if it happens," he said.

I started back toward the main room, and Paul followed along. "I'm just telling you ahead of time, I'm not happy about this one." I told him.

"Noted. But I think you'll find that you enjoy helping people out this way. You're easing a man's mind for all eternity; isn't that worth something?"

There was a lot less peace and quiet in the main room than when I'd left. I picked up the pace when I realized that a group had gathered in the middle of the room, and the front door was standing wide open. Instinctively, I looked around for Melissa, but didn't see her. I started walking even faster.

I calmed down a little when I noticed Maxie hovering near the ceiling, grinning from ear to ear. Whatever her faults (and I could chronicle them, given the time), Maxie is devoted to Melissa, and would never be smiling if she saw my daughter in any kind of difficulty.

I got to the entry area, Paul just behind me, and tried to sort through the crowd. Melissa was indeed there, looking just fine, but confused. My mother stood near her, but was facing the group gathered in the center of the room. The two guys from the game room and Linda Jane were standing in the center of the room, forming a circle around . . . Who *were* those people?

"It wasn't a real hot tub," said a man I couldn't see for all the people in the way. "It was a much larger tub we had built there, so more of the cast could be seen at once."

"Oh my!" Warren breathed. "It all looked so real!"

"It's real, all right," the man's voice answered. "Everything that happens on camera really happens. We just make sure it looks as good as it can when it happens."

"Excuse me," I almost shouted. "I'm the proprietor here. Can I help you?"

"Oh, Alison!" Jim said. "It's amazing! I'm so glad you didn't tell us it was going to happen—the surprise is wonderful!"

"What surprise?" Apparently, I was surprising the guests with something so secret, even *I* didn't know about it.

The crowd parted, and standing in its center was a man of about thirty, with a haircut that had probably cost as much as the sofa in my main room. He wore blue jeans carefully aged to look as if they hadn't been carefully aged, a polo shirt with a logo so trendy I didn't recognize it, and shoes designed to look extremely casual at about three hundred dollars a pair.

"I'm sorry," he said. "Are you Ms. Kerby?"

Melissa stood up and walked to my side, and instinctively, I put my arm around her, suddenly feeling like she needed to be protected. Mom walked over to stand at my side. The Kerby girls were closing ranks. "Yes," I admitted. "I'm Alison Kerby. Who are you, and how did you get in?"

The young man stepped forward and offered a hand. "My apologies," he said. "I came in looking for you, and we got caught up. My name is Trent Avalon." He produced a business card, and I took it.

The card read, "Trent Avalon, executive producer: *Down the Shore*." It bore the logo, in the top left corner, of VidChannel, a cable network that specialized in reality television and game shows aimed at an audience of teenagers and college students.

But apparently it also attracted some senior citizen viewers, because my guests were absolutely agog over Trent, who had apparently been regaling them with tales of his television exploits.

"Mr. Avalon," I said, "I don't mean to be insulting, but what does your TV show have to do with me?"

Warren's eyes widened. "You're not a fan of *Down the Shore*?" he asked. "I'm absolutely addicted to it!"

"Not everyone is in our target demographic, Warren," Trent assured him, then turned his attention back to me. "I'm here to discuss the possibility of us doing a little business together, Ms. Kerby."

That wrinkled my brow, all right. "I'm in the guest-house business, Mr. Avalon," I said. "You do television. Do you need to have some people stay here at the house?"

"More or less," he said. "Is there someplace we can . . ."

"He wants to have the next season take place *here*!" Warren beamed. "Oh Alison, you really have to say yes!"

Four

"They're going to film a TV show in your house?" My best friend, Jeannie Rogers, four months pregnant and showing just enough that you wouldn't think she'd just gained a little weight, was still walking faster than me on our trek from Stud Muffin, the local bakery café, to the Harbor Haven police headquarters. Jeannie was determined to gain weight only in her baby area and nowhere else, so she had decided to exercise until her doctor told her to stop. So far, her doctor had not told Jeannie to stop.

"Well, I have Larry going over the paperwork, but they're in a hurry, so I'll know by this afternoon," I said. Larry Morwitz is my lawyer, and even though the only time we'd ever done business before was when he represented me in the divorce from The Swine, I knew he could handle reading a contract.

"What's it about?" Jeannie asked. The sun shone brightly on her face, and she drank it in. Within six weeks, it would start getting warm, then hot in the afternoons, and neither of us would be walking this quickly, I'd bet. At least Jeannie would have the baby as an excuse.

"It's something called *Down the Shore*," I told her. "It's . . ."

"Omigod! They're filming *Down the Shore* at your house? I *love* that show!" Jeannie stopped dead in her tracks and stared at me. "How did you manage that?"

I was a couple of steps ahead before I realized she'd stopped. "The house they were going to use burned down," I said. "A show about a bunch of drunken kids looking for sex in our own backyard? You watch that?"

"Oh, it's way more than that," Jeannie answered, waving a hand. She started to walk again, and I fell into step with her, but it was hard to keep up. "These kids put on such an attitude, and they think they're entitled to, like, everything. It's a riot!"

"It sounds disgusting."

"It is. That's the best part. There was this one show where this guy, he calls himself Mistah Motion, he went to the Stone Pony, where Bruce Springsteen used to play, and tried to get onstage to sing 'Born in the USA.' They threw him out the back door into a Dumpster!" She practically doubled over with laughter.

I shook my head. I was getting a tidy sum for me (a pittance in the TV business, no doubt, as VidChannel was sort of MTV's poorer cousin), and was already beginning to question my decision to take it. The world had gone crazy while I slept one night, and I'd missed it. Now I was living in a house with ghosts and senior citizens, and by this evening it was likely to be invaded by four young people, each hoping for fame by being more obnoxious than the other three.

I used to wonder why people made New Jersey jokes. I don't anymore.

Jeannie managed to gather herself to the point that she could ask, "How did they pick your house?"

"Well, the producer said there were two factors," I told her. "First, I, um, had the space available for the next three weeks. They only need one room. And even that is just for show—the 'boys and girls,' as he calls them, will really be living in trailers parked behind my house."

"What was the other factor?" Jeannie asked.

"Well, Trent said he'd asked around town, and people were talking about my house because of . . . you know . . ."

Jeannie looked puzzled. "Because of what?"

"Because of the ghosts."

Jeannie grinned and punched me on the shoulder. "So you put one over on them, too, huh?" Jeannie, despite the most obvious evidence a person could see, still absolutely refuses to believe in Paul and Maxie. Her husband, Tony Mandorisi, however, has interacted with the ghosts, and is now a true believer, even if he can't see or hear them.

"Mmm-hmm." I punted. After a while, there's no point in arguing with Jeannie—she's a force of nature.

"How's it going to work?" she asked. It took me a moment to remember what she was talking about.

"Once the papers are signed, the four 'cast members' show up about six tonight. With the full complement of guests from Senior Plus, I had just the one room open, and they're setting up their operations in there, pretending the kids are living in it all together. The four of them move in after equipment is installed in the room—which the production company insists will cause no damage that they can't repair when they move out. Then I guess this Trent guy figures out stuff for them to do and films it."

"And they can shoot it all in three weeks? That seems fast." Jeannie wasn't asking any questions I hadn't asked Trent the night before, but when he gave the answers, they seemed more reasonable.

"He says they want to air the show during the summer, when people would really be here on vacation. So they film hours and hours and hours of stuff, and then they edit it down."

"Why didn't they start sooner?" Jeannie asked.

"What temperature was it here two weeks ago?" I reminded her.

"About fifty-five."

"A little chilly for the bikini scenes they so desperately need on the beach," I explained.

"These people need to show a little gumption if they want to make it in show business," Jeannie said.

"Gumption is not what they'll be showing."

We walked up the steps to the police station and went inside. At the dispatcher's station, I asked for Detective Anita McElone (that's Mac-el-OAN-ee) and was asked to wait. Jeannie lowered herself into one of the molded plastic chairs (orange) in the waiting area, but I chose to stand. McElone was already considerably taller than me, and I didn't want to give her an added advantage.

Let's just say our relationship, while not hostile, had hardly been friendly.

After a few minutes she appeared in the doorway, straight and rigid, took a look at Jeannie and me waiting for her and let out an audible groan.

"Whatever it is," she said, "I don't want any."

I reached into the canvas tote bag I substitute for a purse (I carry a lot of stuff, and support my local public radio station) and produced my wallet, which I opened. The private investigator license that had been issued to me by the state of New Jersey was prominently displayed therein.

"I just have a couple of questions," I said.

"The Dunkin' Donuts was out of Old Fashioned Cake this morning, so I knew it was going to be a bad day," McElone deadpanned.

"May we come in?" I asked, all professional and everything.

"We?" the detective asked. "Is your pal a PI, too?"

"I'm an expectant mother," Jeannie piped up, standing. "You can't expect me to stay out here with hardened criminals."

"There's no one else here," McElone pointed out.

"There's no one else here *now*," Jeannie retorted. Like I said, a force of nature.

McElone waved us into the squad room and led us to her cubicle, which was kept incredibly neat and had only a picture of her family on her desk. A desk like that is the work of an unbalanced mind, in my opinion.

Her entire body seemed to sigh. "What is it you want to know?" she asked. "You do realize I'm not required to share any police information with you at all, right?"

"I was hoping you'd answer one question out of professional courtesy," I answered.

"Bring in a professional, and we'll talk," McElone muttered under her breath.

"I'm sorry, what did you say?" Jeannie asked.

"I said, 'What is your question?'" McElone replied.

"Have there been any mysterious deaths in Harbor Haven recently?" I asked. "Something at the Ocean Wharf or one of the hotels on the shore, maybe?"

McElone looked at me as if I'd asked whether fish could walk upright. "The Ocean Wharf's been abandoned for six years," she said. "Who's going there to die? And what do you want to know about mysterious deaths for? You trying to drum up business? Is that cursed guesthouse you're running in the red already?" McElone is afraid of my house; she says it gives her "the creeps."

"I thought I was asking the question," I said.

"You can ask all you want," the detective answered. "I don't have to answer unless I'm satisfied that there's a good reason for you to know."

"I have a client who's concerned that something might have happened—an accident, maybe—and I'm trying to find out whether it did or didn't. Is that so sinister?" Minus the comment about it being sinister, that's exactly how I'd explained it to Jeannie. Trying to tell her I was representing a ghost would have been pointless.

"With a mysterious death involved? Yeah, that's pretty

sinister," McElone said. "Now, what do you know about this supposed incident at the Ocean Wharf?"

"*Did* something happen there?" Jeannie insisted.

McElone looked at Jeannie, then at me, then back at Jeannie. "You sure you don't have a detective's license?" she asked Jeannie.

"No, but if you don't answer Alison, I might have to go and get one."

The detective considered that, then turned her attention toward me. "When did this thing happen, according to your client?"

"Six days ago. Last Friday, not sure what time."

"Friday was seven days ago. Today's Thursday."

"Do we count today? I'm never sure." I started counting backward on my fingers. "Wednesday, Tuesday, Monday . . ."

"Never mind. Last Friday." McElone punched up some information on her desktop computer screen. "No calls to that area at all on Friday."

"Could a body have been discovered Saturday, or any day since then?"

"A body?" McElone shook her head. "If there was a dead body somewhere, I'd have heard about it."

"So nobody named Arlice has died mysteriously lately," I reiterated, just to confirm.

"Arlice! You mean Arlice Crosby?" McElone asked.

"I don't know. How many Arlices are there in Harbor Haven?"

"Mrs. Crosby is the only one I know about," she said. "Must be close to eighty."

"And she hasn't died recently?" I wanted to report back to Paul without any hesitation and have this whole Scott McFarlane thing behind us as quickly as possible so I could concentrate on the coming onslaught of hard bodies and empty heads about to take over my quiet little guesthouse.

"Not that I've heard about," McElone said. "If she did, it wasn't considered suspicious."

"Do you have her address?" Maybe I could swing by and visit Mrs. Crosby to absolutely confirm her aliveness.

"We're the police," McElone said. "We have *everybody's* address." But she didn't move to write it down, and she didn't say anything else.

"Well, can we have it?" Jeannie asked, scratching her belly, which seemed just a little larger than when we'd sat down.

"Hell, no," McElone answered. "Get it out of the phone book. Google it. Call her up on your cell phone. I'm not going to invade Mrs. Crosby's privacy by giving her address away to every nut job who walks into the station."

We pressed (Jeannie even attempted to go into labor), but it did no good. But even as McElone dismissed us and we scurried off into the mid-morning, I felt better about this affair. Scott McFarlane hadn't killed anyone after all.

Probably.

Five

"Arlice Crosby." Phyllis Coates, editor and publisher of the *Harbor Haven Chronicle,* sat back in her squeaky chair in her cramped office and rubbed her eyes with her thumb and forefinger. "You've lived in this town all these years and you don't know Arlice Crosby?"

Phyllis and I go back to my days delivering papers on my bike for her when I was thirteen years old. Before that, she was a crime reporter for the *New York Daily News,* and before that, she was probably in kindergarten. Phyllis was born to dig up the dirt and then print it, though always in a classy way.

"I took a few years off when I was married," I reminded her. "I haven't lived here *all* this time. Come on. You know everybody. Who's Arlice Crosby?"

Jeannie had begged off the visit to the *Chronicle* office, or she might have been able to intimidate Phyllis, although I doubt it—Phyllis is pretty tough and usually amused by the goings-on in our town. Besides, Phyllis wasn't McElone; she was perfectly happy to share information, especially if there was the possibility of a good story coming out of it.

She didn't disappoint. "Arlice Crosby is the widow of Jermaine Crosby, who died at least thirty years ago. He made a fortune in the amusement piers here, in Seaside Heights, Wildwood Crest and Asbury Park, and then he died young. Ate too much of that boardwalk food and had a series of heart attacks. Today they might have been able to save him, but not back then.

"It was while I was working at the *News*, so I wasn't around for it, but Arlice grieved, I guess—she holed up in that big house and essentially became a philanthropist, tending to Jermaine's fortune so she could give plenty away but still keep a lot, too. Turns out she's some kind of financial whiz, and she's never lived like a rich lady, just a very comfortable one."

"So, she's a hermit now?" I was learning, as an investigator, to read between the lines when people spoke to me.

"Oh no," Phyllis said. "She's a fixture at the cultural commission, at the arts center over in Ocean Grove, places like that. She even shows up at Hanrahan's every once in a while." Hanrahan's was one of the less refined saloons on Ocean Avenue, our main drag.

Okay, so maybe I needed between-the-lines reading glasses. "Well, where do you think I can find her today?" All I wanted to do was confirm that the woman was alive. I didn't need to write her biography.

"I'm sure she's at the house most of the time," Phyllis answered. "You want the address?"

"I didn't come for the great coffee," I told her. The coffee from Phyllis's ancient hot plate, dangerously close to a few stacks of paper, was not something anyone would stop by to drink.

Phyllis wrote the address of Arlice Crosby's house on the back of a receipt for seven dollars and sixty-three cents' worth of postage dated three years earlier. "You have to keep these things for the IRS," she said as she handed it over, "so bring it back when you're done. What's this sudden interest in Arlice, anyway?"

I told her the same story I'd given McElone, about having a client who wanted to confirm Arlice's well-being, which was true. I left out the part about the client having been deceased for close to eighty years, as I didn't see how that was relevant. And then I thanked Phyllis for the help, promised her an exclusive on the filming of *Down the Shore* at the guesthouse (no confidentiality was written into my contract, I was pretty sure) and got into my decrepit Volvo station wagon to find Arlice's house.

Luckily, I had a portable GPS device. Even as well as I knew the streets of Harbor Haven, this was a part of town I'd never visited before, not even in high school, when driving around town was our major form of recreation and social interaction. This was before Twitter and e-mail, when you actually had to be in the same car as your friends to spend the evening with them.

Clearly, this was an exclusive little alcove that had been constructed for the more well-heeled among Harbor Haven's citizenry. While it wasn't gated, the entrance to the cul-de-sac bore a brass sign that read "Ocean Paradiso," obviously quite old but still polished and shiny, mounted on a concrete pillar. Trees lined both sides of the drive, and looked to be quite well cared for. The grass was freshly mown. I also noticed a video camera on the top of the pillar. The residents in this area were interested in security.

I passed a few really impressive homes, each one overlooking a different view of the ocean and a private beach, but based on the impression of the lady Phyllis had given me, I could tell right away which house belonged to Arlice Crosby: There was an absolute mansion, resembling nothing so much as the main house of Tara in *Gone with the*

Wind, standing apart at the top of the hill with the best view and the best beach. It was also, clearly, the largest and most impressive house.

Arlice Crosby's place was right next to it, a very appealing but smallish Colonial, extremely well-maintained, with a long front porch and a glider, flowers on every windowsill and a few hanging plants, none of which had so much as one brown leaf. It made me think that I hadn't done anything with my own front porch yet, and I should start getting ideas.

I parked the Volvo in front of the Crosby house and thought for a few moments before getting out of the car. If I were a wealthy woman of advanced years, why would I decide to talk to a complete stranger whose sole purpose in coming to visit was to verify that I was actually alive? The only answer I could propose was that it would be nice for someone to show that level of interest. That probably wasn't good enough.

But wait—I had something with me that would serve as a terrific conversation piece in awkward situations. I took it out of my purse and walked to Arlice's front door, where I rang the bell.

It took some time, but the door did open, and behind a screen stood a woman who was impeccably but casually dressed. She had probably been quite tall when she was younger, but age had bent and shrunk her a bit. But she was not one of those older people who seem to carry their ages on their backs; she smiled warmly when she opened the door and looked me straight in the eye.

"Yes?" she said.

"Are you Mrs. Arlice Crosby?" I asked.

"That depends," she said. "Who are you?"

I held up my investigator's license. "I'm a private investigator. My name is Alison Kerby. May I ask you just a couple of questions, Mrs. Crosby?"

"I haven't yet said whether I am Mrs. Crosby, Ms. Kerby," she pointed out. "What are the questions regarding?"

"Well, there have been reports of some . . . strange occurrences in Harbor Haven, and the name Arlice Crosby came up. I'd love to talk to her, if that's possible."

The woman pushed the screen door open and looked me up and down. "You're not carrying a gun," she said. It wasn't a question.

I answered it anyway. "No, I'm not."

"You're an odd sort of private investigator."

I nodded. "This is an odd sort of case."

She seemed to make a decision; she nodded, more to herself than to me. "OK, you got me. I'm Arlice Crosby," she said. "Come sit out here on the veranda. Would you like a lemonade?"

"I'd love one." Anything to get the taste of Phyllis's coffee out of my mouth. "If it's not too much trouble."

"Don't be silly." She disappeared back into the house, and I sat on a wooden rocker near a small table. I felt the glider might be a little strange for this type of visit.

Arlice reappeared in just a few moments, carrying a tray with a pitcher of lemonade and two glasses full of ice; she seemed pretty spry for a woman in her late seventies. Or was I being ageist?

"It's sugar-free. I hope you don't mind. I have diabetes," she said after she'd poured for both of us and sat in a facing chair.

"Of course I don't mind," I said, taking a sip of the lemonade, which actually was quite good. "It's delicious."

A rather sad-looking but enormous black cat ambled its way onto the porch and, without any attempt at niceties, sprung up onto Arlice's lap. She didn't jump at the impulsive move, and simply began stroking the cat while she sipped her lemonade.

"This is Marcus," she said. "He lives with the neighbors

but, confidentially, he likes me better." She produced some kind of treat from her apron pocket and fed it to the cat.

"I can't imagine why," I said.

"Enough of this polite chitchat. Tell me why you're here."

"I have a client who is . . . concerned about you, and asked me to make sure you were all right," I answered. Yes, even after practicing what I'd say the whole morning, that was the best I could come up with.

"And who is this client?" Arlice asked, her eyes showing more amusement than anything else. She just continued to stroke the cat, who purred with some satisfaction and stretched on Arlice's lap like it was a warm spot on the carpeted floor.

"I'm afraid that's privileged information." I've watched a few detective movies in my time.

Arlice pretended to look shocked. "Really! Here someone is so concerned about my well-being, and I'm not even allowed to know who it is? Did your client happen to mention why I might be in some kind of distress?"

I had rehearsed this, as well, but I was still careful with the words I chose. "It's a person"—at least at one point, he had been—"who felt that there might have been an attempt to hurt you, and was concerned that this attempt might have, unintentionally, involved my client."

"Very good, Alison," Arlice said. "Not so much as a gender-specific pronoun. You've given this some thought, haven't you?"

"I'm just starting out as an investigator, Arlice. I can't develop a reputation if I go around giving away information about my clients. Nobody will want to hire me."

"A sound decision," Arlice said, nodding her head in approval. "But I can't verify this attempt to do me harm unless I know what it involved." She produced another treat from her pocket and gave it to the cat, who appeared to think he had indeed died and gone to Cat Heaven.

"Okay. Now, this is going to sound crazy."

Arlice smiled. "Don't worry. I've heard plenty of crazy in my day."

I chuckled a little. "Well, according to my client, it involved a prank that lured you to the Ocean Wharf Hotel, where a figure dressed as a pirate threatened you." I wanted to look away after letting that information out, but Paul was adamant about observing a subject's reaction.

"Oh, that," Arlice said.

I blinked a couple of times. "Oh, *that*?"

She shrugged. "It was no big deal. My lawyer, Tom Donovan, said he'd heard stories about the ghost of a pirate haunting the main ballroom at the Ocean Wharf. Well, I've always loved a good ghost story. I've been on lots of ghost tours, and even followed a few scientists in paranormal studies when they've investigated claims. So once Tom told me about this one, I figured I'd see for myself."

Oh boy. "So you see ghosts?" I asked. Another of the sisterhood.

But Arlice shook her head. "No, no. I've never actually seen one. But I'd love to, you know—it's so exciting, the idea of people living on after what we call death. The idea has always fascinated me."

"So you went to the Ocean Wharf Hotel looking for the pirate ghost?"

She waved a hand in disgust. "A pirate ghost. It was the silliest fake setup you've ever seen. A button on the floor to make moaning noises, can you imagine? And an empty pirate suit that they'd probably bought at a Halloween store. It was even rigged to swing a sword at me."

"A sword!" Best to sound shocked. I didn't want her to have any idea I'd heard the other side of the story— and that the ghost wasn't the least bit fake (except for the pirate bit).

"Yes. It looked quite real, but it just swung over my head and went right into a wall. Knocked Tom right down, though. It didn't touch him, but he was scared to death, the poor man. We left right after that. The thing stopped moving. Silly, really."

Her story was even weirder than Scott's, and he'd been dead since the nineteen thirties. "Who would have set up such an elaborate hoax?" I asked.

"Damned if I know," Arlice said, shaking her head. "Kids, maybe. Someone with too much time on their hands. People need to spend more time trying to do good for others, if you ask me."

The lemonade was almost gone. I stood up. "Well, thank you for your time, Arlice," I said. "You've helped me quite a bit. My client will be pleased that you're all right."

Arlice gently lifted Marcus and put him on the floor of the porch as she stood up. "Go on home, now," she said. "They like you up there, too, you know." The cat did not look back as he ambled toward the larger house slightly up the hill.

"Yes, this mysterious client of yours, Alison." She smiled, then stopped, looked more closely at me and snapped her fingers. "Alison Kerby! You're the one who owns that new B and B everybody says is haunted!"

"It's not a B and B. I don't serve food," I replied automatically. It's practically a reflexive response at this point.

"But it is haunted?" Arlice asked. She sounded so hopeful.

"If you're so interested in ghost stories, and you've heard all the nonsense they're saying around town, how come you haven't been by?" I asked her. All right, so it was a dodge. What's wrong with a dodge when it's used for the kindest of reasons?

"I've never been invited," she said, looking me right in the eye with a dare.

"Well, I'll tell you what," I said, knowing I'd been hooked by a pro. "We're going to have a séance tonight to see once and for all if the house *is* haunted."

"Really!" Arlice waited. She knew if she was silent, I'd have to fill the space.

"Yes, but it's only for invited guests," I said.

She waited a while longer.

"So consider yourself invited," I said.

Arlice clapped her hands. "I'll be there with bells on," she said.

"That could get awfully noisy," I told her.

Six

"What the hell did you agree to?" Maxie's arms were folded across her chest, obscuring her "Take a Picture, It Lasts Longer" T-shirt. "There are people crawling all over our house!"

To be fair, the cast and crew of *Down the Shore* did resemble an infestation of bugs at that moment. Lights were being set up in the main room. Young people in remarkably skimpy bathing suits were standing idly by, doing as much nothing as a person can do while remaining upright. And a few of my more awestruck senior citizen guests—minus Warren Balachik and Jim Bridges, who had weighed the advantages of a cold beer over their clear fascination with the production, and come down temporarily on the side of beer—were watching the nothing happen with something very closely approximating rapture.

The seniors in the house, by the way, had raved about the extra dimension to their vacation—or at least Jim and Warren had. When the two gentlemen weren't raiding the cooler of beer in the game room, they never let the young "cast" out of their sight. Bernice, muttering something about "encroachment" in the den—a room I had not seen her frequent during her stay so far—was still there to gawk. The Joneses could not be reached for comment.

I had not yet been introduced to our reality cast, but was told they'd be "happy to talk with you after they've got a couple of scenes in the can." Right now, until all the technical snarls could be straightened out, the two young women and the two young men were scattered to the four corners of the room, not interacting at all. With anybody. Once cameras were rolling, Trent had explained, there would be plenty of action.

One person's definition of "reality" might not be the same as another's. It's a flexible decade.

I was huddling in the front hall, right near the door, trying to talk to Maxie in such a way that no one would see me having a conversation, to all appearances, with myself. "First of all, it's *my* house, and if you need reminding, I'll show you the deed *again*. Second, I thought you were the one who couldn't wait for this carnival to get going. Something about 'hot guys with no shirts.' Well, there they are."

"I thought they'd just be here hanging out," she answered. "But they brought a whole army with them."

"Who do you think runs the camera and the sound?"

"I don't know," she said. "How can they be spontaneous with all these people following them around?"

I have to admit, I chuckled condescendingly. "Spontaneous? Take a look. What they're doing now? That's their version of *spontaneous*."

"They're not doing *anything*."

"Exactly."

She sputtered, pouted and left. Which was just as well, since Linda Jane was approaching, and it would have been hard for me to cover my conversation with someone clearly not present.

"So this is show business," she said. "It's like the Army—hurry up and wait."

"Were you in the Army?" I asked her.

Linda Jane nodded. "Briefly. I was a medic, actually. But I got an honorable discharge after eight months."

"Why? If that's not too personal."

"Not too personal," she said. She pulled up the left leg on her jeans, and showed me her prosthetic limb. "Grenada— remember that one? I stood in the wrong place at the wrong time. A bomb went off. So did my leg, just below the knee."

I had no skill set for responding to that. "Wow," I said.

"Yeah. It makes for a hell of a conversation piece." Linda Jane lowered her trouser leg. She waited, but I couldn't come up with an appropriate response. "See what I mean?"

"I'm so . . . it's just . . . that's awful," I finally managed.

"After all these years, I'm used to it. But I am sorry I didn't get to serve longer."

"You're a hero," I said.

She laughed. "Yeah, big hero. I was going to the mess tent for a cup of coffee. Anyway, it was a long time ago." She gestured toward all the commotion in the front room. "This is some show you've booked into the place."

"I'm starting to wonder if what the production company is paying me is worth this," I admitted. "I hope the guests don't find it too upsetting."

Linda Jane laughed again. "Upsetting! Take a look. Almost every single one of them is here watching. They couldn't be having a better time."

"Every single one except Mr. and Mrs. Jones," I pointed out.

"I'm pretty sure they're having a good time, too," she answered.

Trent Avalon, having surveyed the situation from the top of the staircase, clapped his hands loudly to silence the assembled mob in the front room. "Okay, people!" he shouted. "Let's make some reality!"

There were actual cheers from the guests. Warren and Jim, now standing in the doorway to the den with beers in their hands (having the best of both worlds), were especially enthusiastic in their excitement. I'm pretty sure those were not their first beers of the day.

"Now, those of you who are not involved with the show," Trent continued, "we're happy to have you watch the filming, but please, don't make noise while the cameras are rolling, and don't walk in front of them. You'll ruin the shot."

The guests nodded their heads, happy to be part of the show business magic that was about to happen. I had a different reaction—I was seriously annoyed. How dare he order my guests to stay away from his cameras? Would the *Down the Shore* audience be so traumatized by seeing people over thirty years old? But I'd wait to talk to Trent when we could be out of earshot of . . . everyone else in Harbor Haven. Crowds of locals had begun to gather outside the house, in the vain hope of glimpsing one of these misbehaving adolescents. You had to worry for the future of civilization as we know it. Or perhaps I was overreacting.

At Trent's first word, the four kids in the cast had ambled over to spots near the French doors that led to the backyard, probably to give the camera a better backdrop. I could see that the lights were positioned so as to avoid glaring directly into the glass. A man holding a boom microphone stood just out of camera range. A gray-haired man in a baseball cap, whom I had assumed was one of the production accountants, clapped his hands twice.

"Okay," he shouted. "Let's settle down, people." Go figure; he was the director. "Roll the cameras."

And the action began. For the sake of my own sensibility, I'm going to replace every obscenity spoken with the word *migraine*. Because that's what I was starting to get.

"I can't migraine believe you migraine hooked up with that migraine slut last night," the taller, blonder girl said to the boy who was sensitive enough to actually be wearing a shirt. "After a whole week of pretending you were migraine into me."

"Hey, I'm here to have a good time," the sensitive boy replied. "I can't help it if you migraine thought I was migraine in love with you. I held your migraine hand for like ten migraine minutes in line for the roller coaster. Grow the migraine up, Tiffney."

The tall, painfully thin (except in selected areas) blonde girl, who I had figured out was named Tiffney, advanced on him like a lion advances on pretty much anything. She raised her well-manicured nails and really, truly appeared to be preparing to scratch his eyes out. "You migraine!" she shouted. "What the migraine do you migraine are, like the greatest thing that ever migraine to women? Let me tell you something, migraine-head. I wouldn't migraine you if you begged me. Not if you migraine *begged* me."

I saw Linda Jane mouth the word *wow*.

The less-tall, less-blonde girl—whose name I knew was Helen, but who preferred to be called "H-Bomb"—shuffled over until she was in camera range. Then, she walked with purpose at the taller, blonder girl. "What are you migraine screaming about?" she wanted to know. "I was trying to get some migraine sleep so I can go out tonight!" I noted that she hadn't been anywhere near the backyard, where her "bedroom" was located, and in all likelihood couldn't have found it without a Sherpa guide, but I didn't say anything.

Tiffney turned on her furiously. "Why do you migraine need to go migraine out?" she demanded. "You can just migraine this migraine right here, like you did last night!"

And that's when I became aware of the presence at my right side. A little bit over, and a little bit down. The presence that had just walked through my front door, much as she did every day around this time.

Melissa.

"You migraine migraine!" H-Bomb screamed back, and

that's when I cleared my throat as loudly as I could, and then yelled, "Excuse me! Cut! Print it!" It was the only movie talk I knew.

"What? Who was that?" The director turned around so quickly his baseball cap ended up pointed to the side, like Charlie Brown.

"Mom," Melissa whispered, "what are you *doing*?"

"I'm handling it, Ed," Trent said, already on his way down the stairs. He walked to me, with every eye in the room watching. "Alison, do we have a problem?" he asked.

"I don't know if you do, but I certainly have one, Trent. I'm not going to allow that kind of language in front of my ten-year-old daughter."

"I've heard those words before," Melissa muttered. Oh yeah? That was something we'd have to discuss privately, later.

"You can't expect our cast to be watching their every word whenever Melinda is around," Trent said. His smile never dimmed, but his eyes were about ten degrees colder than when he'd been trying to get me to sign a contract.

"It's Melissa, and yes, I can."

"This is a reality show," he said. "It's not scripted. I can't tell them what to say."

"Oh, come on. This show is as real as *Scooby-Doo*. And you certainly can tell your 'cast' what to say when you're creating an unhealthy environment for a fourth-grader." My voice was getting a little bit louder. Dolores was staring at me, and I couldn't tell whether her expression was one of admiration for my principles or aggravation over my holding up shooting.

"You can't tell me you expected everyone in the cast of *Down the Shore* to speak PG language," Trent tried again. "Haven't you ever seen the show before?"

"No."

He looked positively astonished. Surely *everyone* knew

what a big deal he and his show were—no doubt critics all over the country had lauded the "raw, unvarnished" quality I'm sure they thought the show must have. Critics like anything they don't understand.

"You're embarrassing me," Melissa sing-songed quietly. "What do you think he's going to do?"

"Wait for it," I hissed at her.

"All right," Trent breathed, deflated. "What is it you want?"

"I don't care what they do when my daughter isn't in the room. After her bedtime, if your little team of degenerates wants to behave like this is nineteen seventy-nine and they're at Studio 54, they can enjoy themselves, provided they do it out of sight of my other guests. But when Melissa is awake and in the room, they're going to watch their language, their behavior and their choice of underwear. Or you can go find another house. Are we clear?"

Trent chewed his lower lip for a moment, then nodded. "We're clear."

"We *are*?" H-Bomb, having scrambled up behind Trent, looked stunned. "You mean I can't say . . ."

"Watch it," I told her, and nodded toward Melissa.

"No, you can't," Trent assured her. "Don't worry. We'll put it back in when we loop the episode."

"But it always gets bleeped," she protested.

"So you'll say it, then we'll bleep it."

"Bleep that," H-Bomb said, then sneered in Melissa's general direction and walked back to the group in front of the camera.

Trent fixed me in his gaze. "Happy now?" he said with only a slight edge in his voice.

"Satisfied," I countered. You never know; there could be other unexpected snags along the way. No sense in limiting my options.

"Okay. Now, here's what *I* want." Trent took my arm and maneuvered me out the front door, away from the crew, the guests and Melissa. "I want you to understand that we're paying a lot of money to use this house, and we expect a certain amount of value for what we're spending."

"What does *value* mean?" I asked.

Trent pointed at me, as a teacher does a student who asks an especially appropriate question. "For our purposes, *value* will mean that we have access to every part of the house, even the other guests' rooms if we need them, assuming the guest signs a release form. We will, of course, stay away from your daughter's room at all times."

"You sure will," I interjected.

He kept going, but nodded. "It also means that for the next three weeks, you will not interrupt shooting when cameras are rolling. If you have an issue, you can bring it directly to me *after* we get what we need on film. Is that clear?"

"I understand it," I told him.

"Close enough. It also means that besides having the cast living here, the crew will be allowed in at any hour that we choose, because this show is all about things happening unexpectedly."

The poor man—I think he actually believed that. "Uh-huh," I said.

"And if we think something interesting is going on here at the house—like, for example, a séance—we'll have unfettered access. Agreed?"

"You want to film the séance? That's just a little activity for the guests. I mean, I don't want a national TV audience to think I run a spook house."

"That's only a problem if real ghosts show up," Trent said. "I told you last night, one of the reasons we chose this house was that people were saying it was haunted. We think that adds drama."

He had no idea. "Okay," I said. "But the séance won't be effective with bright lights flooding the room. You're going to have to shoot with natural light."

Trent nodded agreement. "Absolutely. I'll tell Ed. I think it'll look better, anyway. I'm glad we had this talk, Alison." He walked back into the house to relay our conversation to the director and to reassemble his cast for more "spontaneous" filming.

And I sat down on my front step and wondered what I'd gotten myself into.

Seven

"This is ridiculous."

My "favorite" guest, the indomitable (and I could think of a few other words) Bernice Antwerp, was enjoying herself in her favorite fashion—she was complaining.

I'd been walking through the front room, about to begin our séance, when Bernice, whom I'd been trying to avoid, had buttonholed me to run down a list of all the things that had been insufficient since she'd arrived. I'll give you the summary:

Everything.

Now she was on a tear about the evening's entertainment, which she considered a waste of her time. I bit back the temptation to suggest she lock herself away in her room like Mr. and Mrs. Jones.

"A bunch of grown people standing around pretending they're in contact with ghosts. It's undignified," Bernice went on. I'd stopped listening sometime around when she'd explained that I was a bad hostess because the toilet paper in the bathrooms was rolled with the edge on the back, not

the front, so her dissatisfaction with the séance was hardly
cutting me to the quick, especially since she'd claimed to
be one of the guests most interested in seeing ghosts to
begin with.

"I'm sorry you feel that way," I answered. "The tour was
quite clearly advertised as a trip to a haunted guesthouse,
and you have seen the way the ghosts make themselves
known every day."

She sniffed. "Simple tricks. I don't for a moment believe
there are spirits in this house."

"Oh, but there *are*!" Dolores Santiago, the most ghost-
obsessed guest, appeared behind Bernice like Paul or
Maxie might, only with a less transparent body. "I've gotten readings on my instruments that absolutely confirm the
presence of two entities in this house." She reached into her
purse. "I think I have the readouts here. . . ."

"Honestly!" Bernice exploded, and walked away. But I
noticed she walked toward the den, where the séance was
to be held.

"Thanks for the help, Dolores," I said.

She looked up, confused. "What help?"

"Never mind. I appreciate it, anyway."

I looked toward the front door, because even while
people were gathering in the den (and the *Down the Shore*
crew was hooking up its power to a truck parked in my
driveway), Arlice Crosby was arriving there, looking thor-
oughly enthralled with the proceedings.

Dolores's eyes widened when she saw Arlice. "What is
she doing here?" she asked.

"I invited Mrs. Crosby earlier today," I said. "Do you
know her?"

"Not really. I've seen her around town. I think. Is she
going to stay for the séance?"

"That's why she's here," I answered.

Dolores shook her head. "Too many people," she said.
"Too many distractions." And she shuffled away toward

the staircase, which was just as well—I was hurrying to greet Arlice.

"I hope I'm not late," she said. "I'd hate to have missed it." I noticed her car parked at the curb—a Prius.

"We would have waited for you," I said. "We're honored to have you here with us."

Arlice waved a hand. "Oh, go on with ya, now," she said. "Let's see some spooks." I nodded, and turned toward the den. "Oh, Alison, wait," Arlice said, seeming to remember something.

She reached into her purse and pulled out a small royal blue box covered in velvet. "It's rude to come to a friend's house empty-handed," she said. She handed me the box, and I opened it.

Inside was a lovely silver amulet, in the shape of a slightly asymmetrical triangle with lettering in an unfamiliar alphabet on one side, on a chain. It took my breath away.

"It's lovely," I said to Arlice, "but I can't possibly accept it."

"Don't be silly. I'd be horribly offended if you turned it down. I would have brought a proper gift, you know, but the invitation only came this afternoon." She grinned at me.

"This is much more than a proper gift," I said. "Are you sure . . . ?"

"It's been in my family for generations," Arlice answered. "I don't have any children, and I never wear it. Time for it to start some new traditions, no? Is that little girl I saw over there your daughter?"

I nodded. "Melissa," I said. "She's ten."

"You can pass the amulet on to her, then." Arlice knew she had me with that.

There just wasn't a way for me to tactfully reject what must have been a very expensive gift, so I let Arlice clasp it behind my neck, thanked her more than profusely, and headed upstairs to change for what I was already thinking of as "The Show."

* * *

"May I request absolute silence. The spirits will not approach if they are distracted or frightened by noise." I stood on a platform—okay, a stepstool left from when Melissa was four years old—at one end of my den, the largest room in the house. I was wearing an old terry cloth bathrobe I'd stolen from a hotel almost thirteen years ago on my brief honeymoon (The Swine had to be back in New York after the weekend to attend a meeting on how to get elderly people to give you their Social Security money), which was the closest thing I had to a flowing gown. I had my arms raised in what I thought was the proper pose for an active medium (although I was more of a small).

The *spirits* of the house—having been given a report on Arlice that I was told had been passed on to Scott McFarlane—were hovering around the ceiling, taking in the crowd with what looked like amusement on Paul and annoyance on Maxie.

I was grateful for the space in the room, because it was packed to the rafters. Besides Arlice and the Senior Plus tour guests (minus the Joneses, who had not emerged from their room but who must have been still breathing, based on the reportage of Linda Jane, who was in the room next to them—"believe me, I can hear them through the walls— they're alive, okay"), the cast of *Down the Shore* was present, watching and feigning excited fascination, since the cameras were rolling. In fact, four cameras, but no lights, were being employed, working with the abundant candle-light in the room and nothing else. Trent hadn't been happy that I wasn't using the chandelier, but I argued that it would spoil the mood, and he had relented.

Arlice had a place of honor directly to my right. She'd seemed quite pleased with the activity, and heartily amused at the appearance of the *Down the Shore* cast, in their best pierced and tattooed finery.

Also in the room, watching me make a spectacle of myself, were four cameramen, Ed the director, Trent the producer (sorry, *executive* producer), two sound men, a guy with headphones whose job was a mystery to me, Melissa, Mom and, at the extreme far side of the room, Jeannie and her husband, Tony, who were barely disguising their amusement.

And Paul and Maxie.

"Frightened by noise?" Maxie, hovering near the ceiling to take in the crowd with no obstructions, glowered at me. "What do you want them to think we are, wimpy ghosts?"

I didn't answer her, of course. Instead, I went on with my ethereal rant. "I am calling out to the spirits inhabiting this house. We have people here who have questions for you, spirits. There is no reason to be afraid." I stared directly at Maxie while saying that. "We all welcome you here. We ask you to share your wisdom and your suffering."

"Suffering?" Paul asked. "What suffering?" He was actually standing near the window, staring out into the backyard. He'd said that Scott McFarlane might come to the house tonight to reassure himself that Arlice was alive, but so far Scott hadn't arrived. I didn't know what Paul was afraid could have happened to Scott, but he appeared concerned.

"I am beginning to sense the presence of spirits," I reported to the gathering, stuffed as they were into a room whose temperature appeared to be going up by the minute. Warren and Jim, ubiquitous beer bottles in hand, stood at the wall to my left, with satisfied, dazed grins on their faces.

Bernice, dissatisfied (of course) with the lack of adequate seating in the room (despite being given a prime spot on the sofa), was looking annoyed and had complained before I'd begun about her inability to "see anything" from the lower vantage point of the sofa. When I'd informed her that I thought there would be little to see and much to hear, she'd sniffed with discontentment, folded her arms and made a face daring me to produce ghosts.

"Yes," I continued. "There are definitely—two!—spirits in the room right now! Can you speak to us, spirits? Can you tell us who you were?"

"Abbott and Costello," Maxie said. Melissa, who thinks Maxie is a riot, giggled.

I ignored her and looked at the crowd. "They say their names are Paul and . . . Hortense."

"Hortense!" Maxie spat out. "I don't have to stay here for this!"

I turned to her. "Yes, Hortense. What is that you're saying? You're thrilled to be here? Well, we have a *whole crowd of people* who are just as happy to hear from you. So glad you didn't *disappoint* them."

"How do we know they're really here?" Bernice demanded. "You could say you hear anything. Why should we believe you?" H-Bomb nodded her head in agreement; in her capacity to be underwhelmed, she was practically a Bernice-in-training.

Luckily, I had anticipated that question, because it was actually one I would have asked a charlatan as obvious as myself. "Ask for a sign, something to be manipulated in this room, and it will be done," I assured her.

"I've seen stuff flying around all week," Bernice countered sourly. "Let's see these ghosts of yours do something that you couldn't have arranged ahead of time. Let's see them—"

She didn't have time to finish the sentence, as Maxie reached down and took Bernice's eyeglasses off her face, then started to rise toward the ceiling with them. Bernice stopped in midsentence and gasped. "Stop that!" she yelled. "Those glasses cost me four hundred dollars!"

One of the camera operators—a woman, I was pleased

to see—had been assigned to follow any "freaky" ghostly happenings (the other three—all men—were focused lovingly on the *Down the Shore* cast).

But the demonstration had certainly gotten the desired effect: All the guests were openmouthed as Maxie returned Bernice's harlequin glasses, and they broke into a round of applause when it became obvious that Bernice herself was unable to think of a complaint to voice for the occasion.

Dolores, the most studious of the guests, watched the most carefully, placing a wand approximately the size of a surge suppressor for electronics (which I secretly believed it had once been), painted black with red and green lights running up and down one side, on the small end table next to her. It was being used to "measure the vibrations of the paranormal presences," she had explained. The lights were heavily into the red category right now, so maybe it was really measuring something. Like the strength of the batteries Dolores had placed inside it. She wedged herself in between me and Arlice, determined not to miss any vibrations or further evidence of our nonbreathing visitors.

"What's that?" Tiffney asked, pointing at Dolores's thingamajig.

Before Dolores could launch into the technical specifications of the thing, I answered, "A Ghostometer. You can't have a séance without one."

Dolores clucked her tongue. "Honestly," she said, rolling her eyes.

"Are there any others who doubt?" I asked. "Do we have any requests for further demonstrations of our guests' reality?"

All the way in the back of the room, I could see Jeannie mouth, "Wow." But my mother did not appear pleased. Normally, she believes that everything I do is absolutely wonderful (and trust me, that's not as nice as you might think), but her mouth was clenched in disapproval and her eyes narrowed. She was protective of the ghosts, and clearly believed I was exploiting them. I decided to get on with it.

"Not seeing any further objections," I said, since my mind was apparently racing back to my days as recording secretary of the Ecology Club at Harbor Haven High School, "do we have any questions for our friends from the other side?"

The older guests in the house felt the need to raise their hands and wait to be recognized, but H-Bomb didn't have that problem. "What's it like being dead?" she yelled out.

Paul began to respond, "It's an odd sensation, a little flat. . . ."

But Maxie, grinning, shouted over him, "It sucks!" I passed that information along to the group, who laughed. Except Dolores and, of course, Bernice.

"Is there sex after death?" shouted the larger, more pumped-up guy from the cast, whose name was apparently Rock Starr.

"We don't know," said Paul, getting into the spirit (please pardon the expression) of the proceedings. "We don't like each other that much."

Again, chuckles when I relayed the responses. But I wasn't going to let my core audience get overrun by these impetuous kids. I nodded at Dolores. What the hell; she'd been waiting her whole life for this.

"Yes!" she shouted. "What is the proper bandwidth for . . ."

She never got the chance to answer, because a shout from just beside her stopped everyone in the room. It wasn't a squeal from one of the girls on *Down the Shore*, and it wasn't a shout of terror from someone rattled by the ghosts.

It was a scream of pain. And even before it had stopped echoing through the room, Arlice Crosby fell facedown to the floor, bouncing off a cameraman's leg on the way down.

I jumped off the stepstool and tried to turn her over, but

even before I could, Linda Jane was up and trying to revive her. But based on what I'd seen, I had no doubt in my mind that Arlice was dead.

And floating directly behind her, at just about an average man's height, was my red cloth napkin, folded into the shape of a bandana.

Eight

"So, let's see if I've got this right." Detective Anita Mc-Elone wasn't happy about being in my house—she never was. But now someone had died here without explanation, and she had insisted that no one leave the room. (The Joneses were being questioned in their room, an interrogation I probably could have sold tickets to and made enough for the season.) "You were holding a séance, and Mrs. Crosby just keeled over and died?"

"That's exactly what happened," said Trent Avalon. "She was standing just about . . ."

McElone cut him off. "I was asking Ms. Kerby. Believe me, I'll get to you as soon as I can."

The EMS technicians had taken Arlice's body after getting the okay from McElone. There had been no preliminary word on cause of death, of course, but nobody could see a wound on her anywhere, and there was no blood on the floor or on Arlice. She had not seemed frightened, according to everyone who had been standing near her, but I guess a heart attack can be instantaneous and unexpected.

McElone was being thorough, in her own way, which was predictably a somewhat confrontational way.

"What did *you* see?" she asked me.

"I wasn't looking at her when it happened," I said truthfully. "But I heard her scream, or yelp, or something, and the next thing I knew she was on the floor. By the time I got to her, Linda Jane Smith had already said she had no pulse. She tried doing CPR for a while, but Arlice didn't respond." I had taken a class in CPR before I applied for my innkeeper's license, but Linda Jane was a medic and an RN, and she'd done all she could until the ambulance arrived ten minutes later.

A medic in the house, and there wasn't a thing we could do for Arlice Crosby. It had already occurred to me that if I hadn't invited her into a dark, crowded, hot room, she might've been alive and enjoying a calm evening sitting on her front porch with the neighbor's cat, looking at all the larger houses owned by people without as much money as she had.

"Did anybody near her make any sudden moves before she fell?" McElone asked.

I shook my head. "Not that I saw. I was looking for the next question."

"Arlice," McElone echoed. "Funny how tight you got with her after asking me who she was just this morning."

"We bonded," I said. "She insisted I call her Arlice."

"Interesting," McElone said. "Did *Arlice* say anything to you during the . . . event?"

"She didn't get a chance to ask the ghosts a question, if that's what you mean," I answered.

McElone pursed her lips. "Uh-huh. Ghosts. I'm going to go talk to some living people now, okay?"

"Just trying to help," I said.

"Yeah. And by the way?"

"Yes?" I asked.

"Nice bathrobe." Then McElone turned her attention

back to the crowd. So I wandered through the room, being barraged by everyone I passed.

"What happened?"

"Is she dead?"

"When can we go back to the game room?" Attaboy, Warren.

I did what I could to reassure everyone that this was a routine inquiry by the police after an unexplained death, but the fact was, it didn't feel like one. Maybe it's because I've been involved in such things with McElone before, but her demeanor was definitely more suspicious than if she'd thought it was a simple heart attack. Maybe losing one of the wealthiest citizens in town and a patron of the arts for two counties in any direction had something to do with the detective's grumpy attitude.

By the time I got to the back of the room, where Mom and Melissa were talking to Jeannie and Tony, I must have looked like I'd been through a prize fight with Mike Tyson.

"Why are the police still here?" Mom wanted to know after clucking over me. "Your friend the detective is questioning everyone in the room."

"She's not my friend, and I don't know," I answered. "McElone is acting like something criminal happened here, and I don't like the way she's looking at me. Did any of you see anything?"

"I couldn't see over everybody's backs," Melissa said. "I was watching Maxie, because she was up near the ceiling."

"Who's Maxie?" Jeannie asked. Then she remembered, nodded, and condescendingly told Melissa, "Of course you did, honey."

Tony gave me a significant look. He believes it's easier to indulge Jeannie's fantasy than to try to convince her otherwise. I was tired and upset and shook my head while I exhaled.

"I feel terrible. I invite Arlice here, and then this happens." When you're feeling sorry for yourself, the best thing is to sound pathetic when talking to your mother. She'll always do what she can to make you feel better.

"Yes, I guess it could have been the closeness of the room that did it," Mom said. "Or the excitement of the moment. You know, you were really putting on a show."

Thanks, Mom.

"I don't think it was anything like that," Tony said. "I was looking at Arlice just before it happened. I did some contracting work for her a few years ago, and I was trying to catch her eye, say hello, you know. But she was enthralled. She looked very happy. And then something happened, her face changed, she started to turn behind her, and then she dropped."

"What do you mean, something happened?" I asked.

"I don't know. One second she was smiling, then she grimaced, like something hurt."

"Like in her chest?" Melissa asked. Her health class, which the schools insist upon for one quarter of the year instead of letting kids run around in gym, had recently been tackling the issue of heart disease, because the fourth-graders didn't have enough to be afraid of yet.

"No," Tony said. "Something seemed to be hurting her, but she didn't put her hand up to her chest. She looked behind her."

"Go tell that to McElone or one of the cops," I instructed him. "Right now." The last thing I needed was for the detective to think I was letting someone hold back significant information.

"She'll get to me," Tony protested.

"NOW!"

Convinced, he walked over toward McElone.

The night progressed as McElone and two uniformed officers debriefed every person in the room. Slowly but surely, it started to empty out. She made a point of telling Trent that she wanted to see every frame his crew had shot, and after he protested that you didn't measure digital video in frames, he agreed to turn over the footage. But he insisted that the police make copies and return it to *Down the Shore* before any news organization could get its hands on what he called his "exclusive intellectual property."

A woman's death was his intellectual property? The mind reeled.

After a while, the only ones left in the room were Melissa, Mom, Jeannie (protesting at how cops had held "an expectant mother in a crowded room for hours" despite her sitting on a very comfortable armchair), Tony and me.

And three ghosts, waiting for the cops to leave so we could talk and Jeannie could pretend they weren't there.

By one o'clock in the morning, Melissa was asleep with her head on my lap (McElone had said she'd question her the next morning, but Liss wouldn't go to bed), I was sitting on the area rug next to Jeannie's chair, Mom was in another armchair facing it and Tony was standing. The ghosts were hovering overhead when McElone dismissed the two uniformed cops and walked over to our sorry crew.

I stood up, careful not to disturb Melissa, who slept right through. McElone and I are often at odds, although I think she's a good cop and she thinks I'm . . . insane, and I didn't want to give her the height advantage in my own den. "What have you found out, Detective?" I asked.

"You don't seriously think I'd tell you?" she answered.

"No, but it was worth a shot."

"Until we get a preliminary report from the medical examiner, I'm assuming this was a death due to natural causes. That means you're free to continue having guests here and operating as a public convenience." McElone said *public convenience* like she meant my place was a large restroom.

It brought out my natural Jersey antagonism. "That's sweet of you," I said in a voice dripping sarcasm.

"It's also standard operating procedure. But if we find that there was any foul play involved, things might change quickly. Are any of your guests scheduled to leave tomorrow?"

"No. They'll all be here until Wednesday."

"All right. If anything that affects you comes up, I'll let you know," McElone said. "In the meantime, if you think of anything you saw or heard, or if one of your guests or . . . the television people . . . remembers anything, call me. You have my number?"

"Memorized. I'm thinking of putting you on speed dial."

"Take a business card anyway," she said, giving me one, and left, nodding toward Mom. McElone clearly believed in respecting her elders, if not their daughters.

As soon as the door closed behind her, I looked up at Tony. "Get this pregnant woman out of here," I told him. "She needs her rest."

Tony looked like he wanted to say something else, but he nodded. "Come on, Jeannie," he said. "Alison says you need your rest."

"She couldn't have said that two hours ago?"

They headed for the door, and Tony made the "call me" sign with his hand as they left. And the second they were gone, I pointed my gaze upward, where Paul, Maxie and (presumably) Scott were hovering, looking like they were about to explode.

"Yes," Paul told Scott. "They're gone. Alison can talk now." He looked down at me and scowled. "I'd been hoping to give Scott *good* news tonight," he said.

"Well, he got good news," I answered. "He didn't kill Arlice." Then I thought about seeing the red bandana behind her when she fell. "Did you?"

"Of course I didn't!" the blind ghost shouted. "Why would I do such a thing? *How* would I do such a thing?"

"The old lady just keeled over," Maxie said, as if we hadn't all been thinking about what had happened for hours. "I guess it was just her time."

"Just what time?" I asked. "Was it just *your* time?"

Maxie made a rude noise with her lips and vanished.

"You know, sometimes you're too hard on Maxie," Paul told me.

"Me? Arlice Crosby wasn't just some old lady; she was a real living person until not too long ago. Maxie was the one being insensitive."

Nobody said anything for a long moment. Melissa snored a little.

"I guess her heart just gave out," Mom said to no one in particular.

"That's not what Tony said," I reminded her. "He thought she was taken by surprise somehow. It doesn't make sense."

"There wasn't any blood. There wasn't any wound. She wasn't killed," Paul said, and then shook his head. "There's something very wrong with this."

"I'm tired," I told them. "I'm going to wake up Melissa so she can go up to sleep, and I'm going up, too. If you think of anything that explains what happened tonight, feel free to let me know in the morning."

There were no further comments from the assembled group. Mom got up as I walked to where Melissa lay sleeping, and we admired my daughter together for a moment.

"She's so dear," Mom said. Grandmothers talk like that.

"I hate to disturb her," I answered. "Do you think I can just leave her there on the floor until it's time to get up for school?" Friday, now today, was still a school day, and Melissa didn't like to miss for any reason, even if she was tired.

"I don't know," Mom said. "Some of your guests will probably be up before Melissa, and you don't want them to wake her up early."

I nodded; she was right. I bent down to pick up my daughter and tried to move both slowly and smoothly as I put my arms under her and scooped her up. Mom saw I had her safely in my arms and nodded a good-bye. She walked out the front door as I turned toward the stairway up to the bedrooms, noting that ten-year-olds are not as light as five-year-olds.

But children aren't quite as pliable as any of us would prefer, so Melissa woke up just a little as I was carrying her up the stairs. "Where's the detective?" she asked hoarsely.

"She left, Liss. It's very late at night." I was trying to step as lightly as I could on each stair, especially the ones I'd had to repair when I was renovating the house last fall. "Go to sleep. You can brush your teeth in the morning." So I'm a bad mother, and I promote tooth decay; go ahead, bring me up on charges.

"Did you tell her about the . . ." I couldn't hear what Melissa was mumbling, but I decided it was best not to rouse her just to finish a sentence.

"Shh . . ."

She shook her head a little as we reached the top of the stairs, and I maneuvered her toward her bedroom. She was getting so big. Why can't they stay tiny forever?

"Did you tell her about the lady?"

"What lady, honey?"

"The lady who bumped into Mrs. Crosby just before she fell over. Did you tell the detective about that?"

I opened the door to Melissa's bedroom and lay her down on her bed. "What lady bumped into Mrs. Crosby?" I asked quietly. Maybe I hadn't heard her right.

"The lady. She walked behind Mrs. Crosby just before she fell, and bumped into her in the back. The lady with one leg."

Linda Jane Smith.

Nine

Melissa got up late for school the next morning, with just barely enough time to throw on clothes and be at the front door when her BFF Wendy's mother picked her up. After everyone had gotten up and started the day and Melissa was safely at school, I called McElone. If she wanted to question my daughter, the detective would have to wait until after three o'clock.

But I'll admit that while I was straightening up before most of the guests went out for breakfast, I was keeping an especially close eye on Linda Jane Smith.

She wasn't doing anything special, just getting herself together to go out to the café for a muffin and coffee or something, but her every move seemed suspicious to me. Even putting on lipstick (just to go to the Harbor Haven Café?) looked odd.

And Linda Jane seemed to notice me noticing her. "Is something wrong, Alison?" she asked as she was adjusting the shoe on her artificial limb. "I didn't freak you out when I told you about the leg yesterday, did I?"

"Oh no," I replied, because in fact, I was not upset by her story so much as awed by it. "You didn't freak me out. I guess I'm still unsettled because of what happened *last night*."

"Yes, an awful thing. That poor woman. I guess when it's your time, there's nothing you can do about it." Linda Jane shook her head, *tsk-tsk*ed a couple of times, and then headed out for a nice warm breakfast.

My newfound suspicions of Linda Jane were already working on my head—how could she be so casual after she might have done something nefarious toward the lovely Arlice Crosby last night? I wondered.

And then the good little angel on my shoulder asked, *Would you be this sure Linda Jane had something to do with Arlice's death if it hadn't been Melissa who'd seen something?* Little angels can be great big pains when they do stuff like that.

I didn't ponder that any longer, because ten o'clock was already on the way, and I wanted to make sure Paul and Maxie hadn't forgotten about their performance in the wake of the eventful night we'd had and the early morning that followed it.

To be honest, I also wanted to ask if they'd heard at all from the spirit of Arlice Crosby. There was so much she could clear up if she was around, and I'd certainly feel better about having invited her if I knew that, after dying, she was still all right.

Jim and Warren were in the library, for once not drinking beer. They were, in fact, having coffee and looking subdued. For them.

"Rough night," Warren said when I poked my head in. "You must feel awful."

"I do," I admitted. "But there wasn't anything I could have done about it."

"Well, you could have stopped that kid from bopping her from behind," Jim said. "You were the closest one, I guess."

"*What* kid?" I, well, demanded. "What are you talking about?"

"You didn't see it?" Jim asked. "That bikini bombshell from the TV show, Tiffney. The one with the . . ." He gestured with his hands in front of his chest.

"Arthritis?" I suggested.

"Exactly. She slithered up behind the poor lady while you were calling ghosts around, and did . . . *something* when she was there that made the lady turn around. Next thing I knew, the lady was on the floor, and then Linda Jane was trying to revive her."

I sat down, a little overwhelmed. "Wait a second. You're telling me that Tiffney did something to Arlice before she collapsed?"

Jim looked at Warren. "I'm speaking English, right?"
Warren nodded.

"Yup," Jim said. "That's what I'm saying."

"So did you tell the police about that?"
They looked at each other.

"They didn't actually *ask*," Warren mumbled.

"But you just mentioned it to me," I pointed out.

"You own the place. You need to know. We don't have to talk to the cops, do we?"

There was no answer to that other than to point out that McElone could use that information as well, but the two men seemed so uncomfortable with the idea of the police that I didn't press the issue. I had every intention of ratting them out to the cops the first chance I got, however, and foresaw a future for them that included yet more questioning from the local detective.

Now, I *really* had to find Paul and Maxie. Well, Paul.

I got up and excused myself and headed upstairs. The ghosts were most often to be found on the second floor this time of day, unless Maxie was in what she now referred to exclusively as her room, aka the attic, which I was still planning on converting into a usable space. She could deal with her adolescent temper tantrums once there was wallboard and a solid floor up there. Then, I was sure, she'd give in to the impulse to design the decorations for the suite, and I'd be gracious enough to allow her to consult on the matter. I could be generous when necessary. Unless, of course, she decided to thwart me at every turn and paint things bizarre colors or "lose" crucial tools.

Oh, it had happened before.

Truth be told, Maxie's decorating ideas could be outré, but they were usually better than mine.

Before the guests had taken up residence, I could scream for Paul at the top of my lungs, and he would appear, looking sheepish, as if he should have known I wanted him before I called for him. Now, however, I had to be more circumspect in my search, because I needed to have a private conversation with Paul, not one that every guest in the house could hear. I walked up to the second floor, checked to make sure no one was in the hallway and said in a conversational tone, "Paul."

No answer. I walked down the hall, passing two guest rooms that both had their doors closed (the Joneses, and Jim and Warren's). When I got to the corner, I said Paul's name again, and again was not rewarded with a response.

That was a little odd. So I made a right turn and continued on past Melissa's bedroom and my own (the room for Bernice and the one ostensibly for the *Down the Shore* personalities were on the first floor, as far from each other as possible). Twice more, I said "Paul" as if in conversation, like I was mentioning a friend's name to someone else. Once, I even pretended to laugh, in case anyone had overheard and thought I was talking to someone else.

I got to the emergency fire exit at the end of the hallway (municipal regulations, you know) and turned back. I frowned. It wasn't that anything could actually *happen* to the ghosts, but it was unusual that I couldn't find them when necessary. I looked down the empty hallway again.

"Paul."

"Yes?" he asked from behind me. I screamed so loudly that a few moments later I actually saw the Joneses' door open, but no one looked out. Then the door closed, just as abruptly.

I turned to Paul. "Don't *do* that!" I hissed at him.

"Do what?"

"Show up unexpectedly like that." It was a losing argument, and I knew it, but it had to be played out.

"You called me. Wouldn't you expect me to answer?" See what I mean?

"Whatever. Listen, have you heard anything from Arlice Crosby yet?"

He gave me an odd look. "Not even a postcard. Why?"

"I'm not sure that what happened last night was a heart attack. And I thought if she had shown up—you know, like you—maybe you could contact her on the Ghosternet."

Paul's face had gotten serious when I'd mentioned my suspicions, and now he nodded. "I'll give it a try later. But I'm pretty sure it took some time for Maxie and me to become like we are. A few days, at least, by my judgment."

"Okay. Listen. I have a detective question for you."

Paul brightened visibly; he loved to be consulted on investigative business. "How can I help?" he asked as earnestly as possible.

I quickly explained the stories I'd gotten from Melissa and Jim about Arlice's sudden death. Paul listened well; he put his fingers together in a pyramid and watched my face as I spoke. He nodded a few times but never betrayed any surprise, even when I mentioned the dueling observations and how neither of them explained Arlice's death, but that both pointed to something other than a naturally induced heart attack.

When I was finished with my epic tale, I waited for Paul to digest the information. He didn't say anything, so I finally asked, "What do you think I should do?"

"That's simple enough," Paul answered. "You tell Detective McElone what you just told me. Then she investigates. Your responsibility in this affair is completed; you have no client to serve."

"But it happened in my house, under my roof, to a guest I invited," I argued. Later, I'd have time to note that it was usually Paul trying to talk *me* into investigating something, and not the other way around. But at the moment, I was simply puzzled and irritated that Paul wasn't picking up on my sense of outrage.

He started to answer, "There's no reason for you . . ."

Suddenly the door we were standing in front of opened, and Dolores Santiago walked out. She'd let her hair down, and it fell almost to her waist, gray and thick. And she was wearing what I could only describe as a gown, but not one for a formal affair. She looked, for all intents and purposes, like she'd been summoned to the graveyard by her lover, Count Dracula.

"Are you talking to one of the spirits?" she intoned.

What the hell. "Yes, Dolores. I am. But he's gone now," I lied. "May I help you with something?"

"You were talking about Arlice Crosby's death last night, weren't you?" she asked, as if I hadn't spoken.

"Yes. It's such an awful thing."

Dolores nodded. "Yes. A terrible loss. And so unnecessary."

"I agree. It was . . . what?"

"Unnecessary. She didn't have to be here last night at all, and then the whole thing probably could have been avoided, I would say."

"What whole thing? Are you saying Mrs. Crosby wouldn't have had a heart attack if she hadn't come here last night?" The faraway look in Dolores's eyes was having an effect on me—it was making me regret having eaten breakfast.

"Arlice didn't have a heart attack," Dolores said. "She was murdered by a spirit wearing a red bandana."

Ten

Dolores's reasoning, of course, bordered on the incomprehensible. But from the babble, I managed to glean the following: Dolores had been monitoring a "level of spectral activity" in the room with the gizmo she'd had in her hand, and it showed the presence of two spirits (because that's how many I'd told the crowd were there). I'm guessing she picked up this particular box of flashing lights at the dollar store, because it didn't seem to serve any function other than to fuel Dolores's fantasies.

Okay, so there really *were* ghosts in the room, but call me a cynic, I was still convinced that thing would have found ghosts in any room on the planet.

But there was a key difference in Dolores's rant, and it was disquieting: Unlike Tony, or Melissa, or Jim, she did not mention anyone bumping or annoying Arlice to make her spin around just before she'd died. But Dolores alone, in a room crowded with people, had looked above the considerable commotion and noticed Scott's red bandana floating in midair, and she assumed that the spirit had "decided to take Arlice home." Of course, it was equally possible that the guests and the TV crew, having grown accustomed to seeing objects fly around here, just hadn't considered the hovering bandana all that unusual.

Paul leaned back, not exactly against the wall, but with a good vantage point. He liked to get a good look at "witnesses giving testimony," as he described it. He believed in the power of the vibe—you could read a transcript of the person's words and not really have the same experience as listening and watching when she spoke.

He did not look pleased.

"Ask her if she saw a weapon," he suggested, and I passed the question along without mentioning it was from someone else hovering in the room.

"Oh, the spirits don't use weapons," Dolores answered with a tone that indicated I might as well have dropped out of school in the third grade. "I'm sure one icy finger placed on her shoulder the right way would do the trick."

Paul rolled his eyes and made a face. "Icy finger," he said. I know for a fact that Paul's touch is more like a warm breeze. But we're just good friends.

"So you didn't see a weapon," I said, in an effort to be completely clear.

"Didn't you hear what I just said?" she asked.

"Just wanted to make sure. You say you saw a red bandana floating in the air?" I said. "Couldn't it have just been blown there?"

"In that room? The air was as thick as cheese," Dolores said. *As thick as cheese?* "Besides, things blown by the wind don't just hover still in the air."

"So you didn't see it move before Arlice died. Like it was stabbing . . . *tapping* an icy finger on her shoulder?"

"No, I can't say I saw it, but it stands to reason. I mean, a spirit that close to the woman at the moment she passed? That can't be a coincidence."

"Well, thank you for the information, Dolores. I assume you told this to Detective McElone last night?" I walked toward the staircase, hoping Paul would follow so we could discuss this further, but when I looked up, he truly had vanished. The coward.

"I tried to, but the detective didn't seem at all interested in the ways of the spirit world." Dolores pouted.

I was glad to hear it. But I would need to talk to the detective very soon, if only so she couldn't later accuse me of withholding information in . . . a homicide?

I called McElone's office, but she wasn't in, so I left a message that I assumed would not be returned anytime soon. McElone seemed, for reasons I couldn't entirely explain, to consider me a nuisance. Me. Imagine.

After the morning performance (today's featured the downstairs lights going on and off, and spooky noises courtesy of an accordion I'd found in the basement), most of the guests headed toward town, and the Bikini Brigade headed for the beach. It was only sixty-two degrees, but those who seek fame and fortune must suffer a few goose bumps along the way, I guess.

Before I'd gotten a chance to start straightening up, though, my cell phone rang, and the caller ID showed Phyllis Coates's number at the *Chronicle*.

I should have seen that coming.

"Arlice Crosby died in your house last night, and you didn't even call me?" she hollered when I picked up. "Didn't I teach you *anything* about reporting?"

"As a matter of fact, no, you didn't. You taught me about throwing the paper onto the porch and not into the bushes."

"Well, I meant to." Phyllis's voice was already returning to its normal decibel level. "Still. You didn't think to call me? After all my help yesterday?"

"You put out a weekly. There's still plenty of time to talk about it. But I don't want my name in the paper. I'm on deep background." This was not the kind of publicity I wanted for the guesthouse. Keeping the whole ghost angle under wraps was tough enough around this town—there had already been plenty of talk about the "haunted guesthouse," and now I was going to be known for holding a séance where a prominent citizen of the town dropped dead? This was not turning out to be the kind of opening week I'd hoped for.

"Fine," Phyllis said. "We'll meet in an underground parking garage wearing trench coats. Alison, you're the owner of a business where someone died. What did you expect—that nobody would notice?"

"I guess I didn't think it through. What do you want to know?"

"Tell me what you saw, first of all," she said.

"Not much," I admitted. "I was running the show, you know, playing up the haunted house angle because people like that, apparently." Phyllis has never acknowledged the idea of ghosts in my house; at least, she's never said whether she believes the stories she's heard or not. I find that extremely reassuring, since Phyllis is not about to judge me as crazy anytime soon. I think it's her journalism training—Phyllis doesn't care about the rumors until she can prove the facts.

"So why does that mean you didn't see anything?" she asked.

"Well, I was busy looking at one of the other guests, who was asking a question just when Arlice collapsed. So in the moments before she fell, I wasn't looking at her."

"Interesting." I could pretty much hear Phyllis licking her pencil and frowning. She's an old-school newspaperwoman who doesn't so much interview you as lets you talk and writes down what you say. So she didn't ask another question right away, and as she might have expected, I filled the silence on my own.

"She hadn't said anything about feeling ill beforehand,"

I continued. "Arlice and I had a very nice conversation just before we went inside, and she gave me a silver amulet on a chain." My index finger reflexively went to the amulet, still around my neck. I'd decided to keep wearing it as a memorial to Arlice.

Phyllis jumped on that. "You came into my office yesterday asking about Arlice Crosby as if you'd never met her," she said.

"I hadn't," I told her.

"Yet by last night she was giving you what must have been a reasonably expensive gift?"

I defended myself. "We hit it off, I guess, when I went to visit her. I liked her, and she seemed to enjoy my company. She was very excited about coming to the séance last night, and I guess that was her way of being nice to the hostess."

"What else? You're holding back." Phyllis is a terrific reader of voices.

"Look, this is off the record, or I simply won't say it. Agreed?"

Her tone indicated she didn't care for the conditions, but she didn't have a choice. "Agreed," she said. "What's going on?"

"Since last night, a few different people who were there when Arlice fell have given me different stories about someone doing something to her just at that moment. And each of the stories had someone else bothering her just as she collapsed." I detailed the claims Melissa and Jim and Tony had made (naming no names, of course), and left out Dolores's story entirely, since I didn't want to start implicating a ghost while talking to Phyllis.

"That's weird," Phyllis said. I could hear the pencil scratching against her paper.

"I said it was off the record," I warned her.

"I'm taking notes. I'm not going to quote you, and I'm not going to use it unless someone else corroborates, okay? Don't tell me my business."

"It's just . . . it's one thing to have a heart attack. I didn't have any control over Arlice's health. But if someone I have in my house did something to make her ill like that, that's another story. That's something I could have prevented if I'd have seen it coming."

"How could you have seen that coming?" Phyllis asked.

"I don't know. But it's under my roof, and that means it's my responsibility."

"Uh-huh." Again, the silence, but this time I wasn't playing. After a while, Phyllis asked, "Any other reason to think it was anything but natural causes?"

"I guarantee you've already talked to the police and to the medical examiner's office," I said. Phyllis rather famously has a "friend" at the ME's office, and I don't like to think about how they worked out their arrangement. "So you tell me—*is* there any reason to think it was anything but natural causes?"

"Hey, who's asking the questions here?"

I didn't like the sound of that. "You've heard something, haven't you?" I asked.

"I haven't heard back from Detective McElone yet," she admitted, "but I did talk to my friend, and he says Arlice didn't die of a heart attack."

"She didn't?"

"No. She died after falling into a diabetic coma. Her insulin level was way too high."

"Well, how does that happen? Did she inject too much before she came over?" I hadn't seen anything like that happening, and quite frankly, had forgotten until now that Arlice was diabetic.

"No, you don't understand. The amount of insulin in her system, to kill her that fast, would have had to have been about fifty times the normal dosage." Phyllis let me have a moment for that to sink in.

"So Arlice overdosed? Accidentally?"

"Standing there in a room with a group of people waiting for ghosts? No, Alison. Think again. All the stories about someone bumping into Arlice and causing her to turn around. As if something stung. As if she were getting a shot."

"Somebody killed her."

Eleven

Detective McElone called back a half hour later and very curtly requested (or more specifically, *ordered*) my presence in her office immediately. And she also made a point of telling me to "bring that TV guy with you."

I found Trent in the kitchen, trying to talk to his breakout star, H-Bomb, who appeared to be having some sort of meltdown, pulling at her hair and actually stamping her foot when I arrived.

"I *won't* do it!" she screamed at the harried-looking producer (sorry, *executive* producer), her black roots screaming for attention while the blonde hair hanging down in her face created a sort of bead-curtain effect in front of her eyes. "There's no way you can make me!"

"Be reasonable," Trent attempted, as if that phrase had ever resulted in reasonable behavior from anyone to whom it was spoken. "We're in our second day of shooting, and we're already behind schedule. All I'm suggesting is . . ."

"I know what you're suggesting," H-Bomb shot back. "You're suggesting I let that skank Tiffney overshadow me on this show, and I'm not going to let you do it. That's *my* spot, and I'm doing it!"

With that, she turned on her heel and walked out through the back door to her trailer, giving Trent a poisonous look.

"Hard day at the office?" I asked.

"That's why they pay me the big bucks," he said smiling, but the smile held no joy. "What can I do for you?"

I informed him of Detective McElone's summoning of the two of us to her office, and Trent wiped his brow, although I didn't see any sweat there. "Give me five minutes, and I'll meet you outside," he said. "I have to talk to Ed." And without waiting for a response, he walked out to the den, where I heard him calling for the director.

Having been effectively dismissed, I went out the back door and into the Volvo, which had had a rough winter and was now happy the warm weather was back. It started up fairly easily, and I sat and listened to a Carole King CD while I waited for Trent.

He showed up ten—not five—minutes later, got into my car and started rubbing his temples with his thumb and middle finger. Then he composed himself and put on his professional smile as I drove down the driveway.

"You like the oldies, huh?" he said, pointing to the CD player as if I didn't know where the music had been coming from.

"I like women who have a point of view," I said. "Too many of the ones singing now have a point of view that begins and ends with their wardrobe."

"You don't think women can be stylish and intelligent?" Trent asked.

"Depends. Which one is H-Bomb?"

"Touché."

Carole was especially insistent that I get up every morning with a smile on my face and show the world all the love in my heart, so I turned the music off. "What was she complaining about before?" I asked.

He chuckled, again with more annoyance than amusement. "You wouldn't believe it if I told you." He didn't wait for me to protest. "She's concerned because she doesn't have to work on the boardwalk at the ring toss game tonight."

I was driving, so doing a double take seemed too reckless to consider. "How's that?" I asked instead.

"Exactly. See, we set the cast up with jobs on the boardwalk, the idea being that we get to see how they respond to responsibility and a structured schedule."

"Which they had when they were in high school, like, fifteen minutes ago."

Trent looked truly amused this time. "You'd be surprised. There's not one of them under the age of twenty-four. H-Bomb is almost thirty."

"You're kidding. And their idea of a job is working a fixed water-gun race at the boardwalk in Wildwood?"

"No, their idea of a job is being a great big TV star, which is why each of them signed on for the show. They think if they act outrageous enough, it'll be their ticket to acting, or modeling, or designing their own fragrance, or something like that."

We were about halfway to police headquarters, and I was in no rush to see McElone's scowling face, so I was observing the local speed laws and keeping the Volvo under twenty-five miles per hour, which probably was a source of relief for my engine. "And if they act like complete and total jerks on national television, that's going to get them a career?" I asked.

"Stranger things have happened."

"So why is Helen so upset about not working the game tonight?" That part didn't seem to fit in. Wouldn't she want to avoid work and concentrate on wearing as little as possible in front of the boys?

"Ooh, careful—don't let her ever hear you call her anything but H-Bomb," Trent warned. "If you think that little tiff we had was something . . . Anyway. It's not that she wanted so badly to be working the game tonight. It's that I changed the schedule and gave her spot to Tiffney. H-Bomb thinks that means I'm favoring Tiff over her and that I'm going to give Tiff the better segments to shoot, and she'll end up being shoved to the side."

"So, no H-Bomb fragrance."

"Exactly. Can't have that." Trent closed his eyes and leaned back.

"So why do you put up with her? Why not tell her to take a walk?"

He didn't open his eyes to answer. "She tested the highest in last season's focus groups. Everybody hated her. She's my star."

"The one everybody hated is your star?"

"Welcome to my world," Trent said.

"So why don't *you* quit?"

He sat up and opened his eyes wide. "What? And give up show business?"

By the time we got to the police station, I'd heard as much about "reality" television as I'd ever want to. More, actually, since I didn't want to know anything about it. But Trent no longer seemed like a shallow, uncaring slick-talker. He actually showed signs of intelligence and wit. I'd have to be very careful with him or I might find myself becoming attracted to a TV producer who was going to be here for all of three weeks. Not a great idea for a single mom. I'd gone out on exactly three dates since divorcing The Swine. I did not want to find myself mooning over a visiting TV producer who probably had no romantic interest in me anyway.

McElone looked impatient even as we arrived and treated us as though we were late for some very formal appointment she'd confirmed with us weeks before. The truth of the matter was that it had taken us almost twenty minutes to show up in her office.

"I've screened all the tape you shot last night," she said

to Trent after we settled into her extremely neat, but still undersized, cubicle. "And aside from some movement in one corner of the screen when Arlice Crosby fell over, there isn't a single shot of her in the lot. How do you explain that?"

"Simple," Trent replied. "The camera operators were instructed to keep our cast in frame at all time. We also had a camera on Alison because she was running the séance. Everyone else was focused on our cast. In fact, they were told to avoid shooting the houseguests or anyone else at all if possible."

"Why is that?" McElone asked.

Trent shrugged. "We make television for an audience of twelve-to-twenty-four-year-olds. Do you think they're interested in watching a bunch of people in their seventies and eighties? Besides, anyone shown on-screen has to sign a waiver, or I'd have to spend money pixelating their faces out of the scene. I wasn't interested in getting everybody there to sign off unless it was completely necessary."

"You didn't know something was going to happen that you wouldn't want to show on camera?" McElone was stretching, for sure.

Trent's face practically inverted. "Of course not. If I knew someone was going to die right there in the room while we were talking about ghosts, don't you think I'd have had a camera and a light on her? It's already going to be my highest-rated show of the year."

Television people have an interesting idea of morality.

McElone turned to me. "I assume by now your network of spies have told you Mrs. Crosby did not die of natural causes."

"Network of spies? This whole town thinks I'm a lunatic who believes there are dead people hanging out in her house. Who's going to join my network of spies?" I crossed my arms and sat back like a petulant thirteen-year-old.

McElone blew out some air. "You know Mrs. Crosby didn't die of a heart attack, right?"

I tilted my head and nodded in what I've been told is a sheepish manner, although I've never actually studied sheep body language. "Right."

"So we're considering her death a homicide, and that means someone in the room with you last night was responsible for it." McElone stood up from her desk and put her hands on her hips. She looked at Trent. "Every witness—and the videotape—places you nowhere near Mrs. Crosby when she died," she told him. Then she turned to me. "Has anyone in the house said anything to you that might give us a direction? Did anyone see anything they didn't tell the police, but did tell their friendly innkeeper?"

There was no sense in holding back. "As a matter of fact, a number of people have told me they saw something, but nobody knows exactly what, and no two stories match at all."

McElone reached into her desk drawer for a pad and pen. She seemed surprised, as if she hadn't expected me to offer anything of note. I'd show her. "Who said something, and what did they say?" she asked, sitting back down behind her desk to take notes.

"Well, you know that Tony Mandorisi said he'd seen something change Arlice's expression immediately preceding her death," I started.

"Yes," McElone agreed, nodding her head. "Mr. Mandorisi told me that last night. But he didn't see anything that could be considered suspicious, exactly."

"Let me finish," I insisted. I was going to be of use to this woman if it killed me. Or she did. "Then, late last night, my daughter, Melissa, told me she'd seen one of my guests walk behind Arlice and that Arlice seemed to react, and then fell over."

"Which one of your guests?"

I frowned. "Do I have to say?"

I got a sharp look from McElone. "No, this is the police department. We don't want you to do anything that might cause you the least bit of inconvenience, especially if it might help solve a prominent citizen's murder. Of *course* you have to say. But I promise I won't tell your guest where I got the information, unless it amuses me to do so."

That wasn't very reassuring. "Linda Jane Smith," I grumbled.

"The one-legged ex-Army medic?"

"You're very tactful. Yes."

"Why would she want to kill Arlice Crosby?" McElone asked.

"How would I know? I'm just telling you what Melissa said. And then another guest, Jim Bridges, said he saw Tiffney pass behind Arlice at just about the same moment Melissa said Linda Jane was there, that Arlice looked startled, and then she collapsed."

"Wait a minute!" Trent started. "If you're trying to implicate Tiffney . . ."

"Tiffney got a last name?" McElone was taking notes.

"Warburton," Trent said. "She's one of my cast members. But she prefers just Tiffney."

"I'll bet."

I could almost see the wheels spinning in Trent's brain—was it better for the show for Tiffney to be a suspect, or wrongly accused? It took a moment before he said, "And I can tell you, she had no reason to want to kill Mrs. . . . Mrs. . . . ."

"Crosby," I reminded him. "It's touching how you remember."

"Doesn't mean I don't care," Trent said. "Besides, you've seen all the footage, Detective. I'm willing to bet you saw nothing to indicate Tiff did anything wrong."

McElone and I ignored him.

"Why didn't I hear this last night?" she wanted to know.

"Well, Jim and his friend Warren seemed to want to avoid the police, but didn't have a problem talking to me. And Melissa was asleep."

McElone regained her composure and nodded. "Why didn't *you* tell me earlier?"

"I left a message for you. I figured you'd get back to me when you wanted to hear what I had to say."

She stood up again. Either she couldn't sit still, or McElone was doing the slowest aerobic exercise routine in history. "Okay. Thank you for your cooperation, both of you. You're free to leave."

A swell expression of gratitude for all I'd given her, but I was happy to get out of there. Trent and I stood up and gathered our meager belongings (my purse, and his nothing) in preparation for exiting the premises.

"There's just one thing," McElone said, as if just thinking of it that moment. "This is not the death of an ordinary citizen. Arlice Crosby was very, very wealthy, and that means a lot of people might have thought they'd benefit from her death. Since this is now a homicide investigation, and the crime took place in your guesthouse, I'm going to have to insist that no one leave the house, at least not permanently, until we have had the opportunity to investigate further. So tell the guests they're staying with you until I give you further notice."

It was my turn to bulge my eyes and cough, and I probably turned purple at the same time just to make it more colorful. "What?" I managed to choke out.

"You heard me," McElone said. "Until we figure out who the killer is, nobody's leaving your house."

Twelve

Not surprisingly, neither Trent nor I said much on the ride back to the house. I imagine each of us was thinking about the effect McElone's investigation—and her latest pronouncement—would have on our jobs. At least I know I was.

Technically, McElone didn't have the legal authority to keep everyone in my house, but she could require that they not leave the state until she had managed to sort out what happened to Arlice Crosby. Since the Senior Plus guests were scheduled to leave Wednesday, still five days off, it wasn't imperative I tell them right away, but if there were travel plans to be changed, it was probably better they knew in advance. I girded myself to break the news, especially to the always sunny Bernice Antwerp. Maybe I'd start with Linda Jane first.

Slightly more worrisome from my business perspective was the fact that two more guests—who weren't part of Senior Plus Tours—were due on Tuesday, a day before everyone else was moving out, a couple I'd booked before I knew Trent would be taking the downstairs bedroom to not film his cast in. Rance would let me know if Senior Plus was sending anyone else my way after he saw the evaluation forms my current guests would fill out. I was trying not to think about those.

With more guests on my mind, converting the attic was making more and more sense to me. Sure, it wouldn't be ready by Tuesday, but hey, the next time there was a murder in the house, I'd be ready.

I looked over at Trent, who was back in his "exhausted producer" mode, leaning his head back on the rest, eyes closed, with an expression so put-upon that Job himself would probably have offered the guy a cookie.

"So it's fun being a TV producer, right?" I asked.

No answer. I shut up and drove.

When we got back to the house, I headed to the room Linda Jane and Dolores were sharing and found neither there. Not surprising—the guests (minus the beyond-belief Joneses) didn't spend much time in their rooms; they were in other parts of the house or out exploring.

I eventually found Linda Jane in the library, brushing up on her Steinbeck. When I told her about the police investigation and McElone's requirement that she stay in New Jersey, she nodded.

"Can I stay here?" she asked. "I don't want to have to move to a hotel or something, and besides, if we have to remain beyond Wednesday, I should stay in the house until Senior Plus sends another RN, in case of an emergency with the guests."

"Sure, I'll work it out," I said, wondering how in hell I'd do that.

"It's an awful thing about poor Mrs. Crosby. That someone would do that to her deliberately. I hear she was something of a local celebrity, but she wasn't famous enough to make it to Kansas. I never even spoke to her. She seemed like a nice woman, though."

"She was. And I just met her yesterday."

"I was standing almost right behind her when she fell," Linda Jane volunteered.

"Did you see anything? Anyone near her?"

"To tell the truth, I was looking at you," she said. "I didn't even know Mrs. Crosby was down until someone yelled, and then my medical training took over."

There wasn't much more to say. I was tempted to ask Linda Jane if she'd pass on to Dolores the news that they were both under house arrest, but I knew I had to suck it up and be a good innkeeper and tell her myself.

But first, I went to pick up my daughter from school. I told Melissa that McElone wanted to talk to her, and she asked why.

"Because of what you saw last night," I told her.

Melissa stopped and thought for a moment. "You mean about Mrs. Crosby falling down like that?" she asked.

There was something odd in her tone. "Yes, honey. The detective needs to ask you what you saw when that happened."

"Did somebody commit a crime when she fell?" Melissa asked. I was starting to wonder if she and I were having the same conversation.

"Yes, baby. I'm afraid so. Someone killed Mrs. Crosby." I guessed Melissa went to sleep thinking Arlice had died of a heart attack, but then why had she made a point of talking about Linda Jane?

Melissa gasped. "Really? That's so sad."

"I'm afraid so. And Detective McElone will want to ask you about what you saw just before she died."

"Is she asking everyone?" Melissa looked a little scared; she didn't want to have to talk to the police.

"Well, she spoke to most of the people in the room last night while you were sleeping, but she didn't know it was a murder then. I imagine she'll want to talk to some of the rest of us again, as well."

"What should I tell her?" Melissa asked.

"Tell her the truth. Always tell her the truth. Tell her what you told me when I was carrying you up to bed." I didn't want to be accused of coaching my daughter, but it seemed she was really confused about what McElone might want to know from her.

"When you were carrying me up?" Melissa asked. "What did I tell you?"

"You don't remember?" Uh-oh.

"No. I just remember waking up in my bed this morning. I don't really remember you carrying me up." Now she looked scared.

I patted her on the hand. "Don't worry, baby," I said. "Just answer the detective's questions, and you'll be fine." Maybe a little coaching wouldn't be an awful thing, after all. "Just tell her about seeing Linda Jane."

"The lady with the metal leg?"

I nodded. "Yes. Tell the detective how you saw her bump Mrs. Crosby right before she fell over."

Melissa narrowed her eyes—she calls it "crinkling"— and lowered her head a little. That wasn't a good sign—it meant she was thinking. After a long pause, she asked, "Is that what I told you when you were carrying me upstairs?"

I just nodded. This wasn't going the way I had anticipated.

"I don't remember that, Mom," Melissa said.

Despite myself, I gulped. "You don't?" I asked.

"No. I think maybe I was dreaming."

Double uh-oh.

Thirteen

"You sure you want to make just one room?" Tony Mandorisi and I were taking a look at the attic, which is code for "I got Tony to come and tell me what was practical and what wasn't." He stood in the middle of the space, one foot on each of two beams. "There's plenty of space here for two."

"I'd have to go back to the town for approval to have more than two more people in the house," I told him. "It requires a different license. Besides, I want to market this as a luxury suite, so I can charge more for it and only rent it out when someone *really* wants a special vacation." I thought of the Joneses; what they'd do with a space like this was something I preferred not to imagine.

Tony nodded. "Well, clearly the first order of business is at least a plywood floor, and you should be doubling your insulation anyway, because at some point, you might have guests during the winter, and besides, you live here. You want to keep your heating bills down. During the summer, air conditioning is going to be expensive up here. Insulation is job one."

"Yeah, and then I have to put up walls. Tell me the stuff I wouldn't figure out on my own."

He wrapped his arms around his chest like he was hugging himself. Tony's not that starved for affection; that's just what he does when he's trying to envision a project completed.

"Well, with the sloping roof, you don't have tons of headroom on the sides, but a lot in the center," he began. "So if you want to make it a real suite and put in a bath up here, you could do it near the side, where you don't need that much headroom, and even put in a skylight if you wanted."

Maxie, wearing a pair of red overalls over another in a series of black T-shirts, floated up through the floor near the window and spied us immediately. "What's *he* doing here?" she grumbled. Maxie had developed a little crush on Tony when she'd first seen him, and when it sunk in that his reciprocating was both physically impossible and (more appalling to Maxie) completely undesired on Tony's part, she decided to resent him. I ignored her and instead watched Tony as he looked around the whole open space.

"If you really want to get a high-end clientele, particularly one that's younger than your current crop, you might put a loft bed in here," he went on. "It would make for a little nook underneath, make it feel like an apartment, but you'd have to make sure it was for people who don't mind climbing up a little."

"What's this about?" Maxie demanded. "I thought we'd decided you weren't doing anything up here."

"*We* didn't decide anything," I told her, and Tony immediately looked alarmed.

"Is she here?" he asked. He can't see the ghosts, but he knows about Maxie in particular, and she scares him. With good reason.

"Maxie is not pleased that I'm considering renovations in the attic," I informed him.

Tony's eyes widened, and he started walking in circles, careful to always step on a beam. Once a contractor, always a contractor. "Where is she?"

"Over there." I pointed, and just to be contrary, Maxie moved closer to Tony. I did not revise my estimate, so he looked where she used to be.

"I *told* you I don't want anyone up here," Maxie whined. "This is my room."

"You don't *get* a room," I insisted. "I have to make enough money to keep this house and send my daughter to college."

"She's ten."

"Right, which means I'm already about ten years behind on saving for her education." I walked past Tony, who was staring up into the rafters. "Look Maxie, I understand you need some privacy once in a while, but I need to be able to house more guests so that we can keep the guesthouse going. You can understand that, right?"

"No, I can't," Maxie pouted. "You already have all those people downstairs. That's enough."

"What's she saying?" Tony wanted to know. "Is it about me?"

Maxie rolled her eyes heavenward. "Men."

"No," I answered him. "It's about her selfish desire for a dusty attic weighed against my need to generate income. *Some* of us," I directed at Maxie, "don't have to worry about such things."

"Yeah, being dead's a real relief," she groused. "If you need the extra room so badly, fix up the basement."

"Have you *seen* the basement? There are posts holding up the ceiling and, oh yeah, a furnace down there."

"You're so negative," Maxie said.

"By the way," I asked, since she was there anyway and because I wanted to change the subject, "has Paul said anything about hearing from Arlice Crosby?"

"Who?" Maxie can exhibit a terrific capacity to not think about anyone besides herself.

"The woman who died here last night," I reminded her.

"He didn't say anything to me. Why, are you expecting a message or something?" Maxie's outfit changed into her typical blue jeans with chains hanging off the belt, black boots and a black T-shirt, this one bearing the slogan "Will Build to Suit." I had no idea what that meant.

"I was hoping she might give us some insight into who killed her," I said.

Tony had been ignoring my conversation with Maxie, but now he turned toward me. "So I was right?" he asked. "Somebody did something to her before she died? It wasn't just a heart attack?"

I filled him in on everything I'd learned, including the conference with Detective McElone. "Apparently someone gave her a very large injection of insulin, enough to cause her to collapse on the spot, and that's gotta be big." WebMD is so helpful when looking up such things.

"Well, it should be easy enough to find out who did it," Maxie suggested.

"Really! Why is it that easy?" I answered, and then explained to Tony what I was answering.

I'd never seen a ghost look so smug before. Maxie pursed her lips while smiling, which I didn't think was possible, and put her hands on her hips. "All you have to do is figure out who had a great big bottle of insulin they could get their hands on," she said.

"Oh, please," I started to answer. The problem was, suddenly her response made a lot of sense. "Actually . . ."

Tony looked at me. "What did she say?" he asked. So I told him. "I hate to say it, but . . ."

"I know. She's right."

"Why doesn't anybody want me to be right?" Maxie wanted to know.

"Go find Paul," I said.

"Who, me?" Tony asked.

"No, not you. How are you going to go find Paul?" I looked up. "Maxie . . ."

But she was already gone.

"You think someone in the house is smart enough to inject Mrs. Crosby with a lethal dose of insulin in front of a roomful of people while not being seen, but stupid enough to leave the syringe lying around so we can find it?" Paul was "standing" in my bedroom as he usually did (about eight inches off the floor). I'd decided my room was the only area in the house where we could have some semblance of privacy.

"It seemed like a good idea when I first heard it," I said.

"And who suggested it?" Paul asked, with a tone that intimated he knew the answer.

"I did," Maxie announced proudly, hovering over the dresser in a pose that was supposed to look like she was sitting. Problem was, she was so excited over having had this great insight that she couldn't hold still and kept bobbing up and down into the furniture.

"I rest my case," Paul said, which I would have considered cruel if I hadn't been thinking it myself.

"Geez!" Maxie said, and she vanished in a huff.

Melissa had spied me heading into my room with Tony and saw Paul and Maxie slide in later, so she'd known something was up. She was now sitting on the bed. "That was mean, Paul," she said.

Paul lowered his eyes and nodded. "Yes, I guess so. I'll apologize to Maxie later. But it doesn't change anything. There's very little reason to think that searching the guests' rooms would do anything more than infuriate them and make them feel like they're not trusted here. I doubt the person who injected Mrs. Crosby kept the syringe or the vials of insulin after you all went to bed last night."

"Then, what should the next order of business be for the investigation?" Tony asked.

"The next order would be to let Detective McElone do her job," Paul reiterated. "She's the professional, and we do not have a client asking questions about this murder."

"What about Scott?" Melissa wanted to know. "Isn't he worried about what happened to Mrs. Crosby? He seemed to really care when he thought he'd done something bad to her."

"Yeah," I asked, remembering Dolores's odd assertion. "What about Scott? Have you heard from him since last night?"

Paul shook his head. "I get the general feeling that he's brooding, but no direct messages. And before you ask, I haven't heard anything from Arlice, either. If she shows up in a form . . . like me, I doubt it will be for at least a few days."

"Until we can get her to show up, I have to figure out where I'm going to put two extra guests come Tuesday," I whined. "The TV people are using my only open room to not sleep in."

"The new people can stay in my room," Melissa said. "I can sleep in your bed."

"No," I answered, making a rule I didn't know I'd decided upon already. "No guest ever puts you out of your bed, Liss." She smiled. She was being a good citizen, but she really didn't want to leave her room.

"One problem at a time," Tony said. He's good at injecting sense into a chaotic situation; it comes from working on construction sites and being married to Jeannie. "The biggest thing right now is to figure out who killed Mrs. Crosby."

"No," Paul argued, "that's a job for the police. Alison's priority should be her business here in the house."

Tony answered after I relayed the message. "They're one and the same. Until the murder is cleaned up, Alison won't be able to run the guesthouse the way she wants to."

"Alison can run the business perfectly well while Detective McElone does the investigating," Paul said. "But this is the first group of guests in the house, and there's already been an incident damaging her reputation. She has to address that and make sure things operate as close to normally as possible." Paul had the advantage of not having to wait for me to tell him what Tony had said. I, of course, had the option of *not* telling Tony what Paul had said, but that seemed unfair. So I looked for a way to end the debate.

"Alison can—" Tony began.

"Does anybody want to know what Alison thinks?" I asked.

They both turned toward me with the same combination of surprise and sheepishness. I had to hold back my laughter.

"I'm very touched that both of you are so concerned for my welfare, but I'm a grown-up now, and I can make my own choices," I began. "I decided to move back here to Harbor Haven after my divorce because I always wanted to run a guesthouse here. Now, after a *lot* of hard work, I've got that guesthouse up and running. I know, I just met Arlice Crosby yesterday, and she seemed like a very nice woman. But I can't let her death change my priorities. There's no reason on earth for me to do anything but run my business and let the police do theirs. And that's exactly what I'm going to do. I'm not investigating anything, Tony. I'm concerned with making sure my guests have a good time, don't get run over by insane television crew members trying to catch a glimpse of a girl running down the beach with no bra—cover your ears, Liss—and seeing to it that nobody else dies on my watch."

"All well considered, Alison," Tony said. "And I agree. But you're forgetting one thing."

"Yeah?"

"Arlice Crosby was murdered by someone in your den

last night. And all the suspects in your den last night are staying under your roof."

It was already closing in around me, but I was trying not to acknowledge it. "So?" I said.

"So whoever killed Mrs. Crosby is still here." And then Tony did something so unconscionable, it's amazing I still consider him my friend.

He looked at Melissa.

"What?" she asked.

I'm sure my voice was a little icier than I intended. "Melissa is just fine, Tony. Don't worry. I never let *anything* keep me from protecting her." But the seeds of doubt were already planted in my mind. "I'm doing that now by not investigating a crime the cops can handle."

"There's nothing that can change your mind?" he asked.

"Nothing."

Tony put up his hands, palms out. "Good enough," he said. "You know what you're doing."

There was a knock on the door at the same time Maxie flew up through the floor (and, consequently, the bed). "Hey, there's some guy—" she began.

I opened the bedroom door, and there stood my mother.

"Hey, what's everybody doing in here?" she asked.

"We were discussing—" I began.

Mom cut me off. "Never mind. There's a man at the door who says he needs to talk to you. Says he's Arlice Crosby's attorney."

"What does he want from me?"

"He told me he wants to hire you to investigate her murder."

Tony is a good enough friend that he did not smirk as I walked out the door.

Fourteen

Thomas J. Donovan, Esquire, was a distinguished-looking gentleman of about sixty. In a black suit with a dark tie (he was mourning his client, after all), he stood tall and straight in my front room.

All around him, cameramen were following swimsuit-clad twentysomethings determined to show off as much of themselves as was possible without depleting the production company's budget for pixelation. Donovan, distinguished gentleman that he was, managed not to drop his jaw and stare openly. But he did steal the occasional glance, and I can't say as I blamed him. The *Down the Shore* cast might not have been even passably polite, but they sure were a photogenic bunch.

"Can't I show you into the library?" I offered. "It gets a little chaotic here when the crew is shooting."

"This is fine, Ms. Kerby," he answered. "I'm sure you have to keep an eye on the proceedings in your guest-house." Maybe he wanted to keep an eye on the proceedings more than I did, but I deferred to his preference.

After all, rumor had it he wanted to pay me money for something.

"How can I help you, Mr. Donovan?" I asked.

"As you're probably aware, I was Mrs. Arlice Crosby's attorney," he began. "I understand you are a licensed investigator, and I'd like you to look into the circumstances of her death."

Of course, I'd been warned, but it still didn't add up for me. "I'm flattered you thought of me, but I am a bit puzzled. Surely as experienced and capable an attorney as you has an investigator or two he uses on a regular basis. Why take a chance on me with a client this influential?"

H-Bomb was rubbing herself up against the more buff young man in the cast. I think it was Mistah Motion, assuming one could tell which one that was—with all the ab crunches these boys did, it was astonishing they had time to curse and flirt with the girls on camera.

Either way, Donovan was noticing.

"Mr. Donovan?" I prompted.

He forced himself to look away and actually turned his back on the spectacle in the other half of the room. "Sorry. The question?"

"Why me?"

"Of course. The fact is, Arlice herself called me yesterday afternoon to recommend you."

I must have looked like he'd hit me with a brick. "Arlice Crosby called you and said you should hire me in case someone murdered her last night?"

Donovan almost smiled. "No, no. She said she'd just met with you, and was impressed with you as an investigator."

Really? Perhaps I'd underestimated her perception. Or overestimated it.

"Arlice was a real believer in supporting new businesses," Donovan went on. "She championed new artists and often helped finance new business ventures that wouldn't have survived without her help. She thought I should give you a chance. I'm truly sorry that this is the chance I have to give you."

"Again, I'm flattered," I answered as Tiffney wandered into the front room and saw H-Bomb draping herself all over Mistah Motion. I thought her eyes might actually pop out of her head. She made some protest, and the entwined couple turned to "notice" her. Ed the director was chewing on the end of a dishtowel, which I was glad to note was not one of mine. I continued, "But surely the police investigation will—"

"I'm sure the police are doing all they can," Donovan said, cutting me off. "But Arlice was a very wealthy woman, and in such cases it's always possible her estate was the real target. The fact is, you're in close proximity to these people all day and night, and you have more access. You can find out things the police will not."

Why not push it? "Like what you were doing with Arlice at the Ocean Wharf Hotel a while back, looking for ghosts?"

This time, Donovan did smile. "Very good, Ms. Kerby. I can see Arlice's evaluation was accurate. You *are* good at what you do."

"What I do is run a guesthouse, and it is yet to be seen if I'm any good at that," I said. "And you haven't answered my question."

The fray in the other room was getting louder, with a lot of *migraines* being thrown around, but I didn't want to speak up for fear of ruining the scene and making them do all this again, only phonier. "Very well. I went with Arlice to the Ocean Wharf Hotel because she had been told—and I don't know by whom—that the place was haunted. She wanted to find out, because she had developed a very strong interest in such things." He said *such things* in a tone similar to the one I'd use to describe the bats I'd been imagining in my attic.

Suddenly, I noticed Paul's face sticking through the wall

over the piano, about ten feet away. I wondered how long he'd been lurking. I managed not to jump. It takes practice.

"And what happened when you got there?" I asked Donovan. I wanted to see if he'd corroborate Arlice's account of her "meeting" with Scott McFarlane.

For the most part, he did. "We didn't find much of anything there," he said. "A few obvious parlor tricks someone had gone to a good deal of trouble to place there, but not much else. It wouldn't have frightened a six-year-old child."

I think I saw Paul smile.

"And then Arlice said you fell down?"

Donovan didn't get the chance to respond. Behind us the sound of H-Bomb's screechy voice rose to a level that threatened to decalcify the spinal cord of every person in the room.

"Keep your migraine hands off my man!" she screamed at Tiffney. "You keep away from him—*forever*—or I promise I'll kill you! Do you hear me? I'll *kill you*!"

Donovan turned back to look, and I stared in their direction. The three cast members held their terrified (Tiffney), terrifying (H-Bomb) and absolutely vacant (Mistah Motion) glares at each other until Ed the director yelled, "Cut!"

Then, I swear to you, there was applause from the crew. Trent Avalon, who apparently had been just out of sight in the kitchen doorway, walked out toward them, clapping his hands as well. "Very nice," he said. "That's going to be a real moment for you, H-Bomb."

But he was still behind his star, and couldn't see her face. H-Bomb had not relaxed when the lights went out, as the other two had done. She was still staring daggers at Tiffney, until she broke the eye contact, pivoted a full hundred and eighty degrees, and stomped her way out of the room.

As she passed Donovan and me, I could hear H-Bomb mutter, "I'll kill her." And she didn't sound like she was acting. I'd seen her when she was acting. This was a lot more convincing.

I told Tom Donovan I'd think about taking the case and that I'd call him the next day with my decision. He told me how much he would be willing to pay for a successful conclusion, and that was going to make it more difficult for me to decline.

My mother appeared as soon as Donovan left, which led me to believe that Paul and/or Maxie had been relaying messages up to my bedroom while I was downstairs negotiating. She walked to a cabinet I keep near the front door, reached in and pulled out an honest-to-goodness picnic basket she must have stashed there when she'd arrived.

"Thought you might like some home cooking," she said.

I defended myself. "I can cook."

"I know, Ally, and you're wonderful at it, but you just don't have the time. So I prepared a little something. I hope you don't mind."

She went into the kitchen to heat up whatever it was she'd made, with specific instructions not to make anything smell too delicious until most of the guests were already outside, heading for a restaurant. Meanwhile, I wanted to confer with Paul but was waylaid by Dolores on my way to the stairs.

"Linda Jane says we are not to leave town," she began.

Oops. I knew there was something I'd forgotten to do.

"I'm sorry, Dolores. I was looking for you before. You see, the detective investigating Mrs. Crosby's death—"

But she didn't let me finish. "I think it's *marvelous*," Dolores gushed. "This will give me that much more opportunity to locate the spirits living in your house."

"Of course it will."

"Will there be an extra charge if we have to stay past our scheduled departure date?" Dolores wanted to know.

That was a good question; I hadn't considered it before. "Let's see how long the extra stay might last, and I'll reassess," I told her. This, in the guesthouse business, is called *procrastination*. "I'll talk to you about it on Tuesday."

She looked positively tickled as I walked away.

Jim and Warren were heading out the front door, dressed for a night out (their white pants and white shoes were especially festive). Warren, the taller of the two, looked over his shoulder and saw me. He stopped and walked back over.

"Alison," he said, smiling. "There's a slight problem with the felt on the pool table."

"What's that, Warren?"

"I sort of . . . tore it." He averted his eyes, apparently worried that I would tell him he had to go to bed without supper.

"And how many beers did you have before you sort of tore it?" I asked him.

"Maybe one or two." Still not looking at me.

"Well, suppose I take a look, see how bad the damage is, and find out what it's going to cost to repair. Then we can figure out what to do, okay?"

Warren smiled and looked me in the eye. "That sounds good, Alison. I'm really sorry."

"It happens," I said. It especially happens when you have your first beer at eleven in the morning, but it would have been supremely ineffective to mention that. Warren joined Jim and waved as they headed off. I shook my head a little and waved back.

I was going to head into the kitchen to help Mom with dinner, but now I guessed I should check out the damage my first guests had done to the expensive pool table I'd picked up used.

Tony walked into the front room as I went toward the game room. Toolbox in hand, he was getting ready to head home. Just his luck—another few seconds and he would have made it, but I caught sight of him and beckoned him over.

"What's up?"

"How much do you know about pool tables?" I asked him.

"You usually have to bank your shots," Tony answered. "And you're supposed to hit the black ball in last."

"Come on. We have a repair job to assess." And I didn't give him the option of refusing, because I'd already turned and proceeded toward the game room.

The room was empty, of course, since Jim and Warren were the only ones who ever came in, and they were out in search of something to soak up the alcohol in their systems. But they had at least cleaned up after themselves; there were no empties anywhere to be found in the room, and the pool cues were carefully placed back on the rack I'd mounted on the wood-paneled wall. (Maxie had practically thrown a fit over the paneling, but a game room with a pool table made such old school décor a necessity.) The Coca-Cola Tiffany-style lamp over the pool table was still turned on, and the barstools I'd put in for those not currently shooting were scattered to the corners of the room.

"Uh-oh," Tony said.

He pointed. Sure enough, the green felt covering of the pool table had a very long vertical gash in it, reaching across for at least six inches, with a horizontal tear, only an inch or two, at the bottom of the gash.

"That doesn't just sew up, does it?" I asked.

Tony snorted a bit and shook his head. "The whole thing needs to be replaced," he said. "You can't do this yourself; you don't have the equipment. You need to get someone to come in."

"Price?"

"Not cheap." Tony raised the flap at the bottom of the tear, and then let it drop. "But the table is useless if you don't get the repair done."

I moaned, but just a little. There's a cost to doing business, and if you want to stay in business, you pay it. "Do you know anyone who does that sort of work?" I asked Tony.

He started looking underneath the table. Contractors do stuff like that; even if they're not going to make the repair themselves, the construction of the piece fascinates them, and they try to figure out how they'd do it if it were indeed their task.

"I don't, really," he answered, his voice muffled under the table. "But I can ask around. Hey, what's this?"

"What's what?"

Tony's voice sounded concerned, even though I couldn't see his face. "You'd better take a look at this," he said.

I dropped to my knees and looked where Tony was pointing, at the underside of the pool table, in a specific spot, not far from the rail that returns the ball after it drops into the pocket. I had to get very low to the floor to see what he was showing me.

There was something taped to the underside of the slate base of the pool table.

"What's that?" I asked.

Tony reached into his tool belt and pulled out a small flashlight. He turned it on with his teeth (men are so macho) and pointed the beam at the object attached to the table.

I gasped.

Taped to the bottom of my pool table, with plain cellophane tape that had not yet yellowed, was a small glass vial.

Like the kind that could contain insulin.

Fifteen

"I'm glad you knew enough not to touch it," Detective McElone said. She didn't even grunt as she rose up from a low squat under my pool table. On top of everything else that irritated me about her, McElone was in really good shape.

"Of course I knew not to touch it," I said. "But I doubt whoever left it there was stupid enough not to wipe it off first."

"Oh, I don't know," the detective answered. "They were stupid enough to leave it where it could be found instead of throwing it away or destroying it. You can't ever tell with criminals. Some of them are really dumb."

She had already questioned Tony and me about the way we'd discovered the vial and seemed vaguely suspicious of Tony's explanation of why he was underneath the table to begin with. I believe her comment was "The felt's on the top part, right?"

"It's attached underneath," he'd explained.

"Tony was helping me with the pool table," I'd told her. "Contractors like to check out every part of a job."

"Are you fixing the torn felt?" McElone asked Tony.

"No," he admitted. "I don't do that kind of work."

"Uh-huh."

Now, wearing latex gloves, McElone had gotten back down and was actually lying on the floor under the pool table. Tony remained standing, but I dropped down to watch what she was doing—if I was going to carry an investigator's license, it couldn't hurt to watch a professional investigate something.

She carefully removed the tape on one side of the vial and held her hand under it when it dropped. But the tape on the other side held tight, and the vial did not fall off the slate.

"Oh, come on, Detective," I said. "You don't really think Tony killed Arlice Crosby. In fact, there's a whole roomful of people who can testify to the fact that he was all the way on the other side of the room when she collapsed. If the insulin killed her instantly—"

"You're right," McElone said, slowly removing the tape on the other side, using a pair of tweezers. "I don't think Mr. Mandorisi killed Mrs. Crosby."

"That's good," Tony said.

"Then why are you being all suspicious about it?" I demanded.

The tape came loose and McElone pulled the vial free, holding it with the tweezers until she could rest it safely in a plastic evidence bag. "I'm suspicious for a living," she said as she stood up, considerably more smoothly and quickly than I did. "It's sort of my job."

"What about *my* job?" I asked. "Is this now a crime scene? Can I still have guests and exhibitionist TV personalities in my house, or do I have to file for welfare?"

"Relax, you can keep your little hotel going here,"

McElone said. She liked to refer to the place as anything but a guesthouse when she was trying to get under my skin, but only because it worked. "But there's a problem."

I wasn't crazy about that pronouncement. "What?"

McElone waved the evidence bag just a little. "This vial couldn't hold nearly as much insulin as the ME found in Mrs. Crosby's body," she said. "So I'm thinking it wasn't the one that was used to kill her, or at the very least, not the *only* one."

"That's your problem," I told her, exhaling. "Not mine."

"Well, see, in this case, what's my problem is also your problem," the detective said with a less-than-warm smile. "Because I have to assume that this is not the only vial the killer used. And so—"

"Don't say it."

She said it. "—now I'm going to have to run a very thorough search of this entire house. To see if I can find any other vials or diabetic supplies that might have been used in the crime."

There was a deep sound in the back of my throat that I didn't recognize. "So you and a team of CSI wannabes are going to swarm all over my house and inconvenience my guests, is that it?"

"Not CSI wannabes," McElone answered. "The real thing. I'm going to call the county's crime-scene team in on this."

"Swell. So I can expect a real professional going-over. Can't wait."

"Good. Because they'll be here within an hour."

She was as good as her word. The crime-scene team, three men dressed only roughly like storm troopers, showed up less than fifty minutes later and immediately dispersed themselves around the house. The sun was going down, and my guests would soon be returning to their vacation home away from home, only to discover people going through their underwear drawers looking for evidence of a murder they'd witnessed the night before.

I didn't think this was going to play well with Rance's company. Good-bye future Senior Plus tours.

McElone cleared Tony to leave with an unnecessary warning not to stray too far from home. Tony was an expectant father and had work lined up in Harbor Haven, Lavalette and Seaside Heights over the next few weeks; the probability of him leaving for parts unknown anytime soon was pretty low.

But Mom, who had stuck her head into the game room while McElone was questioning us and been told to go away (all right, so the detective actually asked if Mom would "please wait until I can get a clear picture on this") was not far from my side anytime thereafter. She had, it turned out, retreated to the kitchen to heat up the massive meal she had brought in her picnic basket.

"You know, my Uncle Nathaniel was a diabetic, and he used to have all sorts of things to, you know, keep his sugar in the right range," she was telling me as Melissa came into the kitchen (after McElone had spent ten minutes asking her about the "dream" she'd had regarding Linda Jane) and started setting the table, as requested.

"Was that how he died?" I asked, taking Mom's picnic spread out of the oven.

"No, he was in a three-car pileup on the Cross Bronx Expressway," Mom told me.

She had brought—no joke—a whole roasted turkey, mashed potatoes, gravy, broccoli, cranberry sauce (which I secretly hate, but couldn't tell her because it would hurt her feelings) and bread stuffing, all in that picnic basket. Well, some of it might have been carried in that backpack Mom wears whenever she goes out, like a sixth-grader.

"Well, hopefully the crime-scene team can get this done quickly, because the three of us are going to have to go through all the guest bedrooms as soon as they're done and straighten up," I said. Mom nodded.

Melissa, on the other hand, looked disgusted. "I'm not

going through some socks and stuff"—(with an actual shiver on the word *stuff*)—"from people I don't even know."

"Yes, you are. We're making sure they're disrupted as little as humanly possible," I told her, with a look that indicated no back talk would be accepted.

"Excuse me." Linda Jane Smith stuck her head in through the kitchen door. "I don't want to intrude on your family dinner."

"It's okay, come in," I said. "I'm always available to a guest and, besides, we have way too much food."

Mom beamed; she loved being accused of overgenerosity.

Linda Jane walked in. Now that I knew about her leg, I noticed the slight limp that I guessed I should have seen all along. She really was very good at not letting her prosthesis slow her down.

"Thank you, but that's not necessary," she said, although her eyes were drifting toward the turkey and did not look uninterested. "I just wanted to ask about the police officers going through the house right now."

I grinned. "I'm not sure if any of them are unmarried, Linda Jane."

She smiled, too, but not as widely. "I'm sure I can find out if I want to," she said. "But I assume they're here to investigate Mrs. Crosby's death last night, and I'm wondering what they might be looking for."

I told her what McElone had instructed me to say, and what I'd told the other guests before I'd come in to eat: "They haven't told me anything. In fact, they wouldn't tell me. I get the impression they won't know what they're looking for until they find it. Please, sit down and eat. Liss, get another plate."

Linda Jane tried to protest, but Melissa was up and at the cabinet before she could open her mouth. "That's awfully nice of you," Linda Jane said. As soon as there was a plate in front of her, Linda Jane started to load it up, and I was glad that Mom *had* brought too much. The woman could eat.

"Was there something you were concerned about?" Mom asked. "Something you're afraid they'll break or something? We can ask them to be careful around a certain object, if that's what's bothering you."

"Oh, it's nothing," Linda Jane answered. "I was just worried they might be looking for insulin. I have some in my drawer; it's part of my medical kit."

Everyone's fork but hers froze in midair.

"Is something wrong?" she asked.

Sixteen

Linda Jane stared at us for a very long moment until I regained the power of speech. "How . . . what makes you think they might be looking for insulin?" I asked her.

She waved a hand. "When I was trying to revive Mrs. Crosby, I noticed the calluses on the tips of her fingers, where she'd probably used lancets to check her blood-sugar levels. And she was wearing an insulin pump, for goodness' sake. When I first took a look, I thought she might be in a diabetic coma, but that wouldn't have killed her that fast."

I stared at her again for a while. Linda Jane just went on eating.

"Isn't that what happened, Mom?" Melissa wanted to know.

I stumbled over words for a few seconds, before I managed to get out, "Well, I don't know that much, but I did hear it was diabetes-related."

"The cops wouldn't be all over this place if they thought this was a death by natural causes," Linda Jane argued, as if trying to make herself sound like a suspect. "If they're looking for insulin, it's possible someone injected her with too much and sent her into a hypoglycemic state, but it would take a *lot* to do it that fast."

"I bet," Mom said.

"The thing is," Linda Jane went on, "most vials wouldn't hold enough. Very strange."

"Yeah, but . . . they didn't tell me that's what they were looking for . . . or anything," I stammered, sounding so ridiculous that even I didn't believe me.

"Would you pass the gravy?" Linda Jane asked. Melissa reached over her grandmother and picked up the gravy boat to give to her. "Anyway, if they find that supply in my medical kit, I'll just have to explain it to them, I suppose."

"I suppose," I said. "If that's what they're searching for." I wasn't going to get off the "I don't know" train, no matter how far off the tracks it was veering.

"Do you know the detective in charge very well?" Linda Jane asked.

Mom and I exchanged glances. "I've had . . . dealings with her before."

"What's she like?"

"Sometimes she's not very nice," Melissa said. "But that's just because she really wants to solve the crime, and she gets mad when she can't." Don't ever think children aren't good judges of character, or that they don't see what's going on.

I heard the kitchen door open again and turned to look. "Wow, turkey!" Jeannie stood in the doorway, Tony behind her. "Is that for everybody?"

"No, but *you* can have some," Mom told her. "It's good for the baby. Sit down."

I made the introductions between Linda Jane and my married friends and watched as Tony pulled up a chair for Jeannie and a stool for himself, as we were running out of seating options. "What are you doing here?" I asked

Jeannie. I pointed at her husband. "I sent that one home a while ago already."

"He said there were armed men storming your castle," Jeannie said, sitting down behind the plate Melissa had fetched for her. "I figured you'd need us to run some defense."

"So far, they've been leaving us alone," Mom said. "We haven't needed any defense."

"Good," Tony answered. "Because I saw those guys, and I couldn't take them without a power drill and a sack of cement."

"You want some cranberry sauce?" Mom asked me, noting its absence on my plate.

"No, I'm good," I said. "I'm trying to lose some weight."

"I used Splenda," she said, and plopped some down on my plate, ruining some perfectly good stuffing. "Besides, you look perfect."

Melissa and I exchanged our "that's Grandma" look, and she actually took a little of the cranberry slop off my plate when Mom wasn't looking.

"So, fill me in," Jeannie said. "What have I missed since last night?"

I gave her the *Reader's Digest* version of the day's events, including the visit with McElone and the drive with Trent. Jeannie's eyes lit up at the reference to a single man in whom I might be interested, but I cured her of that misconception with a simple "Don't." Melissa, contrary to my expectation, did not look the least bit puzzled.

Once she was completely informed, Jeannie looked at her cleaned plate, sighed and said, "Being pregnant feels like it should give you license to eat as much as you want."

Mom pushed the mashed potatoes in her direction, and Jeannie did not resist.

"Okay," Jeannie said when she could speak again. "Let's go around the table. Who do you think did it?"

There was a stunned silence.

"I beg your pardon?" I asked.

"Who's your candidate? You're an investigator. This is a good way to get all the ideas out there and start to zero in on the most logical person."

"It's really not," I said. "It's wild speculation, it's irresponsible, it's uninformed and it's . . ." I thought Linda Jane would be offended, but she didn't seem to think of herself as a suspect, and was looking thoughtful, as if she were wondering what she'd say when it was her turn to speak.

"I think it was that girl Tiffney from the TV show," Mom said. "Anybody who'll walk around like that without underwear is capable of anything."

"It's called 'going commando,' Grandma," Melissa informed her. I began to doubt I'd sleep that night. Had she been watching *Down the Shore*?

"She had no motive and nothing to gain beyond a higher Q rating, and she'd never met Arlice before," I pointed out. "It seems extremely unlikely she was mentioned in Arlice's will."

"What seems unlikely?" Paul rose up from the basement and took up a position near the cereal cabinet, where he was unlikely to be disturbed. I flashed my eyes in Linda Jane's direction, and he nodded. I couldn't answer him directly.

But Mom hadn't gotten the memo. "It seems unlikely that the girl from the TV show killed Arlice," she said.

"But you just said you thought she did it," Linda Jane protested.

"Well, yeah, but I was just answering—"

I gave Mom a stern look.

"I was answering Alison's argument," she went on. "She convinced me I was wrong."

"Well, who do you think did it?" Jeannie asked Linda Jane.

She put down her fork and Paul suddenly looked more attentive. "If her death was insulin-related, then it has to be someone who had access to large quantities, someone with knowledge of how much insulin it would take to kill her," she said, seeming to think out loud. "And it would have to be someone who was standing nearby at the time." She looked serious for a moment and said, "Honestly, my best candidate would be me. But I have no motive, and I know I didn't do it."

We all gave Linda Jane the laugh she was looking for, but it wasn't exactly mirthful. There were odd glances all around the table and up near the cereal cabinet.

"So, since I know it wasn't me," Linda Jane continued, "I'd have to say the next most logical candidate would be someone else who's also a type 1 diabetic. They'd have the drug and the means of administering it."

"Are there any other diabetics among the guests?" I asked, based on Paul's prompting. "You're the RN; you would know."

"It would be unethical for me to disclose that information without the patient's stated consent," Linda Jane pointed out. "But yes, there is another diabetic in the house. I won't tell you who." I looked at Paul, who shook his head; no, it wasn't the time or the circumstance to press her on the subject.

"What about you, Melissa?" Jeannie asked. "Who do you think is the killer?"

"Whoa, Jeannie." I tried to put on the brakes. "Melissa is not—"

"I think it was someone we're not thinking of," Melissa piped up. "Somebody in the room last night who knew Mrs. Crosby, but didn't say anything. And they were real mad at her, so when they saw she was coming for the séance, they figured out a way to kill her without making it obvious that it was them."

That was actually, as speculation goes, fairly coherent. Paul beamed as I complimented Melissa on her detective skills. "But you still have to finish your math homework, young lady, so let's get this table cleared."

Jeannie started to rise to help clean up, but Tony, traditional guy that he is, told her to stay seated. He started to clear dishes, as did Mom. Linda Jane, looking mournfully at her empty plate, joined in as well.

"Nobody asked *me*," Tony said, "but I think that one of those two beer-drinking guys did it. I bet one of them had a grudge against Mrs. Crosby for some reason. They were awfully quick to start pointing fingers this morning, trying to deflect suspicion. They don't want to talk to the police. I'm saying: You grill them long enough, one of them is going to roll over on the other."

Paul folded his arms, then raised his right hand to stroke his goatee. It was his best pretentious "thinking" look. His mouth flattened out, and his eyebrows lowered. He must have thought Tony had made a decent point.

"I think you're reaching, honey," Jeannie told her husband. "You're guessing too much about the people you're accusing."

"I'm not actually accusing," Tony protested. "This is just a parlor game. And it was your idea."

"Alison," Jeannie said, doing her best to ignore Tony, "you're the only one who hasn't answered the question. Who's your candidate? Who do *you* think killed Arlice Crosby?"

I didn't get the chance to say that I didn't have a candidate (although I was secretly starting to suspect the Joneses, just because they were sneaky enough to get in and out of their room every day and never be seen), because at the very moment we had cleared the table and filled the dishwasher, the kitchen door opened. Detective McElone walked in, followed by two of the CSI storm troopers.

"Oh, you're not going to take my whole kitchen apart, are you?" I protested.

"What do you care?" she shot back. "You don't serve food here."

"We still eat," Melissa told her. Melissa has no fear of grown-ups. She might not develop one until she's a grown-up herself.

"Good point," McElone acknowledged. Turning to me, she said, "Yes, we are going to search this room. It's the last in the house that hasn't been inspected." She gestured to the two officers, who started to open cabinets and remove their contents. It was going to be a long night.

Linda Jane walked over to McElone. "By the way, Detective, I was just telling Alison that if you were looking for insulin, you'll probably find some in my med kit. I'm a nurse, and I have some in case a patient requires it."

McElone shot me a nasty look, probably thinking I'd gone around the house telling everybody an insulin search was on. I held up my hands, palms out, to begin to deny it, but she cut me off.

"In fact, we did find some insulin in your bedroom, Ms. Smith," McElone said. "We found three vials."

"That's odd. I only have two." Linda Jane looked genuinely puzzled.

"In your kit, yes," the detective nodded. "Thank you for giving us the key." She handed a key to Linda Jane, who nodded an acknowledgment and put the key in her pocket. "We also found a vial taped to the back wall of your closet."

"I don't understand," Linda Jane said. "I only had the two and no reason to hide another one."

"Lieutenant!" one of the storm troopers called over from the pantry. "There's a vial here stuck under one of the shelves."

McElone walked to the pantry and ducked down to look. Tony handed her his small flashlight, the one he carries in his pocket. "Very good," McElone told the officer. "Save it as evidence, like the others."

"Hang on," I said. "Besides the vials in Linda Jane's room, how many others have you found?"

"Eighteen," McElone said. "The fact is, we found at least one in every room in your house."

Seventeen

McElone's pronouncement had something of a dampening effect on the evening. Despite their offer to "stay and offer a defense," Jeannie and Tony went home when Jeannie decided she wanted a hot dog from a local place called the Windmill. I didn't mind; there was very little left to defend against.

Luckily, I wasn't the one who'd had to deal with the cast of *Down the Shore*, since I'd heard considerable shrieking and a few thumps outside my back door, where the CSI team had gone to search the cast's trailers. H-Bomb at one point shouted loudly that she would "stand like Rosie Parks" against the onslaught, and as far as I could tell, not one crew member had so much as guffawed.

Mom stayed for a while, waiting until the dishes were washed, dried and put away. She helped Melissa and me clean up the damage the CSI team had done to the guest bedrooms, then got into her Dodge Viper and hit the road at the legal limit of twenty-five miles per hour. She'd be home within the hour, her townhouse being less than eight miles away.

When I had the chance, I asked Paul if he'd gotten any Ghostograms from Scott McFarlane, but there had been no further communication from our erstwhile client. I was starting to wonder why I was this deep in this much trouble.

I went back out to the front room to talk to the guests a bit. They were agitated because of the police activity, but most of them seemed to find the whole experience exhilarating. I have no idea what the reaction of the Joneses was, of course, since they had once again retreated to their chamber to do . . . I prefer not to think about it.

Jim and Warren, unaware their names had been prominent in our earlier speculation, peppered me with questions about the investigation, almost all of which I answered with, "You'll have to ask Lieutenant McElone. The police don't tell me anything." Which was almost true.

After most of the guests went back to their newly tidied rooms, I forced Melissa to go to bed and started repairing the damage in the rest of the house. Every single book in the library had to be reshelved, a concept that left me close to tears. I started on one shelf, got emotional, and decided to finish the task in the morning.

The front room wasn't as badly disorganized, so I concentrated on that area for a while, then moved on to the den. Maxie hovered over the fireplace, a delighted grin on her face at my inconvenience.

"You really got yourself into something this time, didn't you?" she crowed. "I can't believe you let that old lady die here in our house, and now you can't figure out what to do about it."

I was putting knickknacks back on shelves, and couldn't remember where they belonged. "You can manipulate physical objects," I reminded her. "How about helping me clean up?"

"This isn't my room. The attic is my room." So we were back to that one.

"Fine." I went back to rearranging, putting things where

I was sure Maxie would find them objectionable. "What do you want?"

"Why do I have to want anything?" she asked. "Can't I just be here?"

"You can be in your precious attic. You don't like me. Why come where I'm cleaning if you're not going to help?"

Maxie floated, considering. She picked up a small figurine, one that I'd picked up in an antiques store in New Hope, Pennsylvania. It was a sea captain, sitting back in a rocking chair, smoking a corncob pipe. I didn't care for it very much, but I thought it was a good idea to have some sea-oriented decorations at a shore house. I fully intended, someday, to replace it with something less kitschy. "Yeah, I can see why you'd be worried that this might not find its way back," Maxie said.

"If you don't want to help, don't help. Some people would simply pitch in out of friendship, but don't you feel obligated." I was trying to remember why I wanted most of this crap out where I could see it, anyway.

"Friendship? Are we friends?" Maxie seemed genuinely surprised.

Okay, so maybe *friends* was stretching it a bit, but if Maxie was going to be in my house for, as far as I could tell, the rest of my life (if not longer), I might as well try to make a stride or two toward civility.

"We're not enemies. At least, *I* don't think we are."

"You don't like me," Maxie replied.

"What makes you say that?"

She sputtered. "Everything."

"Melissa likes you. That's enough for me," I said. "The kid has unerring judgment."

"Where do you want this?" Maxie asked, holding a decorative mug with the seal of Monmouth University emblazoned on it that I'd bought when I was a student there. The idea that Maxie would ask instead of just deciding where she'd put it—or, more commonly, to "accidentally" drop it so it would no longer offend her sensibilities—was extremely unusual.

"Why are you here, Maxie?" I asked again, ignoring her halfhearted attempt to be helpful.

She put the mug on the mantel over the fireplace, pretty much the last place I'd have wanted it. I guess two could play at this game. She looked around the room and found a photograph of Melissa and me, a copy of one taken as a gift for my mother on Mother's Day when Liss was about six years old. Maxie floated over and picked it up. "It's my birthday next Wednesday," she said.

"What?"

"My birthday. I'm going to be . . . *would've been* thirty years old on Wednesday." Maxie didn't look at me. She swirled around to the other side of the room, moved around some things I'd placed in unacceptable spots, and then vanished up into the ceiling, leaving me to wonder what the hell that had been about.

Usually, I liked being alone when the house was quiet like this, but it had been an unbelievably long day, and now all I wanted was to get to bed. So I straightened up just to the point of acceptability and then turned to head for the stairs, and bed. I'd do the rest in the morning.

When I turned around, Dolores Santiago was standing in the foyer by the staircase, her gray hair down to the waist of her long flannel nightdress and without her usual inch-thick eyeglasses.

"Something I can help you with?" I asked her. Inside, I was thanking my lucky stars it wasn't Bernice; another complaint right now might put me in the fetal position and on the floor until September. The look in Dolores's eyes, however, was chilling—she was staring straight ahead and appeared to be in what I could only call a trance. Was she sleepwalking?

She walked directly toward me, but never made eye contact. I repeated my question, but she didn't answer me, and when we were only a foot apart, she reached up and touched the amulet hanging from my neck. The silver one in an uneven triangular shape.

The one Arlice Crosby had given me the night before.

Dolores cupped the amulet in her palm and caressed it with her thumb.

"Are you all right?" I asked her. "Is there something about my necklace that you want to know?"

"It's a family secret," Dolores intoned. Then she pulled hard on the amulet and snapped the chain right off my neck.

"Ow!" I shouted. "Hey!"

But she had already turned and headed for the stairs. Luckily, being forty years younger, I still moved more quickly than she did, and stood between her and the landing. "Where do you think you're going?" I asked. I pulled the necklace out of her hand and stuck it in the pocket of my jeans. It was a tight fit, but better uncomfortable than missing, I always say.

Dolores still didn't answer. She just continued up the stairs as I called to her, and then disappeared into her room.

I gave it a long, hard thought and decided not to think about it again until I'd gotten a good night's sleep.

It had been an unbelievably long day. Or have I said that already?

"Have you seen Tiffney?" Ed the director was walking around my extremely large backyard, his camera crew at the ready, his cast (or most of it, anyway) assembled and his patience, apparently, wearing thin. "Do you know where she is?"

I had no idea and told him so. I wasn't interested in trailing the cast of *Down the Shore* around my property, since the four of them seemed, to my sensibility, a quartet of spoiled brats who needed to be told to sit down, shut up and eat their spinach, or there'd be no tequila, posturing or sex later. You have to have standards, after all.

They were shooting a sequence in the backyard that was meant to show off the cast's athletic skills (and most of their bodies) while they played "beach volleyball." To achieve this, the crew had imported hundreds of pounds of sand to dump on my grass, despite there being an actual beach not three hundred yards away that had all the sand you could possibly want. No doubt the sand there didn't look as sandy as this sand. I had been assured any damage done to my lawn would be repaired when the company was finished shooting, a moment I was starting to anticipate almost every minute of every day.

I, in the meantime, was trying to forget all about last night and Dolores's attempt at robbery while apparently sleepwalking. I hadn't seen her this morning and assumed she was either out or hiding in mortification.

I had found the library's bookshelves mysteriously restocked (although very badly sorted) when I awoke this morning; maybe my speech about friendship had gotten through to Maxie after all. So, having rescued the rest of my house from the indignities heaped upon it by McElone's CSIs, and having made it through the first ghostly performance of the day, I was now relaxing a bit in the backyard, watching what was supposed to be filming.

Phyllis Coates had come by at my invitation (and because she wanted some pictures of the *Down the Shore* crew for the *Chronicle*), and we were eating burgers from the Harbor Haven Café that she'd brought with her as payment.

I'd caught Phyllis up on the developments in Arlice Crosby's murder—as many as I knew, anyway—and told her I was still deliberating about Tom Donovan's offer, when Trent Avalon, stonewashed jeans, black T-shirt and two-hundred-dollar running shoes at the ready, raced onto the "set," where a remarkably small volleyball net had been erected on the imported sand.

Trent headed directly for Ed, and they began talking and gesturing. Everything in television, I was discovering, was a crisis. No cold water bottles? A crisis. A pimple on Rock Starr's left (facial) cheek? Crisis. Threat of rain in the afternoon? Massive crisis.

But Arlice Crosby getting murdered in my den while the crew filmed four narcissists flexing their muscles? Great television.

It's a funny business.

"From what I've heard through my police sources, Detective Anita McElone has more suspects and more evidence than she knows what to do with," Phyllis was saying. "I guess it's feast or famine in the police business."

"None of it makes the least bit of sense to me," I told her. "I've been thinking about it. As far as I know, nobody in that room had any reason to want Arlice dead. And yet, everybody seems to be a suspect."

"For all you know, there wasn't a person in the room who *didn't* despise her." Phyllis took a large bite of her burger and washed it down with black coffee. I loved Phyllis, but I doubted her digestive system shared the sentiment.

In the distance, Trent's hands went to the top of his head. He looked like he was trying to keep himself from flying up into space. This must have been a *big* crisis, like running out of H-Bomb's favorite brand of sunscreen.

"I didn't despise her," I said.

"You barely knew her," Phyllis countered. "But it doesn't even have to be someone who despised her; it could just be someone who thought they'd speed up the distribution of her estate. Maybe you should take Donovan's money and do some investigating."

"I'm not a *real* investigator," I argued. "I have the license, but it's not like I know what I'm doing. I'd be taking the money under false pretenses."

"No, you wouldn't. Donovan would get exactly what you've told him you are. You're the one he's asking. You should do it."

"Ah, McElone will have the thing solved before I ask my first question," I said hopefully. "She's annoying, but she's good at what she does. I'd just gum up the works. I'm sure we'll discover this is much simpler than it seems, when all is said and done."

"That's lunch, everybody!" Ed clapped his hands once for attention and shouted so the assembled crowd could hear. "Back here in two!"

The crew, union members all, were gone in the blink of an eye, but the cast seemed puzzled and (of course) annoyed at the sudden interruption. "What the migraine was *that*?" H-Bomb wanted to know. "I've been, like, getting my volleyball skills ready all morning." If by *volleyball skills*, she meant greasing up the area in and around her pectoral muscles, she was being entirely accurate.

They stomped off, no doubt in search of fattening foods that would mysteriously never make so much as a tiny bulge on any of their waists, while Phyllis and I exchanged confused looks. I stopped Trent as he tried to motor on by me by grabbing his arm and holding on for dear life. He had strong arm muscles, I noticed.

"What's going on?" I asked. "You looked like you were just about to shoot."

"We were," he said. "Something came up."

"Something's always coming up," I pointed out. "This must have been a big something."

He looked grim as he nodded. "Tiffney is missing."

Eighteen

Trent Avalon, having heard that in addition to operating a guesthouse I was also a licensed PI, immediately asked me to look into Tiffney's disappearance. He seemed quite disappointed when I told him I was already in the middle of another investigation (having made the spontaneous decision to take Tom Donovan's offer instead) and would not be able to conduct both. As I later told Paul, I was more comfortable taking a case that I knew McElone could solve ahead of me, and besides, I really had no idea how to track down a missing person. And the truth of the matter was, in the back of my mind, I really wasn't all that sorry that Tiffney was gone.

Besides, she'd been gone—what, two hours? That's not a disappearance; in Tiffney's world, that's a bathroom break. But Trent was acting like she'd vanished off the face of the earth two weeks before. I was not interested in getting involved in his craziness.

Worse than that, I was secretly afraid Helen DiSpasio

had done something to her rival, and the last thing I wanted was an angry H-Bomb living on my property and looking for me.

Trent said Tiffney had retreated to her trailer after yet another heated encounter with H-Bomb, something to do with his letting Tiffney wear a blue thong bikini when H-Bomb insisted that was her color. It was like a gang war fought with silicone. After a reasonable cooling-off period, H-Bomb had told Trent she'd go see Tiffney and smooth things over, and no one had seen Tiffney since.

H-Bomb, of course, insisted that she'd left the trailer after having patched things up with her hated rival, about whom she was now sobbing in a corner of my den, wailing that she'd lost her "closest friend, like, ever."

And saying it all directly into the camera while making sure her eye makeup was running just the tiniest bit. Enough to show the depth of her torment, but not so much that she looked like a circus clown. It's an art.

"But I need someone who knows the way the show operates, who knows Tiff," he said. "And I need someone who can keep it quiet."

"That's going to be hard to do," I told him. "You knew that the editor of the local paper was here to write a feature on the show shooting here."

He blanched and looked back through the glass doors to where Phyllis was taking pictures of the two male cast members and Ed, all the while asking them questions that they didn't realize at the time would end up in her report on Tiffney's disappearance. "That's *her*?" he said.

Trent didn't wait for an answer, which was just as well, since I'd already provided it. He strode to the French doors, opened them and shouted, "No more press! That's it, gentlemen! This set is under a news quarantine!"

Even from this distance, I could see Phyllis grinning as she mouthed the words *news quarantine*.

"What's the problem, Trent?" I asked. "I'd think you'd want publicity for something like this. If someone sees Tiffney, you want them to contact the police, don't you?"

"The police!" he practically exploded. "Nobody's calling the police!"

"You're right," I said. "There's no need for the cops. You have a missing cast member who probably just went to an afternoon movie. Why are you so wound up?"

Trent made a visible effort to bring his behavior to normal-human-discourse level. He even—I'm not making this up—put a finger to his neck, trying to take his own pulse and force himself into a calmer state through sheer willpower. "You don't understand," he told me. "This can't get out. For one thing"—now he was breathing more normally—"the police wouldn't consider Tiff a missing person until at least twenty-four hours have gone by. But she'd *never* miss a chance to be in front of the camera. *Never.* Something must be wrong."

Trent went into another litany, pleading with me to investigate Tiffney's vanishing, and I told him I'd take a look in her trailer, but that was all. Paul, hovering just over my left shoulder, followed me outside as Trent offered his rather embarrassed thanks. Trent led me to Tiffney's trailer and started to follow me inside. I turned and pointed at him.

"Stay here," I told him. "I can't do anything with you breathing down my neck." The truth was, I wanted to be able to ask Paul questions, and I couldn't do that if Trent were nearby. Instead, I left him outside with Phyllis, who as we walked away was asking him for a correct spelling of Tiffney's last name. Trent looked like he might be sick.

The crew was striking the volleyball set as I walked into the trailer. No one in the crew besides Trent seemed terribly concerned about Tiffney's whereabouts, and they were working with the usual combination of resignation and good-natured kidding among themselves. Of course, the crew guys never seemed to get upset about *anything*; it was always Trent or the cast who were apoplectic. No one was paying any attention to me, anyway, which was exactly what I wanted.

"What am I looking for?" I asked Paul.

"I'll know it when we see it," he said. "Keep your eyes open and don't make up your mind about anything. Going in with preconceived notions about what you'll find means you'll only find what you're looking for, and not what's actually there."

The trailer, luckily, had been left unlocked after Trent had gone searching for Tiffney and come up lacking. I opened it and walked inside, and Paul just hovered in through the wall, rising off the ground to meet the proper eye level. Sometimes the grace with which the ghosts moved made me feel like being dead had its advantages.

But not that many.

The trailer, as big as the average Manhattan apartment, was luxurious and tasteful, two things I wouldn't have expected from Tiffney. It had a very lovely sleeping area, unadorned by the kind of tackiness I might have expected. There was a kitchenette with a mini-fridge, a microwave oven and an actual stove, which I was willing to bet had never been used. Of course, I'd been living in my house for six months and had turned on the stove eight times, six to heat water for hot chocolate. So I might not be one to judge.

There was also a bathroom area with a shower and a toilet and enough room for Tiffney to have spread out cosmetics on every surface, but either she hadn't done so, or she'd meticulously cleaned up after herself. I tended to believe the former option was more likely.

Then I remembered that there was another whole trailer devoted to makeup, so Tiffney probably didn't need all that much in here.

"It looks like a hotel room after housekeeping has been through," Paul said. He was standing, sort of, in the middle of the space, taking it all in. "What does it smell like?"

"Smell?" I asked.

"Yes. I can't smell anything anymore."

I hadn't thought about it. I took a deep sniff. "It smells clean," I said. "Like you said, a hotel after the maid's been in."

"Interesting," he said.

"Do you think someone cleaned up after Tiffney and H-Bomb had their brouhaha?" I asked.

"Like I said, don't make assumptions," Paul scolded. "Another possibility is that Tiffney herself never really lived here."

"Aha, the plot thickens," I said in a theatrical voice. "Suppose she was shacking up with one of the hunky guys, and H-Bomb found out."

Paul shook his head and sighed, the teacher having to repeat the lesson for a student with, let's say, limited learning capacity. "Or the other hunky guy found out and was jealous. Or Tiffney and H-Bomb were really lovers and one of the guys they'd been flirting with found out. There are hundreds of possibilities, and very few of them end in violence. The only thing we know for sure is that Tiffney isn't here right now."

"That's true," I said. "We don't even know if it's because she wanted to leave, or if someone forced her to."

"Now you're getting it. Don't make any assumptions. Just take a look and see what you can—"

"Hey!" I shouted, cutting off his lecture on the Basics of Detecting for Idiots. "Look at that!" I pointed at a spot on the carpeted floor in the bedroom area.

"What?" Paul asked, but he was already lowering himself down through the trailer's floor so he could get a very close look at the area I was indicating. "Now, don't jump to conclusions, Alison."

On just a few fibers of carpet, right next to Tiffney's bed, was a dried spot of liquid.

Red liquid.

"It's blood!" I said. "Something happened here between

Tiffney and H-Bomb, and the show knows, so they covered it up! Tiffney's not missing, she's—"

"Good thing you're not jumping to conclusions," Paul said. "You know, blood dries brown, not red."

"It does?" But of course I knew that. Any mother who does laundry knows that.

"Yes, it does. My best guess is that this is nail polish."

Men. "I've never seen Tiffney wear red nail polish," I said. "She favors black for a shock effect or, for some reason, green at other times. Never red. Look at a woman's hands once in a while, just for a change of pace, will you?"

"Focus on the task, Alison." Yeah, yeah.

I dropped down to the carpet and performed the same task I had when he'd asked about the air in the trailer—I sniffed. "It doesn't smell like nail polish," I told Paul. "It's dry. It doesn't really smell like anything."

"It could be anything. They might have been having meatball subs and it's some marinara sauce." Paul was already looking around the trailer for another clue.

"It's paint," I told him. "I recognize the texture. It's latex paint."

Paul's head turned toward me. "Really!"

"I've painted every room in a seventeen-room house, Paul. If there's one thing I recognize, it's cheap latex."

He dropped down and took a better look. "You're right. I wonder what they were painting in here."

"I have no idea." I stood up again, my knees cracking, and walked to the far end of the trailer, where the bathroom door was closed. "The one thing we haven't seen is a closet," I said. "There's got to be one."

"There are pantry cabinets in the kitchen," Paul pointed out. "Look for the bifold doors, like those, only larger."

And sure enough, I found the doors, between the sleeping area and a small table with chairs (bolted to the floor, of course), where Tiffney could . . . entertain? I opened the doors and looked inside.

"I think we can rule out marinara sauce," I choked out when I got my breath back.

Paul streaked over and looked. "Yes, I suppose we can."

Inside the closet, sitting in a folding director's chair whose cross-canvas read "TIFFNEY" was a full-size mannequin wearing a cheap blonde wig, a pair of torn skinny jeans, and a sweatshirt from the University of Florida, which I guessed was Tiffney's alma mater, assuming she'd gotten someone to take the SATs for her.

The mannequin's neck was painted all the way around with red paint, sloppily, and some had dripped onto the sweatshirt, the chair, the jeans and the floor. And on the dummy's forehead was written, in red, the word *skank*.

I broke away from the sight, closed the closet door and walked straight to the trailer door. Once outside the trailer, not bothering to see whether Paul was with me or not, I marched directly to the kitchen of my house, where Trent was looking over some paperwork with Ed the director.

"Call the police," I told him. "This case is much too tough for me."

Nineteen

I left the house before Detective Anita McElone could arrive. I knew it was the wrong thing to do, and it was cowardly, but the scene in the trailer was as much as I could handle, and another grilling from the lieutenant was more than I was willing to bear.

Instead, I went to the office of Thomas Donovan, attorney-at-law. And even in the polished-oak environment there, I was admitted without question once the receptionist in the main office let her boss know Ms. Kerby was present. Because it was a Saturday, I'd called ahead and discovered Arlice Crosby's lawyer working in his office, even on the weekend. If the receptionist was annoyed about being there, I certainly couldn't tell through her "welcome to Walt Disney World" smile. Within seconds, I was sitting in a very comfortable, overstuffed chair in front of Mr. Donovan's desk, which was roughly the size of a coffin and just as shiny.

"I'm so glad you've decided to take on the investigation," Donovan said when I informed him of my decision.

He didn't know I was taking it for two reasons: First, he was paying me a very fair amount of money, and second, it was a way to avoid taking Trent Avalon's offer to investigate Tiffney's disappearance, which was looking much kinkier and more involved than poor Arlice's dose of insulin.

In short, I didn't know who killed Arlice, but I knew for a fact that I was afraid of H-Bomb. Never was a girl more aptly nicknamed.

"I just want to be very clear," I answered him. "I'm a new investigator, and I've never taken on a homicide case before." (Not professionally, anyway.) "I still recommend that you rely on the police to discover what happened to Mrs. Crosby, and why."

Donovan nodded. "I appreciate your candor," he said. "But Arlice believed in you, and that means I believe in you. According to the police, someone murdered her, and I don't think she would want us to sit on our hands and wait for someone else to discover what happened."

"All right, then," I said. "Let's not."

He blinked. "Let's not what?"

"Sit on our hands. Let's go to the Ocean Wharf Hotel, and you can walk me through what happened on the day you went there with Mrs. Crosby."

Tom Donovan did the last thing I would have expected to do. He stood up and headed for his office door.

"Yes," he said. "Let's."

The Ocean Wharf, a hulking structure standing right on the beach about a mile and a half from my house, was everything you'd expect out of an abandoned hotel—that is, it was a hotel, and it had been abandoned.

At one time, it had probably been one of the more imposing and luxurious buildings on the shore in this area. As art deco as they come, I could imagine its stucco facade painted pink, its glass-brick windows polished and gleaming, and its neon sign shining aqua over the bar on the veranda and, by extension, much of the Jersey shore.

Now, however, it was another great big piece of the past that had been left on its own for too long and had lost any relevance it once had. Donovan drove his Lexus up to the building through overgrown vines and plants. When we arrived at what had surely been a magnificent entrance portico decades before, we found a pair of glass doors that had clearly been boarded shut but which had since been broken with bricks, rocks or just negligence over the course of many harsh winters and inactive summers.

"Arlice insisted, or I would have driven right back to her house," Donovan said as we got out of the car. "I was amazed the doors weren't locked, but then I realized the locks had been forced out of the doors years ago."

He reached over and opened one of the doors for me, ever the gentleman. The board that had been holding the two together swung open along with it, its usefulness long since gone. I stepped over some broken glass and a couple of discarded beer bottles as I walked inside.

"This is prime real estate, even in a bad market," I said. "I'm amazed no one ever bought the property, even if just to knock this place down and build some condos or something."

"I know," Donovan agreed. "I looked into the ownership for a client once and discovered such a tangle of legal documents that even I couldn't unravel the whole thing before the client decided to move on. The land alone must be worth millions."

The entranceway was enormous but dusty and utterly empty. Donovan pointed toward the right and said, "This way." I followed him toward a pair of dark wooden doors with metal pulls in the shape of an *O* and a *W*. He opened the left door, and we walked through.

"This is where we found the 'ghost' Arlice was looking for," Donovan continued.

"What was this fascination with ghosts?" I asked. "What made Mrs. Crosby so curious?"

Donovan shrugged, which seemed incongruous from a man in such a well-pressed suit. "She had developed this interest only in recent years," he said. "Maybe it was a way of dealing with advancing age, the idea that there's another existence after death. People get a lot of very odd ideas when they have to face their own ends."

Yeah, I thought, *I'll be sure to mention that to the two ghosts hanging out in my house when I get back.*

The room was enormous, surely a ballroom in the hotel's heyday. It was totally empty, except for a rather large rocking chair with rounded armrests and a high back sitting almost perfectly in the center of the room. The chair had seen better times, but was definitely not in keeping with the rest of the building.

"This chair was brought in from somewhere else," I thought aloud. "It's the least art deco–looking piece of furniture I've ever seen."

"Yes, that was my first impression, as well," Donovan said. "Someone was setting a stage here. It was designed specifically for Arlice to see."

"It must have been a really elaborate prank," I said, walking slowly around the room, and seeing tons of nothing. "What do you suppose the purpose was?"

"When it first happened, I thought it was just an odd joke, something that someone had set up to frighten anyone who came by, to establish the Ocean Wharf as a haunted house or something." Donovan wasn't following me around the room; he stayed near the door, as if hoping we'd be using it again very soon.

"You say, 'When it first happened'—did something change your mind?" I asked. There were marks on the floor, running from either side toward the center, just in front of the rocker. When I dropped down to examine them, it became obvious they were only spots where the dust and grime had been cleaned up. Masking tape? Perhaps for the "spooky noises" Arlice was to hear, wires had had to be laid down. In any event, all the equipment had been removed.

"Well," Donovan said, "after what happened to Arlice last night, I can't help but wonder if the whole thing had been set up to try to induce a heart attack in her, or some other kind of fatal incident."

I was almost all the way across the room, quite far from Donovan, and I had to raise my voice to be heard at that distance, which produced an unfortunate echo effect. "So when this ghost thing didn't work, whoever it was went to plan B, using a massive insulin overdose? It seems like an awful lot of trouble to go through."

Again the shrug. "I'm only speculating," Donovan said. "Maybe they didn't have access to the insulin at the time," he suggested.

There was a small set of doors, low to the floor, which I assumed led to a storage cabinet of some kind. I hesitated in front of them.

My recent experience opening a closet door had not been one I cared to repeat.

But Donovan sensed it from across the room. "What's wrong?" he asked.

Now I had to pretend to be brave. "Nothing. Just thinking about this cabinet."

He wrinkled his brow. "Open it."

Easy for you to say.

"Yeah." I knelt down, took a deep breath, and pulled on the cabinet doors.

They were locked.

"That's weird," I said as Donovan came closer. "This cabinet is locked. Wouldn't they have opened it when they were cleaning the place out? Why take everything but leave one cabinet locked?"

"Excuse me," Donovan said. He indicated I should get

out of the way, so I did. And being the Big Strong Man, he got down on his expensive knees and gave the doors a mighty yank. Nothing happened, except perhaps that Donovan strained his biceps a bit.

"Wait," I said. "These are pretty cheap locks." I'd worked at a home improvement superstore before I was married and spent a good deal of time in the locks department. I knew a few things about opening stubborn ones.

Sure enough, putting pressure in certain spots while holding a key between the doors did the trick quickly. The doors swung open, and I forced myself to look inside.

It was, I have to report, both a relief and a disappointment.

Inside the cabinet we found all the crazy gear the perpetrators of the prank had left for Scott McFarlane to wear: a pirate hat, a long blue coat with hook-and-link buttons, an eye patch.

And at the bottom, just as Scott had suspected—a real, clean, sharpened sword, neither a cutlass nor a fencing epee, but something that looked for all the world like it would do some honest-to-goodness damage to someone if it hit her exactly the right way.

"Don't touch it," Donovan said. "We have to call the police." He started to reach for a cell phone in his jacket pocket.

I pulled mine out of my canvas bag faster. "Don't bother," I said. "I spend my whole day doing this."

After an hour of questioning from Lieutenant McElone (which began with, "So you decided to stick around until I got here this time?"), I got back to the house just in time for the four o'clock show, this time with the benefit of a flying ten-year-old girl, who pretended to be terrified, while the ear-to-ear grin on her face told all paying attention that she was having the time of her life.

Mom wasn't joining us for dinner that night, so Melissa

and I ordered Indian food. But as soon as I went back "on duty" after dinner, Trent Avalon walked toward me, cell phone in hand, talking quickly.

"I'm just on my way—we're shooting on the boardwalk in Seaside Heights," he said. "We're shooting around Tiffney, and she wasn't scheduled for tonight. Come with me."

"What?"

"Come with me. I need to talk business with you, and I can't stay here while the crew is eating up money in Seaside. Let's go."

"I can't go. There's nobody to watch Melissa." That was a good excuse. Next, I could rely on "I have paying guests."

"Bring Melissa along. She can play Skee-Ball on the production company's dime." Trent was chewing on a plastic straw. I'd seen him look frantic and harried, but I'd never seen him look nervous before.

"I'm getting my shoes," Melissa said. Who knew she was close enough to hear?

"What business do we have to discuss?" I asked. "I'm not going to investigate Tiffney's disappearance."

"Alison, please!" he begged. It was sort of endearing, in a very unsettling way. But I wasn't buying it.

Then Melissa showed up beside me, jacket on, shoes tied and smile in place. "Ready to go?" she asked.

In the car on the way to Seaside Heights (a half-hour ride Trent's driver was determined to do in half the time), he took another shot at convincing me to look into Tiffney and her strange disappearance. I tried telling him that with the "terroristic threat" I'd found in Tiffney's trailer, McElone was now investigating, but Trent didn't want to hear it. "I don't know what we're going to do without her," he began.

"Isn't this going to create great publicity for your show?" Melissa asked. This is what happens when children have Internet access.

"Not the kind I want," Trent answered in a sour tone.

"If the fans find out there's a possibility Tiffney won't be on the show, I could be finished. Someone from the crew must have talked, because there are already rumors in one of the show's chat rooms. If that grows—and it will—I'm going to need to find Tiff really fast, or they'll replace me with someone who can."

He got such a look of despair on his face that Melissa didn't ask another question, and the car was very quiet until we reached the boardwalk. The driver cut through the relatively sparse crowd—it was only April, after all—and dropped us off right at the entrance to the amusements, which might have been open only because of the presence of the *Down the Shore* cast and crew. Otherwise, this was just too early in the season to bother.

Melissa, armed with a cell phone and a fifty-dollar bill from Trent (over my objections, which admittedly I did not voice too strenuously), headed for the games, and was told to check in every fifteen minutes in the hope that she would check in every half hour. Trent led the way toward the ring toss game, where H-Bomb and Rock Starr were working tonight.

The fact was, no one really had to lead the way. Given the lights and equipment necessary to shoot the completely spontaneous and unrehearsed action, the ring toss game could probably be located with the naked eye by someone standing on Saturn.

And already it was clear the "dramatics" were in full bloom.

Trent took on his "commander of the troops" air as we approached, standing straighter and walking with more purpose when his cast could see him. In the right outfit, and given a corncob pipe, he could easily be seen as General Douglas MacArthur returning to Korea.

The cameras were not rolling, so there was nothing yet to interrupt, but H-Bomb (who else?) was in fine voice and screeching away with wild abandon.

"I don't *care* if he knows how to get people to play," she was braying at a guy in a light blue polo shirt and jeans. "The camera can't see me if he's always standing in front."

The guy noticed Trent and immediately beckoned him over. "I have an agreement with you people," he said as soon as Trent was within earshot. "I let you disrupt my business for three weeks, but they have to work the game. I can't have these constant temper tantrums about who's standing in front. I need them to get people to put down money and play the damn game."

Trent was already in full conciliatory mode. He held up his hands, as if to show he was holding no weapons. "I understand, Bill," he said. "Let me talk to my cast for a moment, and we'll work this out."

"Another night like this . . ." Bill tried to start.

But Trent turned and faced him. "It's April," he said. "Another night like this, with six people on the boardwalk and us paying you a fortune, and you can retire to Boca Raton. Don't push your luck, Bill."

Bill, it should be noted, backed off, holding up his hands in exactly the same gesture Trent had just made.

I didn't stick close enough to hear what Trent had to say to H-Bomb. I didn't want to be there if she was hearing something she didn't want to hear, which happened most of the time. Even from back where I was standing, near the frozen custard stand, I could hear her decibel level and her pitch rise every time she spoke. Something about a shadow on her nose.

Finally, Trent got the conversation down to something approaching a scream and must have said something to tame his star. Rock, meanwhile, was stretched out on the table behind the game, doing crunches. H-Bomb took a visibly deep breath, smoothed out the shorts that barely covered her thong and smiled unconvincingly. The crew applauded, and everybody went back to work.

Trent left the technicians to set up their scene and

walked back to me. "Want to be a TV producer?" he asked. "Because right now you could have my job for a ten-dollar bill and a ride to the airport."

"I'm very impressed," I said. "You know how to handle people."

He waved a hand. "That wasn't me at my best," he said. "Tiffney was the easiest—I could get that girl to do anything. You *sure* you won't help find her?"

"I'm not tracking down Tiffney. Did you see that thing in her trailer? Somebody's seriously deranged."

Trent shook his head. "It's sick, but it's playful," he said. "It's exactly the kind of thing H-Bomb would do. Scare the hell out of her, but do it with cosmetics."

"It wasn't cosmetics. It was interior house paint."

"Lieutenant McElone said it was red nail polish," Trent answered.

I supposed I'd have to tell Paul he was right, but I wasn't going to rush into doing so. Let him think I actually had expertise in *some* field—for a while, anyway.

"Anyway, I don't think it was meant to be threatening," Trent went on. "It was meant to be scary, not violent."

"Well, then it was a complete and total success. I was terrified. And I'm still not taking your case."

"That's not what I wanted to talk to you about, anyway," Trent said. "I have another business proposition."

Immediately, the hairs on the back of my neck stood up. "A business proposition?" I repeated.

"Absolutely. I've been watching what goes on in your house for a couple of days now. The ghosts, the guests. And I'm telling you, there's a really strong reality show there."

It took me a moment. "You want to turn my life into a reality show?"

Trent smiled, and it almost worked. "It's not the way you think. You wouldn't be required to do anything embarrassing or degrading."

"No. I'd just have to have a camera crew follow me

around all day, every day. I'd have to subject my ten-year-old daughter to the kind of scrutiny usually reserved for girls famous for getting out of cars with no underwear on when they're on their way to rehab. I'd have to pretty much give up the business I've dreamed about having all my life to accommodate the comings and goings of technicians, publicists, producers and makeup artists. You're right—that wouldn't be the least bit embarrassing or degrading."

Trent held up his right hand. "Maybe I'm not as good at handling people as I thought," he said. "I give up."

My cell phone rang, and since it was almost exactly a half hour since I'd left Melissa, I figured she was calling in a mere fifteen minutes late. Instead, the caller ID showed Linda Jane Smith's cell number. Was one of my guests having some sort of medical problem? I flipped open the phone.

"I think you might want to come back," Linda Jane said immediately. "Stuff is flying all over the front room."

"Stuff?"

"I think it's entirely possible your ghosts are having a fight," she said.

Twenty

Trent's driver took Melissa and me directly back to the house on Trent's orders. He was also told that any speeding tickets he acquired would be gladly paid by the production company, so it took only about fifteen minutes to go from boardwalk to door.

I'd pretty much had to drag Melissa away from the boardwalk games—there's one involving rolling balls into holes while the theme from *The Flintstones* plays to which she's especially attached—but once I told her Paul and Maxie needed us, she agreed to take her 266 tickets and live to play another day.

We arrived at the house just in time to see a tomato go flying by the front door. It was followed by an apple, which was in turn countered by a shoe traveling in the other direction. Jim Bridges and Warren Balachik were nowhere to be seen, but Dolores Santiago, Bernice Antwerp and Linda Jane Smith were standing in the foyer watching the objects put on a show. At this point, I would've been more surprised if I *did* see the Joneses than I was by their absence. Bernice was in full disapproval mode, and Linda Jane seemed quite amused.

"I don't know what the snit is about, but it's weird to see stuff flying around when it's not ten in the morning or four in the afternoon," she said.

Of course, I could see what was going on. As soon as the front door closed behind Melissa and me, Paul and Maxie stopped tossing each other random pieces of fruit and extraneous decorations, and Paul came down from the upper reaches of the room to talk to me.

"Scott McFarlane is back," he said. "We needed to get you here, so we got someone to call you."

"This is the best you could do?" I sputtered. "A food fight to get my attention?"

"We could have used that little sailor guy statue," Maxie grinned.

"I wasn't talking to you" was the best I could do.

It took some doing, but I got Melissa to agree to get up to bed by promising to give her a full rundown on Scott and whatever was about to happen tonight. The guests who had been watching, apparently deciding the show was now over, applauded and started to disperse. I immediately tried to avoid Dolores, because I still didn't know how to react to the bizarre behavior she'd exhibited the night before.

But of course she sought me out even as I was trying to move to the kitchen, where Paul and I could at least attempt to speak without interruption. She stood directly in front of me and stared some more at the amulet on the chain, which I'd mended and put back on this morning.

"That's a very beautiful piece of jewelry you have," Dolores crooned. "May I touch it?"

I worked very hard at not changing my facial expression into one of utter puzzlement. "You already have," I said. "In fact, you tore it off my neck and tried to steal it."

"Alison . . ." Paul tried to interject. "Not now."

But Dolores had already heard what I'd told her, and her reaction was brief, but telling. There was a pause of perhaps one second when she stared at me blankly, and then she laughed.

"Oh, was this last night?" she asked. I nodded without a word, and she laughed some more, not uproariously, but heartily. "I'm sure it was a somnambulant episode."

This time, *I* stared blankly.

"I was sleepwalking," Dolores explained. "It happens to me sometimes. It's been months. Perhaps I should adjust my medication. Did I do anything inappropriate?"

Most other people would have reiterated that, yeah, trying to walk off with another person's jewelry might be seen as inappropriate, but I am trying to run a business, and Dolores was a paying customer. "Nothing important," I said.

Dolores chuckled. "Well, no harm done, then," she said. "I wonder if I could try to record the spectral vibrations while I sleep." She started to walk away, then turned back toward me and, as an afterthought, said, "I'm ambidextrous, too."

I stood there shaking my head for a few seconds. I couldn't remember whether I'd opened a guesthouse or a facility for treating the mentally ill. If it was the latter, we weren't doing a very good job.

"Alison," Paul repeated. He pointed toward the kitchen. "Can we go now?"

Oh yeah. This wasn't an insane asylum. It was a haunted house. That made tons more sense. I walked slowly toward the kitchen, trying to regain my equilibrium.

Linda Jane appeared at my side as I walked. "That was quite a show," she said. "Frankly, I never believed all this ghost stuff until now. I figured you were working some kind of angle. But if all this stuff can happen when you're not even here, there must be something to it."

"There must be," I agreed. "Please excuse me. I'll be

right back." I walked into the kitchen, leaving behind Linda Jane, who was probably scratching her head and wondering if *I* was on some kind of sleepwalking medication.

In the kitchen, I could see the red bandana, looking a little the worse for wear, hovering just behind the kitchen table. Paul took up a position with a clear view of the kitchen door and the back window. He tended to situate himself like Jesse James in a saloon poker game—he never wanted to have his back to the door. Maxie preferred the bird's-eye view and placed herself near the ceiling. I didn't stop to analyze her choice.

"Okay, Scott," I said in a gruff tone. After all, the ghost had gotten me involved with Arlice Crosby, who'd died in my house, and then he'd vanished (not that I could ever have seen him anway) for more than a day. "Where've you been? What's going on?"

Before Scott could respond, Maxie said, "He says he was going off to investigate Arlice and her murder, and that he feels responsible for bringing her here and maybe for her dying."

"Investigate?" I asked. "How was he investigating? He's a ghost and—sorry, Scott—blind as well."

"True, but it means my hearing is all the more acute," Scott replied, unoffended. "I went back to the Ocean Wharf to see what would happen, and I was there when you came in with the lawyer, Tom Donovan. I recognized his voice as the one who was there with that unfortunate lady."

"I didn't see you there," I said. I was taken aback that he'd been there without my knowledge, and as I occasionally did these days, I wondered how often a similar situation was the case.

"I wasn't wearing the bandana," he replied.

Paul watched intently as Scott answered. I knew he was reading Scott's face, but since I had no idea what the blind ghost looked like, it was impossible for me to picture him.

Paul would have to give me his impressions—which were usually pretty well observed—later.

"So you don't know anything that I didn't already know," I answered. "We're no better off than before."

"That's not so," Scott said. "After the lady detective let you go, I waited for Tom Donovan to be questioned, and his story changed. He told her that he had never been there before, and that it was you who was asking a lot of questions about Mrs. Crosby's will. He said that amulet you're wearing was a valuable gift you'd coerced Mrs. Crosby into giving you."

My mouth was suddenly dry and my eyes wouldn't blink. "He said *what*?"

"I followed him back to his office later on and heard him go to his computer. He was sending a . . . computer message . . ."

"An e-mail," I corrected, unsure why I was bothering to correct his techno jargon.

"Yes," Scott said. "He's one of those men who says out loud what he's typing. Whoever he was talking to must have wanted to know how the visit went, and whether the police had believed his story. He said they did."

My head was vibrating now. "Paul . . ." I began.

"Something is very wrong," Paul agreed. "But I can't believe McElone bought that story, or she would have been looking for you all day."

Instinctively, my hand went into my pocket and brought out my cell phone. I hit the button for messages, and found four from McElone.

"I think things just got a lot worse," I told him.

"On the contrary," Paul answered. "I think we just had our first break in this case."

Scott agreed, at my suggestion, to go back to wherever it was he usually stayed and not to come back until the morning. I needed the time with Paul and Maxie alone, and I think Scott understood that, although I certainly couldn't tell through his facial expression.

As soon as the red bandana vanished, I looked at Paul and asked, "How much do you trust this guy? How well do you know him?"

"You think he's lying?" Maxie asked. "A blind guy?"

"There's never been a liar who couldn't see? Paul, how do you know him?"

Paul frowned. "He responded when I sent out a . . . message about our willingness to investigate for those like us."

"You're advertising me on the Ghosternet?" My head was swimming. McElone would probably be by to arrest me by morning. Who'd watch Melissa if I was in prison?

"I was simply letting those like us know there was someone they could depend upon," Paul countered. "But to answer your real question, I have no reason to distrust Scott McFarlane."

"Do you have any reason to *trust* him?"

He stroked his goatee, thinking, then raised his hands in frustration. "No."

"Terrific."

"He seems like a pretty nice guy," Maxie offered. Coming from Maxie, that was practically a case for canonization, but it didn't really tell us anything, and I said as much. She puffed out her lips, but she didn't dispute my logic.

"We need to mobilize," Paul said. "We've been sitting on our heels on this case for too long. It's time to take some offensive action."

"I like that," Maxie said. "Who can we offend?"

"Aren't you the one who kept telling me to let McElone handle the investigation and that I shouldn't get involved?" I asked Paul, ignoring Maxie entirely.

Paul looked distracted. "We didn't have a client then. Now, we do."

"Yeah, one who's trying to get me arrested. Thanks for getting me into the detective business, by the way."

"This isn't getting us anywhere," Paul said.

"I've had enough," I told him. Suddenly, my mind was as clear as clean water. "Here's what we're going to do."

Paul's eyes widened, and Maxie looked positively amazed, but neither of them interrupted me.

"Paul, you need to get me really up to speed on the art of surveillance and what is or is not admissible in court. I'm going to be seeing what's up with our trusted client, and I don't want him to know I'm doing it."

"What about me?" Maxie wanted to know. Wow. I must have really sounded authoritative for her to react like that.

"You're going to use your computer skills. Get my laptop out of my bedroom and go up to that beloved attic of yours. There should be a perfectly good Wi-Fi signal up there."

"What am I researching?" she asked.

"I want a complete write-up on every person who was in that room when Arlice Crosby died. I want to see why any one of them would want her out of the way. Think you can handle it?"

Maxie shook her head. "I'm better at taking revenge."

"I know, but this is the job."

"Can we discuss the attic if I do it?" Maxie never did anything without extracting a price.

"Discuss, yes, but that's all I'm committing to. You're going to have to give me a much stronger argument than 'It's my room,' understand?"

Maxie actually brightened. "Understood. What else?"

I drew a deep breath. "Something neither of you can do for me, I'm afraid."

Paul's brow furrowed. "What's that?"

"I have to call my mother."

Twenty-one

"Of course I didn't think you were asking Donovan about Arlice Crosby's will, and that business about the necklace was just silly." Lieutenant Anita McElone gave me her best look of disdain. "*I* was asking about the will. When a woman that wealthy is murdered, a cop has to be an idiot not to find out where the money is going. But you'd met Arlice that day. How the hell could you have gotten into her will that fast? Tom Donovan was trying, and very badly at that, to make you look suspicious."

"Well, that's horrible," my mother said. We were sitting in McElone's cubicle Sunday morning, and none of us was happy to be there. McElone had been especially grumpy when I'd called her back the night before, something about having to miss church because she needed to see me first thing. "There should be a law against saying something like that."

"There is," McElone informed her. "It's called *slander*. If you want to sue him, feel free."

"I don't want to sue Tom Donovan," I told McElone.

"But if you know what he told you isn't true, why are we here?"

"I'm trying to figure out why he'd implicate you," the detective answered. "And the question I keep coming back to is: What was the point of getting Mrs. Crosby up to the Ocean Wharf to show her a bad magic show? I mean, did they really think that was going to kill her? And what has that got to do with you?"

I sat there for a moment, expecting her to go on, but she didn't. "You think I have answers for all that?" I asked.

"I was hoping you might have answers for *some* of it," McElone said.

"Here's what I know," I told her. "I know I met Arlice Crosby exactly three days ago, and we struck up a friendly acquaintance. She expressed an interest in coming to my house that night for a séance, and I invited her."

"Wait," the detective said. "Mrs. Crosby asked you about the ghost show?"

"Yes," I answered. "She said she had a real interest in the afterlife, that she'd been hoping to come into contact with real ghosts and that she'd heard I had some at my house."

McElone made a rude noise with her lips. "Real ghosts," she scoffed.

"Hold a civil tongue," my mother warned her. "Some of my best friends are ghosts." In fact, Mom claimed to be in periodic touch with my father, who had died almost five years earlier, but I'd been unable to contact him myself, and not for lack of trying.

"What is your mother doing here?" McElone asked me. "Don't you usually use that friend of yours to try to intimidate me?"

"Jeannie has an appointment with her obstetrician," I explained.

"On Sunday?"

I shrugged. "Dr. Liebowitz is Orthodox. He's closed on Saturday and open on Sunday."

"What am I," Mom wanted to know, "chopped liver?"

"By the way," I said, desperate to turn the conversation around, "what have you found out about Tiffney's disappearing act?"

McElone gave me her patented "are you crazy" look. "Why should I tell you?"

"Because Trent Avalon keeps asking me to investigate, and I don't want to. If I can tell him you've found out something, maybe he'll trust you and leave me alone."

McElone rolled her eyes a bit and took a breath. "You tell him that her credit card hasn't been used, her cell phone has no activity on it since she left and her mother doesn't know where she is but says she's not worried, because 'Tiff knows kung fu.' Is that enough to gain Mr. Avalon's trust?"

"I don't know," I said. "All that tells me is that you don't know where she went, and you have no leads."

"I'm not even supposed to be looking yet. We usually wait forty-eight hours, but this is going to get press because she's a *big TV star*. But frankly, I don't like the idea that this girl decides to vanish right after there's a murder in your house, and I'd like to talk to her. Anyway," McElone went on, clearly tired of the turn the conversation had taken, "Mrs. Crosby told you she wanted to come to your house that night, and you invited her."

"That's right," I said, taking the opening. "We were going to have the séance anyway, but Arlice showed up just before we began, and she was very excited. She gave me this amulet." I showed it to McElone, who actually put on reading glasses to see it clearly.

"That's very interesting," she said. "Does the shape mean anything?"

I shook my head. "Not that I know of. She said it had been in her family for a long time, and she had no children to pass it on to, so she gave it to me. I thought it was very generous of her, maybe too generous, but how do you refuse a gift like that?"

"You don't," Mom interjected. "You were brought up to be polite."

McElone took a packet of aspirin out of her top drawer and took two with no water.

"Anyway, since I already told you everything I know about the night Arlice died, the next thing was that Donovan showed up at my house yesterday asking me to investigate her murder." I looked at McElone, waiting for the inevitable crack about me being a sham as a detective, but she sat back in her chair and closed her eyes.

They stayed closed as she asked, "Did he say why he wanted you? There are plenty of detectives in the phone book."

"He said Arlice believed in supporting local businesses, especially new ones, and that she had recommended me the day she died for any business he might have coming up."

McElone opened her eyes and rubbed them with her thumb and forefinger. "Whose idea was it to go back to the Ocean Wharf?" she asked me.

"Mine, but he picked up on it in a second, like he was waiting for me to suggest it," I said. "I thought it was a little weird that he was in his office on a Saturday, but he made his secretary come in, too. And then he sent her home after he got back from the Ocean Wharf." Oops.

McElone's eyes narrowed. "How do you know what he did when he got back? You left the hotel before he did."

Telling her that I had a ghost operative on Donovan's tail probably wouldn't have earned me any plausibility points with the detective, so I scrambled and took the responsibility myself. "I followed him back and waited outside his office door," I lied. "His secretary came out just a couple minutes later, and then I listened at the door and heard him sending an e-mail. He told whoever he was sending it to that the plan had gone well, and that the police officer on the case had bought his line."

"You *heard* him send an e-mail?"

"He talks when he types," I explained. At least that part was true, according to Scott. "I figured you were too smart to fall for that line, but I let him believe you had."

I thought giving McElone the opportunity to congratulate herself would have slowed her down a bit, but I had underestimated her. "Why didn't you tell me this yesterday?" she asked.

I'd anticipated this question. "I couldn't be *sure* you didn't suspect me, and I didn't want to come in until I had something to say to you."

McElone flattened out her mouth in thought. "*Do* you have anything to say?"

I nodded. "I think we should work together to find out who Donovan's accomplice is, and what role they might have played in Arlice Crosby's death."

"Why should I work with a civilian on a homicide?"

"Because he already thinks he has leverage with me, and he thinks so because he underestimated you," I said. "If we let him believe both those things, I think we can smoke him out, and it might be the key to the whole case." Paul had briefed me well.

McElone thought about that for a moment, then leaned forward and put her elbows on her desk. She held her hands up in front of her and rested them under her chin. "The only way this is going to work," she said, "is if you don't get all full of yourself and start behaving like you know what you're doing."

"I'm perfectly willing to concede that you have a lot more experience doing this than I do," I told McElone. "I'll listen to you every step of the way."

"All right," she answered. "Let's get to work."

Mom looked at the detective, then back at me, and beamed.

"You're so smart," she said.

* * *

McElone wanted to delay the investigation a day so she could get to church and have a day with her family, but I felt it was imperative to get to Donovan quickly, so we reached a compromise: McElone got me a tiny recorder to bring to my meeting (she felt wearing a wire would be "overkill") and ordered me to keep in touch. She gave me her cell phone number and her best wishes.

Mom wanted to come with me to Donovan's home, the address of which McElone had provided. But I draw the line at bringing my mother along on ghost-driven missions, much as I don't bring my daughter (Melissa was at her best friend Wendy's house for the day). It's a business policy, I'd decided.

So by the time I dropped Mom off at the house, where her car was parked, and told Paul about the plan—which he loved—it took me about ninety minutes to get to Donovan's house in the Volvo. That gave Paul the opportunity to get a message out to Scott McFarlane over the Ghosternet, which he assured me had been received.

I took a moment after I'd parked in front of his house to get myself into the moment. I'd taken an acting class once when I was at Monmouth, and had never really learned how to be a tree or a whisper or any of the other crap they wanted me to be, but I *had* learned about how to prepare properly for a scene. And this was, without question, going to be a scene.

I started by thinking about my father (I was a Method fraud, after all), and how angry I was that he had passed away when his granddaughter was only five years old and hadn't really had many memories of him yet. Then I moved on to thinking about The Swine, which was really all the motivation I needed to dig up some decent anger. Steven had started out as a good man with a warm heart, and he could be awfully charming when he wanted to be, but then his business had taken him over and he'd become, well, a swine. One who'd abandoned his wife and young daughter for a Malibu girl whose name, if there was justice, would have been Barbie.

Yeah, that hit the spot. I could go in and be angry now.

I stormed up the steps to Donovan's very tasteful house, a brick number with actual pillars outside the entrance. I considered ringing the doorbell, then pictured The Swine lying on a beach in Malibu, and banged hard on the door. A number of times.

It didn't take long before the door opened, and there stood a plump little lady of about sixty-five, looking as much like Merryweather (one of the good fairies in the Disney film *Sleeping Beauty*) as I would have thought possible. Damn. That punctured my angry balloon in a hurry.

"Can I help you?" she asked.

This was no time to lose my nerve. Lives hung in the balance. Well, maybe some lives had already been taken, but there could still be others in the balance. In any event, this was serious business. I had to play my role, even if it meant being rude to this Mrs. Butterworth incarnate.

"Where's Donovan?" I rumbled.

"You're looking for Mr. Donovan?" she chirped, unaffected by my gruff demeanor.

"Yeah. Where is he?"

The little cherub turned toward the interior of the house and called, "Tom? There's a young lady here to see you."

"Thanks," I mumbled. Sometimes, it's impossible to undo thirty-six years of good manners all at once.

The lord of the manner appeared over her shoulder, tall, thin and dressed as a man of leisure, in Bermuda shorts and a tasteful T-shirt (blue) with a pocket, probably from Land's End. He should have had on a sailor's hat, too, to complete the look, but being inside his own house, was going without. "Ms. Kerby!" he said, as if he were actually happy to see me. "Has there been a break in the case?"

"The case?" the little lady asked.

"Yes, Martha. This is the woman I've been telling you about. The one who's investigating Arlice's death for us."

"Oh my!" she answered. "Won't you come in, Miss Kerby?" I didn't correct her on the name. She probably thought people who said *Ms.* were still burning bras and marching on Washington in support of suffrage. But I did walk into the parlor, which was a very nice one, all done in marble tile. It probably cost more than my still-outstanding mortgage.

"Yeah, there's been a break in the case," I said. "The break is, I'm off the case. And you know why." I gave him a significant look. And thought of The Swine being given a cold drink by Malibu Barbie in the next beach chair, like in those beer commercials where they never say anything.

"Me?" Donovan asked. I thought of asking for some butter, just to see if it would melt in his mouth.

"Yeah, you. Do you want to talk about it here, or in the office I assume you have in the house somewhere?" I thought of spitting, but that would just gross me out more than anything else. There are limits.

Donovan and Martha—his wife?—exchanged looks, and he nodded in my direction. "By all means, let's talk in my office. You can tell me what's gotten you so upset. Won't you excuse us, dear?" he asked the little lady.

"Of course. Would you like some iced tea, Miss Kerby?"

"No." Beach. Swine. Now, Barbie was wearing a tiny bikini.

"All right, then. I'll leave you two to your business." Martha didn't even look puzzled as she walked away. Donovan ushered me toward a room to our left.

It was paneled, of course, in dark wood, with a thick carpet and excellent furniture, much of it leather. There was no head of a conquered animal sticking out of the wall; that would be gauche. But there were photographs on the walls of Tom Donovan with former and current New Jersey governors, state senators and at least one US president. The intimidation was subtle, but it was there.

"So, what can I do for you on a Sunday, Alison?"

I cut Donovan off, not succumbing to his paneling. "Just what do you think you're trying to pull, Donovan?" I barked, using his last name as a way of sounding tougher than I really am. "I just got out of a marathon interrogation with Lieutenant McElone that threatened to turn into waterboarding." I had tried to get McElone to get me some makeup that would look like bruises on my face, but she had refused, something about not wanting to get sent to jail herself. Wimp. "And it was your fault."

One thing that Donovan had going for him was nerve. In this case, he had the unmitigated gall to look surprised. "Mine?" he asked. "How could it be my fault?"

"Don't give me the innocent act," I snarled at him. "You know perfectly well that you told McElone I was asking questions about Arlice Crosby's will when I never said one word about it. You told her you'd never been to the Ocean Wharf before, that I had insisted you go there, and that was a lie. You told her I'd tricked Arlice into giving me this amulet." I showed it off hanging from my neck. "You wanted to implicate me in her murder."

"Oh, seriously. Alison . . ."

"Don't call me Alison!" I yelled. "You doing all that only makes me think you had some role in the murder yourself."

"Me?" The man was the living impersonation of all those lawyer/shark jokes. His teeth were even showing as he spoke. "What motivation would I have . . ."

"More than me," I broke in. "And besides—I know that when you got back to your office after McElone let you go, you sent an e-mail. You told someone the interrogation had gone exactly as you wanted it to, and that McElone suspected me now. Well, she does, and I'm going to see to it that you go back and retract your statement to her. You're going to tell her you were lying. You're going to tell her I had nothing to do with Arlice Crosby before the day she died. And if you're smart, you're going to tell her everything you know about what happened."

Donovan's lower lip turned downward. At first, I thought it was an expression of contrition, but it turned out to be one of contempt. "Don't give me advice," he scoffed. "You haven't a clue what's behind this whole business. I had nothing to do with Arlice's death, and I have nothing to worry about."

"Oh, don't you? How about lying to a police officer in the execution of her duty? Isn't that called obstruction of justice, or is lying to a cop a separate charge all by itself?" I stood up and pointed at Donovan. "You are *not* setting me up on this one, Donovan. Believe me, you don't want to mess with me."

He sat back in his swivel chair and laced his fingers behind his head. "You amuse me, Ali—sorry. *Ms. Kerby.* You're the owner of a little bed and breakfast on the beach, and I'm supposed to be afraid of you? I've been a mover and shaker in this town since before you were born. I know where all the bodies are buried. The police wouldn't come after me even if they were going to take your word over mine, which will never happen. You have nothing to use against me. You have no leverage. If I decide you're going to be implicated in Arlice Crosby's death, then believe me, you will be implicated. And there isn't the first thing that you can do about it."

Donovan's words actually chilled me a little—it wasn't so much what he was saying as the confidence with which he said it, the certainty he had that I was a tiny little thing he could break with two fingers. But then I remembered I was there to be angry, not scared, and I conjured up a picture of The Swine and Barbie I'd rather not share just at the moment, if you don't mind. Suffice it to say it did the trick, and I was perfectly livid again.

But I decided to play it icy instead of volcanic. "There's nothing I can do?" I said, accompanied by what I hoped was a bone-chilling smile. "Apparently, you don't stay as well plugged-in to what goes on in this town as you think."

He looked like the villain in an Alfred Hitchcock movie, so suave and composed he wouldn't break a sweat on an August afternoon in hell. "Really? And what is it I've been missing?" Honestly, James Mason himself couldn't have pulled it off more convincingly.

"You haven't heard the gossip that's been going all around town about my guesthouse?" I asked, playing it mock-innocent. I was starting to think a second career in the theater might not be out of the question, after all.

"Your . . . oh, all that ghost nonsense? Is that what I'm supposed to be scared of?" Donovan chuckled deep in his throat and sat there grinning at me from behind his desk.

"No. *That's* what you're supposed to be scared of," I said, pointing at an area just to his left and a few feet over his head.

Donovan looked up to where I was pointing. And there he saw something he probably had not expected to see.

A red bandana hung suspended in the air, all by itself. Paul's message had gotten through, all right.

"What the hell is that?" Donovan scoffed. "A flying napkin?" He stood up and reached out to grab the bandana. He seemed just a little put off when the bandana moved away from him. Donovan started to look over the bandana, waving his arm in the air.

"There are no wires," I said. "Nothing's holding it up except the head of the person who's wearing it. A person who happens not to be alive anymore. A person who will do anything I ask of him. Now, do you want to go back to McElone and tell her you were lying, or do I leave you here with my deceased friend?"

"This is ridiculous," Donovan attempted. "I'm not going to be intimidated by some cheap parlor trick."

"What would convince you?" I asked. "Does he have to pick up your stapler?" The stapler lifted off the desk and hovered over toward me for a while. Donovan stared at it, mesmerized. "Would it be better if he made the curtains billow?" Naturally, they did. "Or would you prefer that he remove that picture on the wall of you with Henry Kissinger?"

"Wait!" Donovan yelled, before his precious memento had a chance to fly across the room. "I don't believe there's a ghost in this room. I don't believe in ghosts. And you pulling off some kind of trick that you've obviously worked out in advance is certainly not going to convince me."

"Fine," I told him. "Suggest something yourself." I sat in the chair in front of his desk again. "Something over which I clearly have no control. Feel free to indulge yourself. What'll convince you? What would you like to see my friend do?"

"Fine. Let's see your 'friend' lift you up in that chair and make you fly around the room," Donovan said. His voice sounded confident, but he was sweating. This was bothering him more than he wanted to let on. "Let's see that, and I'll be convinced there's a ghost here."

"Be serious," I told him. "Even when he was alive, he wouldn't have been strong enough to—"

And then the chair and I started to rise off the floor and hover around the room. An involuntary impulse caused me to grab the armrests on the leather chair with knuckle-whitening force, and I believe something resembling a shriek escaped my lips. But I was, unquestionably, being lifted around the room.

Which was kind of cool, until I remembered there was a blind man carrying me in a chair through a room with which he was only casually familiar. I stopped breathing for a while.

Donovan, however, looked absolutely shocked. His

mouth dropped open, his eyes widened and his hands unlaced from behind his head and fell limply to his sides.

"Okay, put me down," I told Scott. The chair floated harmlessly to the floor and landed without so much as a bump. Mentally, I marveled at his strength. The old man must have worked out *a lot.*

I gave Donovan the most savage look I have given anyone in my life. Yes, even more than The Swine. "Now," I said in a tone that frightened even me, "do you want that hanging around you twenty-four–seven for the rest of your life? Because, frankly, my friend here has nothing but time."

Donovan swallowed hard. Then he remembered who he was, stood, straightened his shirt and placed his palms on his very impressive desk.

"All right," he said. "Tell me what you want."

I nodded my head just the tiniest bit, to show I'd considered this, and expected nothing less. When I got home, I'd submit the proper paperwork to nominate myself for an Academy Award.

"I want you to show me Arlice Crosby's will," I said.

"That's privileged information," the lawyer attempted.

"Fine. I'll feel honored the whole time you're showing me."

"Why would you want to see that? Believe me, you're not mentioned. Arlice didn't even recommend you before she died."

That stung, although I should have guessed. "I want to see it because you told McElone that I was asking about it. That means there's something there that can make me look bad in the eyes of the police. And as we've established, I don't like looking bad in the eyes of the police. So let's see the will."

"I don't have it here," Donovan said.

But Scott McFarlane's bandana, behind him, told another

story. It was shaking back and forth broadly. "He's lying," Scott said.

"Yes, you do," I said to Donovan.

Donovan looked behind him. Scott immediately stopped shaking his head. Donovan turned back to me. He opened a locked drawer in his desk with a key he took out of his shorts pocket.

"Oh, very well," he said.

Twenty-two

🔑

"So, what did the will say?" Paul was never great at waiting his turn, and now, amid the ubiquitous television crew and tattooed cast members (well, the three remaining ones at least), I was trying just to get through my own front room without being decapitated by a boom mike or ambushed by an executive producer with more investigative assignments to impose on me.

Well, one out of two wasn't bad. I wasn't decapitated.

"Alison!" Trent appeared out of a sea of technicians assembled to record "spontaneity." "We've had a break in Tiff's disappearance!"

"Good," I said, motoring as best I could for the kitchen, which had become our "safe room." "Then you can go find her, and you don't need any help." A good offense is a strong . . . um, something. I don't really like football much.

Trent followed me through the throng. I had greeted Linda Jane on the front porch, and it had suddenly hit me that two new guests were arriving Tuesday, and I had no idea where they'd stay. That appeared to be a problem. It was the very next thing on my agenda—after I talked to Paul.

And that would happen once I managed to ditch Trent.

"You don't understand," he said. People always say that when you disagree with them. It's not that you think they're wrong; it's that you don't understand. I guess people feel better thinking you're stupid rather than thinking you might have a point. "We could get Tiff back by tonight. But I need a professional to handle this just the right way."

I felt like telling him he should find such a professional in that case, but I decided that was probably a bad message to be sending, so I said, "I'm just too busy now, Trent."

He gently took me by the upper arms and maneuvered me away from the crowd, into a corner near the kitchen door. "Alison," he said. "Lieutenant McElone just called. Tiffney's credit card was used to pay for a hotel room in Sea Bright. That means she's spending the night there. All we have to do—"

"All you have to do is wait for the police to follow up, which I guarantee they're doing right now," I argued. "And wait a minute—I saw McElone a couple of hours ago, and she said Tiffney's card hadn't been used since she vanished."

"I guess she just used it. Come on, Alison. I can't wait for the cops. In my business, time isn't just money—it's a *lot* of money." Trent smiled his lady-killer smile, which I have to admit was of very high quality. "I promise I'll make it worth your while."

"Can't you just call down there?" I asked.

"And let her know we're coming? If she's on the run, I don't want to chase her farther away. The fans heard she disappeared on the Web, and now they're threatening to boycott the show if she doesn't return." Trent's gaze bored into my eyes. "We'll go together," he offered.

I wasn't sure whether that made the prospect more or less attractive. "I can't decide now," I told him. "You're going to have to give me an hour at least; I have things to do that can't wait."

Trent let go of my arms and put up his hands, smiling. "Absolutely. Take your time. I'll be here." And he walked back into the mob engulfing my front room. I took the opportunity to finally head to the kitchen.

Paul was waiting for me and tapping his foot, although that had less impact than it might have, since he was tapping it on thin air. "You're not taking our case seriously enough," he scolded.

"It's nice to see you, too. What did you want me to do, set Trent on fire?"

He scowled. "It's an idea," he said.

I poured myself a cup of coffee and sat down. "Do you want to hear about Arlice Crosby's will, or not?" I asked.

"Of course I do!" Paul was easy to irritate; there was a certain amusement to it that was hard to resist. "Did Scott's act work?"

"Like a charm," I grinned. "But I couldn't believe how strong he was—he lifted me and a chair up into the air and floated us around the room. I didn't think he'd be able to handle it."

"It's possible he brought help," Paul said, "but the fact is, people like us can probably do more now than we could when we had actual physical bodies. Something about not having muscles to restrict us, I guess. So—Donovan showed you the will?"

"After that demonstration, he couldn't wait," I said. "I got to read all the way through it, and while I couldn't understand all the legalese, I did get enough of it to know what we're looking for. And maybe who. Is Maxie around?"

Paul looked puzzled. "Maxie? Maxie didn't kill Arlice Crosby."

"I know that. But she's supposed to have been doing online research. Where is she?"

Paul put on a determined expression. "I'll find out." And he vanished straight up through the ceiling.

For a few moments, it was calm. And that was it for the day. In one fell swoop, Paul appeared through the kitchen wall, leading what appeared to be Maxie by the arm. She got stuck on the other side of the wall, yelling, "Stop it! I'm carrying something!" Paul let go of her arm, and in a few seconds, the kitchen door opened wide by itself.

But in addition to Maxie and my decrepit MacBook, Jeannie was standing behind the door. She walked into the kitchen carrying a brown paper bag and smiling. "Breakfast! Bagels!" she shouted. Then she turned and looked at the kitchen door, which was not closing itself. "I guess it's windier in here than it feels." She put the bag on the kitchen table and sat down.

"I'm having a conference right now, Jean," I told her.

Jeannie looked around the seemingly empty room. "Uh-huh."

"Look, you don't want to hear this, but Paul and Maxie are here, and I have to discuss something with them. Feel free to sit in, but . . ."

Jeannie is a pro at not admitting something when she doesn't want to admit it. "If you don't want me around, Alison, you don't have to make up stories."

"I love having you around. But I can't do the pretending thing now." I looked up at Maxie, who was holding the laptop, something that should have clued in Jeannie right then, but she was busy cutting a bagel and looking in my refrigerator.

"Do you have any cream cheese?"

"On the door." I turned my attention to Maxie. "I was about to tell Paul about Arlice Crosby's will," I said. "What have you found out about the people who were here in the room that night?"

Jeannie was halfway into the refrigerator, searching for

something. "I can't tell you anything, except that Tony and I didn't do it," she said.

"I wasn't talking to you."

Maxie, looking even more irritated than usual, put the laptop down on the kitchen counter, across the room from Jeannie. "I've been running as many checks as I can think of on the people we know were here," she said. "I don't have all the names of the cameramen and the techs and all that."

"I'll get them from Trent," I told her.

"Get what?" Jeannie asked. She pulled a carton of orange juice out of the fridge.

I turned in her direction and pointed at a kitchen chair. "Sit down and be quiet. Don't keep asking questions."

Jeannie put up her hands. "I wouldn't dream of interrupting your imaginary conversation," she insisted. She sat down to make herself a snack.

"What have you found out so far?" I asked Maxie.

"Most of them are really dull people," she said. "I mean, some of them don't even show up on Google. Try looking for Warren Balachik sometime and see what you get. The man sells insurance. Honestly."

"Well, let's forget the boring ones and move on to the more interesting bystanders."

"I forget," Jeannie said. "Am I boring or interesting?"

I pointed a finger at her. "What did I tell you?"

She mimed zipping her mouth shut, then opened it to bite a bagel.

"Okay," Maxie went on. "There wasn't anything special about Warren, but his pal Jim Bridges is another story. *He* once accepted a grant from one of Arlice Crosby's charitable foundations."

I waited. Paul waited. Jeannie licked cream cheese off her thumb.

"And?" Paul asked.

"That's it," Maxie said. "That's the connection. He set up a business selling blank media like CD-ROMs and DVDs and makes a very nice living. Not something I'd want to do, but there's nothing wrong with it."

"Tell me there's something more than that," I pleaded.

"I'm just getting started. We also have Dolores Santiago, who has lived in New Jersey most of her life as far as I can tell, and must have run into Arlice at some point."

"I've lived in Harbor Haven most of my life, and I never met Arlice before last Thursday," I told her.

"I haven't had that much time," Maxie said, sounding defensive. "It's a lot of people to search for, and it's more sophisticated than plugging your name into Google, okay?"

"Sorry," Paul said before I could respond with a childish retort. "Did you find anything that looks truly suspicious?"

"Two of them are weird," Maxie said.

"Just two?" I interrupted.

Maxie made a pencil appear behind her ear, so she could pull it out and chew on it. I hadn't noticed that she was now wearing eyeglasses. "There's one," she said. "Very interesting. I looked into the background of your pal Linda Jane Smith."

Some hairs on the back of my neck stood up. "What did you find?"

"I found some lox on the bottom shelf, but I know that's not yours," Jeannie said. "You hate fish. Your mother must have left it." I gave her a dirty look, and she shrugged and looked down at her bagel, which was almost gone.

"It's not what I found," Maxie said. "It's what I *didn't* find. There's no record of a Linda Jane Smith being an Army medic during the Grenada campaign. In fact, there's no record that she was in the Army at all."

A moment passed. "But that doesn't connect her to Arlice Crosby," Paul said.

"Well, wait . . ." Maxie said.

But I jumped in. "Maybe not, but I saw Arlice's will," I

told them. Even Jeannie looked up. "And while two-thirds of her money, a very large sum, was left to the charitable institutions she championed, the other third all goes to a single living relative. Her sister."

"I didn't know Arlice had a sister," Jeannie said. Jeannie knows everybody everywhere, or at least the ones I ask about.

"Neither did anyone else. And this sister is nowhere to be found," I went on. "Donovan says he's searched through all sorts of records and hasn't come up with anyone matching the facts yet, but he's searching for this woman. And here's the interesting thing: The sister is named Jane."

Another moment passed. "Jane Crosby?" Jeannie asked.

Maxie shook her head. "No. Crosby was Arlice's married name. In fact, she changed her name completely when she got married. Her birth name was Alice, and apparently she added the *R* to make it sound more exotic."

"What was her maiden name?" Paul asked.

"That's the thing." Maxie gestured with her pencil, pointing to the computer screen. "Her birth name was Alice Smith."

"So we're looking for a sister named Jane Smith," I thought aloud.

Another long moment. "I don't know where you get this stuff," Jeannie said. "You sure you don't want your bagel? It's an everything."

Twenty-three

I called Detective Anita McElone and told her everything we'd discovered, leaving Paul and Maxie out of the equation for the sake of sanity. She agreed it was interesting but "not nearly enough to warrant an arrest yet." And then she gave me a hard time for not finding out more: Who had Tom Donovan e-mailed after she'd questioned him, and why had he thought he could cast suspicion on me? I *had* tried to force him to tell me those things, but even with the threat of a permanent haunting from Scott, the lawyer wouldn't talk on those subjects. His eyes widened and beads of sweat shone on his forehead. But not a word was uttered.

Clearly, there was someone Donovan feared more than Scott, the police, or me.

In a rare gesture, McElone actually thanked me for my help, assuming that I would now cease my investigation, given that my client—at least, the living, breathing one who was paying me—was a lying jerk who had tried to frame me for murder.

As for Linda Jane Smith, I wasn't really sure how to proceed. She currently seemed to be the chief suspect in Arlice Crosby's murder, and as happy as I was to let the police handle things from here, she was staying in my house. It was inevitable that I would run into her on her way out of the bathroom or reading a book in the library. How should I react? It would be hard not to show my nervousness.

So the logical step was to get out of the house, and the easiest excuse for that was getting into the Volvo with Trent and making at least a superficial attempt at tracking down Tiffney. If I could pick up a little extra money in the process, it was hardly the worst thing that could happen.

And I swear, I was just thinking aloud when I said, somewhere just south of Harbor Haven, "I have people moving in Tuesday, and I have no idea where I'll put them." It had just occurred to me again. Now, my favorite solution would have been to eject Linda Jane and Dolores (who was creepier, if not quite as worrisome) in favor of the new guests, a married couple from Connecticut who'd appear on my doorstep at about two the next afternoon. And they were *not* people looking for ghosts—they were civilians.

It was a little late to call them and say the room was no longer available. Not to mention, I might never see another guest if I did that, and I'd really like to avoid that if possible.

"Well, you can use the room we set up for the cast," Trent said. It startled me, because I'd forgotten I'd said anything out loud about the housing crunch I was about to experience.

"You sure?" I asked. "We have a deal, and I don't want to violate the terms of our contract."

Trent laughed. "You sound so businesslike," he said.

"This is business."

"Don't worry about it. I can shoot around the room for a few days until you get it all sorted out. I can remove the cameras and leave the mounts for them, so we can put them back later. Besides, the cast all sleep in their trailers, anyway. And we're getting most of our best footage anywhere but in the room. Frankly, I only took the room in case it rained a lot and we had to shoot indoors, but the weather's been perfect." He checked the GPS device that was directing us to the Sandy Side Motor Hotel (Harbor Haven did not have an exclusive copyright on all cheesy beach trade names, after all) in Sea Bright. It would be another thirty-eight minutes at this speed, the know-it-all little box suggested.

"You don't make sense to me," I told Trent as I drove. In my side mirror, a white van was keeping a discreet distance, but had been behind us pretty much since we'd left the house. Or was I getting paranoid?

"What doesn't make sense about me?" he said, looking concerned.

"Sometimes you're the guy I'm sitting here with now, this reasonable, funny, down-to-earth man I can talk to."

Now Trent looked downright perplexed. "And the rest of the time?" he asked.

"The rest of the time you're TV Producer Guy, who calls a bunch of spoiled brats his cast and believes that if something wasn't actually written down on a piece of paper ahead of time, that makes it spontaneous. That guy doesn't seem to have a soul and will do whatever necessary to get his show in on time. It's a hard thing to reconcile."

Trent sat back and blinked a few times. "Wow. You really don't hold back when you decide to say something, do you?"

"I don't believe in letting things fester," I admitted.

"I'll say."

The van wasn't getting closer, but it wasn't letting us get too far ahead, either. I couldn't be sure it was following us, but I wasn't exactly tearing up the highway, and the van could have passed me a number of times if the driver had chosen to do so. "I'm sorry if I offended you," I told Trent.

"I don't think I'm *offended*," he answered. "But I've never really looked at it that way. To me, that's part of the job. If I don't get it done, they'll find somebody who will, so I get myself into that mode in order to survive."

"Is *Down the Shore* what you had in mind when you decided to get into the television business?" I asked.

He chuckled with a hard edge. "Of course not. I wanted to make the next *M*A*S*H*. The next *All in the Family*. The next *Seinfeld*. But this is where the work is at the moment, so this is what I'm doing."

"You ever think about getting out?"

Trent raised an eyebrow. "I think about it every morning before I get out of bed. And then I think about it every night when I'm trying to get to sleep. I don't give it a moment's thought in between. I don't have the time."

"Well for what it's worth, I like you a lot better like this than when you're TV Producer Guy," I said. "Maybe you should think about being this guy full-time."

He smiled, and it seemed genuine. "Maybe I will."

I took another look in my side mirror, and there was our constant companion. "I don't want to alarm you," I told Trent, "but there's a possibility we're being followed."

He didn't look back, which I thought showed good judgment. "An unmarked white van?" he asked. "New York plates?"

I checked the plates in the mirror; of course I should have done that already. "Yes. How did you know?"

"It's one of mine," Trent answered. "If we find Tiffney in the motel, I want a camera crew there. It'll make a great moment for one of our sweeps episodes."

TV Producer Guy was back.

Sneaking up on someone while you're being followed by a boom-mike operator, a camera operator and a "grip"—whatever that is—presents a number of unusual challenges. So it was decided that before we attempted that feat, we'd have a chat with the attendant working behind the desk at the Sandy Side Motor Hotel.

The office of this establishment was a room about six feet by eight feet, into which was crammed a counter, a seat behind the counter, a small television set mounted on the wall over the seat, a floor lamp, a plastic tree in a plastic pot and a couch with vinyl cushions on it, just inside the door in front of the counter.

I was hoping they didn't expect us to stay long enough to need the couch.

The clerk behind the counter looked like he'd been born there and had a hard life. He had no teeth missing; I'll give him that. But his hair was thinning and didn't seem to have been anything to throw a party about when it was there, based on the remnants. His skin was pockmarked and his eyes didn't seem especially interested in focusing on the same point in space.

I decided to let Trent deal with him.

I checked out the snack machine, which looked to have been installed during the reign of the emperor Hadrian. It was enough to make a girl swear off junk food. Behind me I could hear Trent's smile, the TV Producer Guy one, even without being able to see it.

"Good afternoon," he began. "I'm wondering if you can help me."

The weaselly little guy probably wondered that himself, but kept his opinion to himself. "You guys from *COPS*?" he asked.

Trent laughed a laugh similar to a chocolate Easter bunny: sweet and delicious on the outside, but hollow inside. "No, no," he assured his prey. "We're shooting a show called *Down the Shore*. Have you ever seen it?"

"Nope, but we only get six channels here," the little guy answered. "The networks and FOX News. You on any of those channels?"

I turned to look at Trent's face, and it was hard to see the crack in his smile, but it was there. "No, we're not, but we have a strong following in the key demographic of . . ." Trent remembered who was hearing his words, and he stopped in mid-sentence and chuckled. "I'm talking in industry jargon. Sorry. Anyway, we're here shooting this show, and we're looking for one of our stars."

The little guy perked up at that. "Yeah? You think a TV star is here?" He looked around at the "lobby" and looked puzzled.

"Absolutely!" Trent said, playing to the guy's perceived weakness. "We think she's right here, in hiding, and we want to film her in the motel and bring her back to the set of the show. Can you help us find her?"

"How can I do that?" the little guy asked. "I didn't see no TV stars walking around here."

"Well, we know she used her credit card when she paid for the room," Trent said. "It's Tiffney Warburton."

"That's no TV star," the guy said. "A TV star is, like, David Caruso or Paula Abdul. *That's* a TV star."

Trent's voice lost most of its patience. "Could you just please look and see what room Miss Tiffney Warburton is registered in?" he asked.

The little guy banged on the keys of a grimy computer first used by Marconi in nineteen twenty-six, and green copy finally appeared on the foot-thick monitor screen. "The card was used for room eighteen D," he said. "Do I get a credit when the episode airs?"

The camera operators and sound guys kicked into gear as we headed up the outdoor stairs to the room where Tiffney was staying. And as Trent and I led the charge, something occurred to me that hadn't before.

"How come the cops haven't been here yet?" I asked. "The locals would have had a huge head start on us; even McElone should have beaten us here. Why didn't the guy at the desk say anything about cops, other than the TV show?"

Trent shrugged. "Maybe he just came on duty and missed them," he said.

"And the previous guy didn't tell him?"

Trent looked annoyed. "How am I supposed to know why the cops haven't been here yet?" he asked. "It just makes it that much more important that we get this done quickly." He gestured to one of the camera operators, who rushed to a room door and set up the camera on his shoulder.

"Hey, I don't want to be on screen for this," I told Trent. "I don't want people to see the crazy ghost lady running up to a sleazy hotel room in pursuit of a girl who doesn't wear much on a good day."

"But it's great publicity for your guesthouse," he said.

"How?"

"Anything that gets you on national television is a plus," Trent answered. "It's like free advertising in every state and a number of foreign countries."

We stopped at the top of the stairs, which annoyed the tech crew. They were in full adrenaline rush and didn't want to pause for any reason. "I'm already going to be seen on nationwide TV in a white terry cloth bathrobe trying to conjure up spirits of the dead while a lovely old woman in the room with me is murdered," I told him. "How much more great publicity could I want?"

"You're sure? You don't want to be seen at all?" Trent seemed truly stumped by this weird character trait I was exhibiting.

"I'm completely sure."

He tilted his head to one side and shrugged. "Okay." He turned to the crew. "No shots of Alison," he told them. "Keep her off camera at all times."

They nodded. They got paid the same whether I was on screen or not.

Trent nodded. "Okay, then. Let's go."

It wasn't hard to find room 18D; it was three doors to the left of the stairway, and there was a sign that would have been easy to read if most of the letters hadn't fallen off during the Reagan Administration. We were in front of Tiffney's door in roughly fifteen seconds.

Once again Trent turned toward the crew, but this time he spoke in hushed tones. I found myself wishing the female camera operator I'd seen at the séance was along; I liked to think she'd have had some compassion for the ambush Tiffney was about to suffer.

"Keep the camera on Tiff, wherever she is," Trent said. "If there's anyone else in there, get shots of them after we're in the door." The camera operator nodded. Trent looked at the sound engineer. "Keep the mike on Tiff, no matter what. We'll add subtitles for anybody else if we have to."

"I think I'll wait in the car," I said in a slightly louder-than-usual tone, hoping to alert Tiffney. "You don't need me here."

"You're the investigator," Trent answered, motioning me to keep my voice down. "If there's any . . . evidence we need to see in there, you're the one I want to see it. You're the professional. You need to stay."

I didn't have time to argue because Trent was banging his fist on the door before I could respond. "Tiff!" he shouted. "Let us in!" But he was already taking the key—a real key, not a swipe card—he'd wrangled from the desk clerk (thirty dollars bought a lot in this neighborhood, apparently) and turning it in the lock. I held my breath. I'm not sure why.

Trent pushed the door open. He let the camera crew in first, but he was hot on their heels. "Tiffney!" he said on his way in. "You scared the migraine out of us!"

I stayed outside the room. For one thing, even if there was "evidence" inside, I had no idea what I'd do about it. For another, I really had no interest in seeing what was going on in the room. I already felt a little queasy.

In a few moments, the tumult died down, and I could hear some kind of grumbling noise in between Trent's questions. I was mentally thanking my lucky stars when he called out to me, "Alison! Would you come in here, please?"

After considering the answer *no*, I exhaled and walked into the room.

It was small and dark, as the room-darkening drapes had been drawn, but even so I could tell this was not the Waldorf-Astoria. The room consisted of a bed and a bed stand with an analog alarm clock that had no radio. At the far end was a door to the bathroom I was hoping I'd never have to look at.

And sitting on the bed, naked from the waist up, blanket covering the areas I was least interested in seeing, was a very dirty looking, middle-aged, bearded, overweight man. He looked annoyed, confused and guilty.

Tiffney was nowhere to be seen. And as I mentioned, I was not about to look into the bathroom.

"I don't know nuthin'," he was saying as I forced myself through the door. "I don't know nuthin'."

"Oh, you know something," Trent said. Facing me, he added, "Alison, can you question this man for us?"

"Question him? Question him about what?"

"If it were me, I'd start with why he's in Tiffney's motel room, and why Tiffney isn't." Trent looked at the camera operator, who pointed the camera directly at me.

I didn't want to look like I was on a perp walk, so I didn't put my hand over the lens, but I did tell Trent, in no uncertain terms, "I'm not questioning anyone about anything until I'm no longer on camera."

Trent nodded, and the camera was pointed back at our less hygienic friend.

Questioning . . . questioning . . . What would Paul ask?

"All right," I began. "What's your name?"

"Darryl," the man said. "I'm Darryl."

"Okay, Darryl." I wanted to make him feel safer, but the last thing I wanted to do was sit down on that bed or touch anything he had touched. "Tell me how you happened to be in this room."

Trying to focus seemed to calm Darryl. Well, that and the two empty bottles of Johnnie Walker Red that my pupils were now dilated enough to notice on the shag-carpeted floor. "I just came in to get out of the sun," he said. "I burn awful easy."

Sure. "You're not in any trouble, Darryl," I breathed at him, talking as much like a TV therapist as I could imagine. "We're not here to bother you or anything. We're not the police."

"This isn't *COPS*?" he asked. I started to wonder if any of the *Down the Shore* crew worked on that show and were unusually memorable.

"No," I assured him. "It's a show called *Down the Shore*. And they're looking for a girl who is on that show. Now, she's supposed to be in this room."

"Ain't no girls here," Darryl protested. "I don't do that kind of thing."

"I'm sure you don't," I told him. "I'm positive of it." In fact, the only thing I was certain of was that this was the kind of thing Paul would say to him. "But here's the thing: That girl's credit card paid for this room here at the motel. Now, how do you figure that?"

Trent was directly over my left shoulder; I could feel him there, leaning in. I wasn't sure what the camera operator was focusing on, but I was willing to bet he was going in for a close-up on Darryl. At this point, as long as he wasn't taking my picture, I had no problem. Darryl would probably sign a waiver form later in exchange for another bottle of Johnnie Walker.

He licked his lips now, possibly thinking about that. "Skinny little girl? Blonde hair?" he asked. "Great big . . ." He made a gesture, probably trying to think of an acceptable word to use.

"Yes," I said, trying to head him off before he came up with one. "That's her. Do you know her?"

"No," Darryl shook his head with conviction, which was probably something he'd had once or twice before. "I just met her the one time."

Trent couldn't bear it anymore. "One time?" he asked. "What time did you meet Tiffney?"

Darryl blinked, confused by the change in questioner. "Why, the time she gave me the credit card," he said.

Darryl's story was simple: He'd been living on the streets in Sea Bright, a town that doesn't really take kindly to people living on its streets. And earlier that day, he'd run into this "skinny blonde girl" who had come up and spoken to *him*, not the other way around. He'd figured she was a prostitute, based on the way she was dressed, but he'd never seen a working girl in this town before, so when she explained that she just wanted to help him, he accepted the gesture in the altruistic spirit in which it was offered.

Or words to that effect.

The girl had suggested he needed a shower and a long nap, and pointed out the Sandy Side, a mere half-block away. When Darryl had protested that he had no money for such luxurious digs, the skinny girl (whom he identified as Tiffney from a photograph Trent carried with him of the *Down the Shore* cast) had helpfully handed over a credit card. She had kissed him on the cheek, he said, and then hopped into a car, whose make and model he could not identify, and driven away.

So after a quick trip to the Liquor Mart, he'd booked himself a swanky room at the motel the girl had so graciously pointed out, had himself a drink or thirty, and passed out cold on the bed. Cut to Trent pretty much breaking the door down, and we had the whole complex narrative completed.

Trent took back the credit card, but assured Darryl he could spend the rest of the week at the motel. I'm relatively sure a certain amount of cash changed hands as well, since Darryl stopped asking if he could also go back to the Liquor Mart. And we headed back down to the waiting van and my Volvo wagon.

"Well, at least we know she's still alive," Trent said as he hopped into the passenger seat of the Volvo, never even considering driving back with his crew.

"We know nothing of the sort," I told him. Hell, if he wanted a professional investigator, I could pretend to be one.

"What do you mean? Darryl identified Tiff from the picture of the cast I showed him." Trent seemed personally offended that I would question the credibility of a homeless man with two quarts of whiskey flowing through his veins.

"Did you see him clearly? Or, for that matter, smell him clearly?" I asked. "He would have identified her if you'd shown him a picture of Mary, Queen of Scots. All we know is a blonde girl with large breasts talked to him on the street and gave him Tiffney's credit card. Assuming he's even telling us that much of the truth. I've never seen such a blatant setup in my life. Someone wanted us here. I only hope it's not because they wanted us away from the house."

I drove a little faster on the way back home. Trent didn't say much.

Twenty-four

Paul found the whole motel gambit fascinating, as I knew he would, and agreed with me that it was meant to attract Trent's attention and lead him (and, by extension, me) to the motel. But he was dismayed by the fact that we hadn't found anything there other than evidence that someone wanted us to go to the motel.

"And you let the guy go?" he continued. "How do you know he didn't kill Tiffney and just tell you some crazy story?"

"There was no body," I countered, though it sounded lame even to me.

"You need to alert the police in Sea Bright, at the very least," he scolded. "Since we discovered that mannequin, Lieutenant McElone is treating this seriously. She thinks Tiffney might really be a suspect in Arlice Crosby's murder. Let McElone know about this, and she can act upon it."

I hate it when he's right.

We didn't have time to argue the point, however. Since I'd left, things around the house had gotten a little bit more interesting. Maxie, at no one's suggestion, had followed Linda Jane around the house all afternoon, and had reported no suspicious behavior of any kind. That in and of itself was not interesting.

But it had left Paul to his own devices, and he had been busy. He'd been floating through every room of the house, stopping to listen to conversations when he could, and checking in on the filming going on in the backyard. Among his reports were that Jim and Warren appeared to have had a falling out (to the point that Warren had been packing his bags at one point) and were drinking beer in separate rooms, but they had recently reconciled; H-Bomb was "going ballistic" over Trent's absence while he was searching for Tiffney in Sea Bright, complaining that she never got that kind of attention and maybe she should disappear, too, just to show Trent what going without a star was *really* like; Mr. and Mrs. Jones had still not been seen outside their room, although a pizza delivery boy did show up at their door at one point, and money changed hands.

But most enticing of all, Paul told me with a crooked grin, was that Bernice Antwerp had been spending the afternoon complaining about the babbling coming from Linda Jane and Dolores's room.

"What's so interesting about that?" I asked. "Bernice would complain about air if she didn't have to suck some in to complain with."

"Linda Jane wasn't in her room when Bernice was doing the complaining," Maxie said. "I was with her out on the front porch."

I stared for a moment. "I'm not getting it."

"Dolores was in the room by herself," Paul said. "I went in to look. She was sitting on the bed, chanting, for an hour by herself. And she had surrounded herself with . . . objects."

"Objects?" I wasn't sure I wanted to know.

"Objects," Maxie said. "Paul made me come up and see

for myself. She had, like, every little metal triangular thing on the face of the planet, all laid out on the bed around where she was sitting."

Little metal triangular things . . . My fingers instinctively went to the amulet around my neck. "Like this?" I asked.

Paul beamed. "Exactly. Dolores was having some kind of spiritual experience, as far as I could tell, with one of those little ghost detector devices going off right next to her bed, and her attention was so focused she didn't even notice it."

"What the heck was that all about?" I asked. "Dolores tried to take the amulet from me the other night, and she was fascinated with it the night—"

"The night the old lady died," Maxie said.

I held the little silver triangle up in front of my face. "What the hell *is* this thing, anyway?" I thought aloud.

"That's what we need to find out," Paul said. "Maxie, fire up Alison's laptop. We need some more research."

Maxie did less grumbling than usual, although she insisted that we start discussing the purchase of a new MacBook if she was "going to have to keep doing this high school homework." I had to agree with her—the laptop was old and slow—in every way but the one that counted: financially. I gave her the amulet to use as a reference in her work, and she put it in the pocket of her jeans. Somehow, putting objects in their clothing seemed to make the things less material for the ghosts, and the items could then travel through walls and such. I'd seen Scott McFarlane do that with his bandana when he left the house.

She vanished up to her attic lair, which I really had to talk to Tony about. I was starting to feel bad about taking Maxie out of the place she seemed to love so much, but I was going to need the money it would bring at some point.

"You know, it's her birthday Wednesday," I said to Paul after Maxie had ascended.

He looked up, perhaps thrown off by the segue. "What?"

"Wednesday. It's Maxie's birthday. She would have been thirty."

"No kidding. Well, I think presents would be somehow inappropriate." Paul was thinking about the case, and could seem a little unfeeling when he was engaged like that. "Why would Dolores be praying to triangles?"

"How would I know?" I asked him back. "None of this business makes sense. I knew Arlice Crosby for half a day while she was alive, and now I know her real name was Alice Smith and she died in my house, and she had a sister named Jane Smith who may or may not be the same Linda Jane Smith currently staying at my guesthouse, and I still have to repair the felt on the pool table."

"What's the felt on the pool table got to do with anything?" Paul asked.

"Nothing. I just happened to remember it. It's on my list of things to do. So, you're the experienced private eye. You tell me what you make of all this."

Paul's ego, when stroked, could grow to the size of the battleship *Missouri*. "Let's go over the facts," he said, playing with his goatee as he hovered over the floor. "We have a very wealthy woman, who no doubt is leaving behind a large estate but is giving most of it to charities. She has a sister—estranged, perhaps—who does not seem to be stepping forward to claim her inheritance. And she left you with an amulet that doesn't seem to be very valuable in monetary terms, but which apparently has some significance for Dolores Santiago."

"There's one thing we're forgetting," I said.

"Just one?" Paul looked amused.

"Remember, Linda Jane told us there is another diabetic in the house, one of the guests, and that person would have to have had access to enough insulin to have killed Arlice. But if that person used all the insulin to send Arlice into an instant diabetic coma that killed her . . ."

"Then that person, being a type 1 diabetic, would need

to replenish the supply of insulin for their own use," Paul said. "That's right. How could we have missed that?"

"I kept hoping McElone would solve the case, and I wouldn't have to think about it," I admitted.

"She still might. I think we need to give her a call."

"What's this 'we' stuff, kemosabe?" I grumbled. "She won't be mad at *you*. What am I asking her now?"

"Have there been any deliveries made to the house since Arlice's death, something in a package for one of the guests, probably a refrigerated package?" Paul asked.

"No," I shook my head. "I'd have had to sign for it if it came here, and I certainly would have heard about it from one of the regular delivery services. There hasn't been anything."

"In that case," Paul said, "you need to ask Lieutenant McElone about where she found vials of insulin in the house."

"We know where," I reminded him. "She found some in every room."

"She found *empty* vials in every room," Paul corrected me. "We need to know where she found *full* vials."

I'd had enough that night, so I didn't call Detective Lieutenant Anita McElone until the next morning. She'd had enough, too—of me, she said—but she agreed to meet me at the Dunkin' Donuts in town before I dropped Melissa off at school.

"You know perfectly well I'm not going to discuss private medical records with you," McElone said, looking down at me over an iced coffee with coconut flavoring in it.

"I'm not asking you to divulge anything you got from medical records," I said, parroting what Paul had instructed me to say. "I'm asking you to tell me about information you got from your search of my house, which you'll recall I agreed to without a warrant."

If a face can look sarcastic, McElone's managed it in that moment. "Nice try," she said. "But I had more than probable cause, I was already inside the house, and even if what you said were true, I'd owe you a grand total of nothing."

I told her what I was thinking about the vials of insulin. What the hell, maybe playing it straight would work. "If I can figure out who the other diabetic in the house is, that person would leap to the head of the suspect list, no? It had to be someone who had quick access to a large supply of insulin. Now, who would have that much? Even a diabetic away for ten days, the longest any of my guests is staying, wouldn't carry that many vials. Who's going to have a large enough supply to inject Arlice with that much insulin?"

"You're thinking out loud," McElone said. She watched as Melissa, working seriously on a Vanilla Kreme doughnut with a Nesquik chaser, sat at the next table, reading an Amelia Bedelia book. "You're trying to work it out all on your own. It's not bad to ask yourself questions, but if you don't have the answers, that means you don't have enough information."

I looked at my daughter, who, by the "sugar high" theory, should have been bouncing off the walls, but was calmly reading a book. I must have been doing something right with that girl.

"I don't have enough information because you won't tell me what I need to know," I pointed out to the detective.

"No, you don't have enough information because you haven't been doing this long enough, and you don't know what you should be looking for." McElone took a sip of her iced coffee and grimaced a little. "The coconut never lasts to the bottom," she lamented. She stood up and put the cup into a trash bin, and she didn't sit back down. "You have some instincts. I wouldn't have said that before, but I'm starting to see it. But the bottom line is: I'm a cop, you're not, and I don't have to tell you anything. It's better for both of us if I don't. I'm sorry."

And she kept walking until she was out the door. I didn't even try to stop her.

I looked over at Melissa. "Paul's going to be mad at me," I said. "Let's go."

Melissa put a bookmark at the page she'd been reading—she'd never dog-ear a page—and stood up, sliding her arms into her jacket. "She's right, you know," my daughter said.

"Who's right about what?" I thought I was about to get a quotation from the wit and wisdom of Amelia Bedelia.

"Lieutenant McElone. She's right about you looking for the wrong thing."

Well, that was a stumper. "What do you mean? What should I be looking for?"

Melissa picked up her little messenger bag and slung it over her shoulder as we headed for the door. "If I were you, I'd be looking for a bunch of little plastic letters with magnets," she said.

"Little plastic letters?" That struck a chord, but I couldn't for the life of me think of why.

We walked to the Volvo and got in. Liss looked at me. "Don't you remember? Scott said that whoever wanted him to scare Mrs. Crosby talked to him with little plastic letters from a kid's set, and that they stuck to a board with magnets, and there kept being more and more. So, whoever has the letters is the person who wanted her to be scared, and probably wanted her to be dead."

I started the car up. "You know, you've got something there. But why would the person"—I didn't want to use the word *murderer* with my ten-year-old; call me old-fashioned—"still have the letters? Why not get rid of them?"

"They weren't expecting Mrs. Crosby to come to our house the night she died—it was a surprise," Melissa reminded me. "Besides, they're just toy letters. They're not evidence or anything. The police don't know about them. And the person is probably pretty sure you don't know about them either. But if you find them, you'll know who to be watching."

I stole a glance at my daughter, just to make sure she was the same girl I'd had to tuck into bed the night she'd first seen *All Dogs Go to Heaven* because "it was so sad." Well, they say kids grow up fast these days. "Are you sure they didn't leave the letters at the house Scott was staying in?" I asked.

"No. Scott said the letters were gone the day after 'the trick,' remember?"

I nodded. "So, wherever the letters are, if they're still around, that's where the person behind the first attack brought them."

"That's right," Melissa said, proud of her pupil. "Find the letters, and you find the killer."

"I didn't even think you were listening to the conversation I was having with the detective," I said. "You were reading a book."

"I was multitasking," Melissa answered.

"You're so smart."

"You sound like Grandma."

It only took a minute to stop at the High Valley Cemetery, since it was between the Dunkin' Donuts and the house. And I told Melissa to stay in the car, so she got out and walked with me.

It wasn't a large graveyard, but it was full of the history of Harbor Haven. The elite of the town, dating back to the eighteen hundreds, were still in residence here.

So, in a very new grave, was Arlice Crosby.

"Why do you want to see her grave?" Melissa asked.

"It's a way of showing respect," I told her. I didn't tell her I still felt a little responsible for what had happened to Arlice. Okay, more than a little. "The funeral was yesterday, and all the important people in the town came. I didn't, because I didn't think I'd fit in. So I'm coming now. It's the way we remember someone we liked who isn't here anymore."

We found the Crosby family plot, with the largest stone, a tiny version of the Washington Monument, devoted to Jeremiah Crosby, who had died seventy-eight years before I was born. Next to him was his wife Henrietta, who had outlived her husband by only a year. Various children and grandchildren were included in the plot.

The freshly dug one, just to the right of the one with a small, dignified stone reading, "Jermaine Crosby, 1929–1980," was for Arlice. I stood there for a moment, mentally apologized to her for what had happened and asked her to drop by sometime and let us know who had killed her. Then I remembered a Jewish tradition of putting a stone on the gravestone to show that someone had been by, and did so. I knew Arlice wasn't Jewish, but I'd forgotten to bring flowers.

Melissa looked thoughtful throughout, but didn't say anything. I'm sure she had at least thirty questions, but she kept them to herself.

Finally, I heaved out a long breath, took her hand, and said, "Let's go." And we turned to walk back out to the Volvo.

As I walked toward the gate, though, I noticed a large stone in a plot about a hundred yards from Arlice's that bore the name "SMITH." Eight people were interred there, with dates ranging from the late eighteen hundreds to only three years earlier.

That grave, the most recent one, had a small, simple headstone, too. And it was for a woman of sixty-one years.

Her name was Jane.

Twenty-five

"Jane Smith is a very common name," Paul said. "It doesn't necessarily have to be Arlice Crosby's sister."

I couldn't talk to him at the moment, but I nodded, acknowledging that the coincidence was pretty, you know, coincidental. But I fixed my gaze on him and very quietly dared him to dispel my suspicion.

"You want the same color?" Bobby asked.

"I want what's cheapest," I told him.

Bobby was a friend of Tony's who ostensibly knew something about fixing pool tables. Tony had brought him over to give me an estimate on mine.

"Do you think it's doable?" I asked him, hoping that Paul, currently in a sitting position in midair, would pick up on the question.

"They're all doable," Bobby said. He had a gut big enough to have its own nickname, but he seemed like a nice man. Tony didn't deal with jerks when he could help it. "The question is whether it's doable at a price that makes it worth doing, and that I don't know yet." He started punching keys on a BlackBerry he pulled off a holster on his belt, presumably to check on the cost of materials.

"There are too many threads to this case," Paul said. "I just don't know which way to go with it. It's almost like we have *too many* clues. The amulet Arlice gave you. The insulin vials. The plastic magnet spelling letters. Now Mc-Elone considers Tiffney a legitimate suspect just because she seems to have fled or vanished right after Arlice died, but I can't even begin to think of a motive she'd have. Tiffney doesn't get any money from Arlice's estate. And I don't know whether we should be looking for Arlice's missing sister, or if that sister is already dead."

"It's going to come to two-eighty for the felt itself, which will come custom cut to fit perfectly," Bobby said after his BlackBerry told him the price.

"It's too much," I said to Paul. Bobby scratched his head.

"I can get the price down a little bit, but we haven't even discussed labor yet," he said.

"I agree," Paul told me. "It's almost like someone is planting clues, trying to lead us in a specific direction. It's making me rethink the theory in which Linda Jane is the only suspect."

"What are our options?" I asked both men.

Bobby, since he didn't know anyone else was in the room besides Tony, answered first. "Well, I can get a slightly lower-quality felt for about two hundred, but I still have to charge you for my time and labor. Now since you're a friend of Tony's, you get the family discount, so all in all, let's say three hundred for the whole job."

I pretended to think it over in order to give Paul time to answer. The truth was, three hundred dollars was considerably less than I had expected to pay to fix the pool table, and I was going to charge Jim and Warren half of that because they had, in fact, caused the damage.

"There's the possibility that Jim or Warren had some motive to want Arlice dead we haven't considered yet,"

Paul said, picking up his cue (not the pool kind, the other kind). "There's also the possibility that Dolores has some strange religious belief that might have led her to do Arlice in. Or, Tiffney could simply be a wild psychopath who's interested in killing simply as an art form and will do random violence to anyone she decides is worthy of it."

"Okay, I'll take it down to two-fifty," Bobby said, I guessed because he thought my pause was a sign of reluctance. "But honestly, I'm not making a dime on the project."

"Alison," Tony said, "it's a fair price. It's *better* than a fair price." I rolled my eyes toward Paul's location so that Bobby couldn't see and Tony could. "Oh," Tony said, nodding. He turned toward Bobby. "Just give her a minute."

Bobby, looking positively incredulous that anyone would need to take this long to consider such a great deal, looked at Tony, then shrugged and took a beer out of a cooler I kept nearby. He sat down and opened it.

"This is not exactly what I wanted to hear," I told Paul as quietly as possible. I took out my cell phone and pretended to dial a number, and Paul swooped down a little to be closer to me, so he could hear the whisper. "Should I send Melissa to Wendy's after school?"

"I don't think so," he answered. "I seriously doubt any of the *Down the Shore* cast are bright enough to plan this kind of crime. I think the other possibilities are much more plausible, which means you and Melissa aren't in any danger at the moment. But we have to focus on which avenue to pursue. And the fact is, Lieutenant McElone is probably investigating all of them except one."

"The spelling letters the killer used to communicate with Scott," I guessed.

"That's right. There's no way she could know about those," Paul answered. "I'll see if I can get Scott back here to talk about it."

"I left him watching over Tom Donovan," I told him. "He's probably still there."

From the other side of the room, I heard Bobby ask in a stage whisper, "Does she know her cell phone isn't turned on?"

"Anything's possible," Tony answered.

"I'll check," Paul said. "But I don't know how much he'll be able to tell you. As far as he knows, the letters simply vanished the day after Arlice Crosby died."

"I know. But he never really knew how the person got in and left him messages. He never really knew why the messages started to begin with. He never really knew what they were promising. No disrespect to Scott, but I think this situation requires a pair of eyes that are still functioning."

"So what can he tell you?" Paul asked, but his smile indicated he already knew the answer to the question.

"How to get to the house he's been staying in," I said.

Bobby stood up and put the empty beer bottle into one of the bins I have for recycling in every common room. "I don't want to rush you, Alison, but . . ." he said.

"I'll take it," I told him. "When can you start?"

Scott McFarlane, being a ghost, could zip along at a pretty decent clip, not having to worry about things like physical laws and where his feet were touching. And he knew how to get back to the house in which he'd been staying pretty much from anywhere on earth, once he could find his bearings. So we worked out a system by which he would wear the red bandana so I could track him, and I would follow behind in the Volvo. The only thing I reminded Scott of before we left was that the town's speed limit on non-highways was twenty-five miles per hour, and he should curtail himself if he didn't hear the Volvo behind him.

I also mentioned that going through trees, buildings or other structures not actually on a road might be a no-no. He had to stick to roads and sidewalks.

It didn't take long to find his home in Avon after only a couple of Scott's excursions into wooded areas when I'd had to honk my horn and warn him back. He stopped in front of a small cottage, one of the older vacation homes that had probably never been winterized. I couldn't tell if he was pointing, but he was certainly trying to get me to notice. Without being able to see more than a bandana, it was difficult to gauge his mood. So why did I think he was showing off his home proudly? Was it something I'd projected onto myself, since I was constantly trying to get people to notice the little touches I'd made to my house?

"He's pointing and nodding his head with a smile. I think he's really proud of the place, and wants you to notice," Mom said.

Oh, did I forget to mention that my mother came along? Well, neither Paul nor Maxie could leave the guesthouse grounds, and I wasn't bringing Melissa on any more investigation jobs (she was back at the house, with Tony as the official sitter of record), so Mom got the nod. Sometimes it's difficult when only certain people you know can see ghosts, especially when one of them isn't you.

"Okay, let's go see," I said.

The house was small and had obviously been abandoned some years before, or perhaps had been bought up in some land development plan that never came to fruition. The front lawn was wildly overgrown, the two steps up to the porch were missing and the windows showed signs of having been boarded up at some point, but were now just broken.

"Do you think he knows what it looks like now?" I asked Mom.

"Of course not. I don't think he knows what anything looks like anymore. It's been more than eighty years since he saw anything. Be pleasant, Alison. Smile."

We got out of the car and walked up the walk, stepping

over the occasional branch or root and avoiding cracked pavement. "It's lovely," I said to Scott. "It's a very cozy little home."

The bandana bobbed for a while, and Scott said, "I'm very happy you're impressed. Please come inside." We graciously accepted, seeing as how that was the point of the whole visit to begin with. I helped Mom up onto the porch, after testing it for my weight, and then pushed open the front door, which didn't require a lot of persuasion to open.

The inside wasn't a vast improvement on the outside, I'm sorry to report. It's not that the house was a shambles; it was just empty and obviously long neglected. It was dusty, and there was water damage from the broken windows and the undoubtedly ragged roof. There was only the living room, a bedroom, and a kitchen on the first floor, and they were each, in a similar way, sad.

"It's very nice, Scott," I told him. "Now, where did you find the messages?"

The bandana started moving very rapidly through the front hall (really part of the living room where the staircase landed) into the center of the living room. Mom and I followed, and I tried very hard not to think about any stray wildlife that might have made the place their home in the years since people stopped living here and Scott started calling the place his own.

There was a closet off the living room, and the bandana stopped in front of it. "I initially found the letters and some other toys for little kids in the closet," he reported. Scott must have opened the closet, because the door came swinging open, and inside there were, as reported, a few old toys. There was a stick horse that looked like Aristotle had ridden it, a wooden jigsaw puzzle (with eight pieces, six of which were still there) of George Washington—which brought up unpleasant memories of another search I'd had to do a few months before—and a Chutes and Ladders game that had probably been played seventeen thousand times, judging by the look of the box.

There were no letters, either plastic or wooden. "The letters vanished right after the scene at the hotel," Scott told us.

"Where did the messages appear when the letters were here? Where did he find them?" I asked.

"Don't talk about Scott like he's not here," Mom scolded. She turned toward the bandana. "She's not really trying to be rude."

"No problem; I didn't take any offense," the bandana said.

"Oh, good. Now Scott, where—" But the bandana was already on the move. In a back corner of the room, near the one completely intact window, was a small easel made of molded plastic. On it was a chalkboard with a shelf at the bottom that was meant to hold chalk and erasers.

"I just bumped into this one day, and it hadn't been there the day before. The messages would appear on this chalkboard, sometimes as often as four times a week, sometimes as little as once a week," Scott said. "At the beginning they were very simple sentences, and then the person who wrote them must have brought more letters, because the messages got more elaborate. The letters had magnets on the back that would stick to the chalkboard, and I could read them with my hands, and then answer in the same way."

"Did you ever stay all night and listen for the messenger?" I asked.

"I did, and even though I didn't hear anything at all, there was a new message in the morning. I asked how it was being done, but never got a response."

"Well, since they were essentially setting up you and Arlice, it makes sense that you wouldn't get an answer," I told Scott. "Tell me, after the letters vanished, did you look through the house for them?"

"I looked all around in this room and the bedroom,"

he answered. "There's not much in the kitchen anymore. Someone took out most of the cabinets before I got here. I couldn't find them anywhere."

"What about upstairs?" I asked.

"I've never been upstairs," Scott responded.

Mom and I looked at each other a moment. I'm afraid we might have betrayed a little too much, but Scott didn't say anything. He couldn't see the look, after all, but he could certainly hear the silence.

"How long have you been here?" Mom asked him.

"About sixteen years."

"And you've never been upstairs?"

The bandana bobbed. "I only need one bedroom. Sometimes, not even that many."

"Did you tell whoever was sending you the messages that you never went upstairs?" I asked.

Scott took a long time to respond. "Now that you bring it up, I think I did mention that once."

I was getting that feeling in my stomach again, the one I'd had just before I opened Tiffney's closet in the trailer. "Okay," I said. "I guess we have to go upstairs."

"Why?" Scott asked.

Mom and I crept up the stairs, Mom because her knees aren't what they used to be, and me because my stomach wasn't ever really strong. Scott levitated up directly through the ceiling, but of course he had no idea where to look, and couldn't see where he was looking. We heard things being knocked over as we ascended, which made me hurry just a little bit more.

At the landing, we followed the destructive sounds down a hall to one of the three doors, constantly testing the floorboards beneath us for strength before stepping firmly down. There were still doors in each of the frames, but a light touch on the one in question and it swung open easily with an ominous creak. This whole house had an ominous creak to it.

There still appeared to be a few sticks of furniture in the bedroom we entered. A dresser with one drawer (of a possible four) left in it was swaying as we walked in, and the bed frame, minus any mattress or box spring, was quivering, seemingly in sympathy.

"Scott," I said forcefully. "Just stand still a moment, okay?"

The movement within the room ceased, and the bandana, as ever, nodded in my direction. I was starting to feel like I had a relationship with what once was one of my cloth napkins.

"Okay," I breathed. "Let's take a nice, *organized* look. Mom . . ." I pointed toward the closet door, because I didn't want to be the one to open it. I pretended to be fascinated by the one remaining drawer, which was actually the third one down on the piece, and the contents could be clearly seen without pulling it out at all.

"Is there anything Scott should do?" Mom asked as she walked—a little slowly, I thought—toward the closet. I was developing what I considered to be a completely rational fear of closets.

"Don't move, Scott," I said. "Get yourself up close to the ceiling, and only swoop down if you hear us scream." The bandana rose up to the ceiling and hovered.

"What's in the drawer that's so fascinating?" Mom asked. I thought she was stalling, but I answered anyway.

"A deck of cards, a map, a pair of eyeglasses and a paperback copy of Dr. Spock," I said. I looked at the cards first, and found they were backed with pictures of women in, let's say, less than complete suits of clothing. "Whoa," I said reflexively.

"What?" Mom demanded.

"Nothing. Someone who lived here had interesting taste in playing cards, that's all." Then I added as casually as possible, "What's in the closet?"

Mom reached over and opened the folding doors on the

closet. She let out a breath. "Nothing," she said. "Absolutely nothing. Except dust. What about the map? Does it show where treasure is buried or something?"

"I'm afraid not. It's a map of Ocean County, and nothing's circled or anything. It's got to be twenty years old."

There wasn't anything under the bed (it would have been hard to miss) or anywhere else in the room, so we decided to move on to the next. That was an even smaller bedroom, with no furniture at all, and the "closet" was actually a cabinet that sat on the floor under the window and surrendered only a blue woolen blanket that had nourished many a moth in its time.

Scott's bandana followed us back out onto the landing. "That's it, I guess," I said. "There's nowhere else to search where the letters could have been stashed."

Mom pointed at the third door. "There's the bathroom," she said.

What the heck; a door's a door. "Okay," I said. "I hope there's a window, or it's going to be dark."

But there wasn't just a window; there was also a stick-up battery-driven lightbulb, clearly installed much more recently than anything else in the house. And sitting in the sink, which bore rust stains but hadn't seen water in quite some time, was an empty vial. A look at its label confirmed what everyone in a ten-mile radius would have expected.

"Insulin," Mom said out loud.

"There's a medicine chest," I noted, and I reached up to open it.

Inside, perfectly positioned on what appeared to be a newly installed center shelf, was a rubberized plastic aspirator, the kind of device you use on an infant who has a cold, to clear out the nasal passages. I know, because using one on Melissa had been one of my first heart-wrenching experiences in the wonderful pageant that is parenthood.

Mom reached over to get a better look. "What is that?" she started to ask.

I grabbed her hand. "Don't touch it."

This one, blue and bulbous, was attached, using medical adhesive tape, to another empty insulin vial.

"I think someone wanted us to know this was here," I said. "I'm starting to feel just a little bit like somebody's playing me."

The red bandana, visible outside in the hallway, nodded.

Twenty-six

"I think I'm going to just follow you around until this case is solved," Lieutenant Anita McElone said. "It would save me all that commuting time."

She was standing in the upstairs bathroom of what I was mentally calling "Scott's house," examining the artifact we'd discovered in the medicine cabinet. Mom and I were outside the bathroom—there just wasn't enough room for all three of us in there—and Scott, bandana safely tucked away, was around somewhere. From the angle of Mom's occasional glances, I took it he was still inside the bathroom, in the vicinity of the ceiling.

"You didn't touch anything, did you?" McElone asked us.

"Of course not," I answered. "Well, we didn't touch the vial or the aspirator, anyway. Before we found it, I can't say we didn't touch anything else in there."

"I touched the sink, I'm pretty sure," Mom added.

"Every time my phone rings, it's you," McElone muttered, or pretended to mutter. We could hear her perfectly clearly.

"Would you have preferred we *not* call you when we found this?" I asked.

"You've had quite a couple of days," the detective responded, not answering my question. "You come to me, you go to see Donovan, you go to the Ocean Wharf Hotel to uncover some Halloween costume, then you're chasing after some reality television bimbo, stop with me for a doughnut, and now you show up here, hunting down a murder weapon that looks like Gallagher put it together." Her eyes narrowed. "What were you two doing here, anyway?"

"My client gave me some information that led me here," I said, having rehearsed the answer to that one. "I didn't know if there was anything to it, so I didn't call you in advance."

"Gee, thanks a heap." McElone, having put on latex gloves, dropped the injecto-matic into an evidence bag. "Wait—I thought Donovan was your client. How'd he lead you here?"

"Since I went into his office and accused him of trying to frame me, I'm no longer in Mr. Donovan's employ," I told McElone. "This is another client, one who prefers not to be mentioned by name."

McElone gave me a long, hard look. "I don't care what your client would 'prefer.' It sounds like you're working for someone with inside knowledge of a murder, and I can start charging you with withholding evidence whenever I feel like it. So how about you tell me what we're talking about. Who is your client?"

I sighed. "I could tell you, but there's no chance you'd believe me. Just accept that there's no way you can talk to my client."

She curled her upper lip and let out a long breath. "Is this one of your crazy ghosty things?" she asked. "A Ouija board told you to come here and look for a vial of insulin with a rubber pump on it?"

"I said you wouldn't believe me."

McElone took another quick look around the bathroom,

which admittedly was small enough that a long look would have been difficult. "The Avon cops let me in here first, but I'm going to send in their fingerprint guy. How much do you want to bet he finds yours and nobody else's? Everybody watches *CSI* now; they know to wear gloves."

We cleared her way out of the bathroom and started downstairs. "You are looking like an awfully good suspect right at the moment, though," McElone said casually.

I almost took a header, and I was only two steps from the landing. "What?" I asked.

"Well, think about it. You invite Mrs. Crosby over to your house, and she drops dead that night. Nobody else knew she was coming. Then the evidence starts showing up all over your house. And once that's done, evidence starts showing up here, and you're the only person who knows about it. You want me to believe that Mrs. Crosby came back from the dead specifically to tell you about it, but left out the one detail about who injected her. How am I doing so far?"

"Lousy," my mother said before I could. "Alison wasn't even looking at Mrs. Crosby when she died; check the video. She couldn't have reached far enough over to inject her. How do you think she did that? And yes, a ghost *did* tell us to come here today. I can have him show himself to you if that'll help." She looked up in Scott's direction, or what I inferred was Scott's direction. I saw a snippet of red bandana appear, seemingly out of the air.

McElone's eyes widened at Mom's offer, and she drew in a quick breath. She does not like talk of ghosts being in the room with her. "No," she said, "that's okay. I was just kidding."

The red bandana vanished again.

We reached the front door, and I saw a black-and-white police car pull up, presumably with the fingerprint duster and at least one other cop. I turned toward McElone.

"I'm starting to formulate a plan," I told her.

Mom beamed. She's never quite so proud as when I do something.

McElone regained her stern expression—the one she uses pretty much whenever she talks to me—and held my gaze. "I'd very strongly urge you not to do *anything*," she said. "I realize you have a license, but you're still really just an amateur. You're not an experienced investigator, and quite frankly—I'm telling you this for your own protection—nobody would hire you if they really wanted the case to be solved. So please, let me do my job, and don't try to help me. Can I count on that from you?"

Mom gasped at what she perceived as McElone's rudeness. I didn't.

The two Avon cops walked into the house, and McElone told them where to search and what to search for. They pounded their way up the stairs looking determined. When they were out of earshot, I drew myself up to my full height, something I learned to do in yoga class years ago, and looked at the detective.

"Lieutenant," I said, "I know you don't see it this way, but I have a lot of respect for you and the job you do. But someone murdered a guest of mine—in my house, as you so clearly pointed out—there at my invitation. I take that personally. And since then, as you also have been kind enough to note, they've taken great pains to make me look suspicious. I'm not fond of that tactic, either. I realize I'm not Sherlock Holmes, or even Larry Holmes, but I'm not going to let some cowardly murderer push me around. Do you understand?"

It took a long moment, but McElone finally nodded slowly. "As a matter of fact, I do," she said.

"Did you kill Arlice Crosby?"

It seemed like a fair question. After all, Linda Jane Smith had a lot of strikes against her: Melissa had seen (or

dreamed) her doing something to Arlice—like stick her
with a needle—just before Arlice had collapsed. Linda
Jane had access to plenty of insulin in her role as a registered nurse. And when Maxie checked into it, Linda Jane's
story about being wounded as an Army medic—in fact,
her Army service entirely—had not been corroborated.

"No," Linda Jane answered. "But I can see why you'd
ask."

We sat in the room Linda Jane shared with Dolores Santiago, who thankfully was not present at the time. After
Mom and I had gotten back from Scott's house, and she'd
taken Melissa to get a pizza, I'd come up here to start questioning people I considered suspects.

Luckily, Trent and the *Down the Shore* crew were on the
boardwalk that evening and were not expected back until
late. I was saving H-Bomb for last and hoping someone
else would confess before I had to talk to her. Tiffney was
really the suspect, but to get the good dirt on her, I'd have
to talk to Helen DiSpasio.

"You know, I looked into your background a little
bit," I said, glancing briefly at Paul, who was standing about
calf-deep in floor just by the door. "I can't find any records
of your service in the Army."

"That's because you searched for Linda Jane Smith,"
she said.

Uh-huh. "Should I have looked for Napoleon Bonaparte?
Because I'm relatively sure he didn't serve in Grenada,
either."

She smiled. "Linda Jane Smith is my married name,"
she said. "I was born Linda Jane Weatherby, and that's the
name under which I served. If I'd have known it was going
to be an issue, I could have brought my dog tags on this trip.
I thought this was going to be a nice little beach vacation."

I looked at Paul, who nodded and rose through the ceiling. He'd get Maxie to work on checking out Linda Jane's
explanation.

"I know," I answered. "I'm sorry. This has become a little trying for everyone. Can you tell me more about the second diabetic? That might help end this sooner."

"I couldn't tell you that if I wanted to," Linda Jane said, shaking her head. "It's privileged information, and besides, from what I've heard, the amount of insulin that was pumped into Arlice Crosby would have been more than even a diabetic would normally carry around. What I can tell you is that when I got back up here that night, the two vials I had were here, but empty. I still haven't gotten replacements."

That wasn't helping. "You didn't marry Arlice's brother or something, did you?" I asked. "Supposedly, there's a sister of hers nobody can find. I thought maybe it was actually a sister-in-law."

Linda Jane cocked her head to one side. "Sorry," she said. "My Howie was just a small-town boy from Kansas. No relation I'm aware of."

Paul stuck his head in from the attic. "She checks out," he reported. "She was Linda Jane Weatherby in Grenada."

I looked back down at the suspect I was interviewing. "So what do you think?" I asked Linda Jane. "Who killed Arlice Crosby?"

"I haven't a clue," she said.

"Would you tell me if you did?"

"No."

"Why not?" I asked.

"What if I were wrong?"

"I certainly didn't kill Mrs. Crosby," Warren Balachik said. "I had no reason to kill her."

That was a good point. Maxie's research had turned up remarkably little about Warren or Jim. But there was something that was bothering me about both of them, and this was officially the time to start putting cards on the table.

"You and Jim didn't want to talk to the police, even after Jim thought he saw Tiffney do something to Arlice when she died," I said. It wasn't a question, but Warren, sitting in the library with a book (not a beer) in his hand, and without his constant companion at his side, knew exactly what I was getting at.

He looked away. "Jim . . . has a record with the police, and he didn't want to bring it back up when all this happened," he said. "We were arguing about it this afternoon, and I think he's coming around. I shouldn't have told you, but you have to know that he didn't kill Mrs. Crosby."

I leaned forward in my armchair while Warren sat straight in his, holding his copy of *Some Like It Hot-Buttered* closed around a finger to keep his place. "What kind of police record does Jim have?" I asked.

"He had a close call with an armed robbery rap a while back," Warren said, still not making eye contact. "He was out of work and desperate, and he held up a convenience store without any bullets in his gun because he didn't want to hurt anybody."

"Jim didn't go to jail?" I asked. I don't know why that mattered in this case, other than to give Paul, once again hovering near the ceiling, something to check with Maxie.

"No, it was his first offense, and like I say, he didn't actually harm anyone, so they worked out a plea deal where he got away with time served. But he knows how it looks if the police check up on him and see a violent crime. They're not going to ask about the circumstances."

Paul vanished up to the research room, and I vamped. "This was how long ago, Warren?" I asked.

"It was nineteen seventy-four," he said.

That left me with little to say, even vamping, for a few long seconds. "That long ago, and he's still worried?"

Warren shrugged just as Paul came back down, again nodding that things had checked out. "He's a sensitive soul," Warren told me.

On cue, Jim walked through the open doorway (in fact, I had taken the door off the library during the renovation, to present a much more open space and to convey that the books were always available) and saw us talking. "Sorry to interrupt," he said.

Warren and I insisted he was doing no such thing, so Jim sat down. But Warren, getting pink in the face and not knowing where to look (so he looked mostly at the rug), was obviously in distress, so Jim asked about it.

"I told Alison about your . . . misadventure," he told Jim.

Jim, in the process of taking a stick of gum out of his pocket, froze. "You did?" he said. He blinked, then started moving again. "Well, I guess there's really no harm in that."

Warren's head sprung up as if a rubber band in his neck had been snapped. "You don't mind?" he asked.

Jim seemed to think it over, tilted his head from side to side and said, "No, I suppose I don't. It was a long time ago, and Alison's not going to hold it against me. Are you, Alison?"

"Certainly not," I said. "You paid the price for what you did, and you never did it again. Right?"

Jim chuckled. "Right."

Then I remembered something Maxie had told me about him. "But I'll bet you didn't mention that . . . misadventure when you applied for the grant you received from the charitable foundation Arlice Crosby underwrote, did you?"

Paul's face became very serious, and he watched Jim carefully for a reaction. Jim looked positively baffled.

"What grant?" he asked.

"In nineteen eighty-nine, he received a grant from the Selective Entrepreneurial Experiment Development Fund," Paul told me. "It helped him set up his business."

I passed that along to Jim, who nodded. "Oh yes, the SEED money. Did Mrs. Crosby have something to do with that?"

I assured him, after checking with my semitransparent friend, that she had underwritten much of SEED.

"I had no idea," Jim said. "But if I *had* known, I would have been more than grateful. That money helped set up my business, the one I sold for six million dollars three years ago. I had no reason to be angry at Mrs. Crosby."

My suspects were clearing themselves with alarming ease. After Paul confirmed the sale of Jim's business through Maxie, I stood up and thanked the two gentlemen for their candor. I promised not to mention Jim's long-ago transgression to anyone, unless it became relevant to McElone's case. They nodded.

I walked out of the library and toward the game room, but I didn't get far. Standing in the hallway was Dolores Santiago, and despite being Dolores Santiago, she was not the strangest thing there.

Next to Dolores, who was staring at it with fascination, was a child's easel, a plastic one of red, blue and yellow. "This is lovely," Dolores said. "Is this how you communicate with the spirits?"

On the easel were black plastic block letters, no doubt magnetized on their backs, spelling out the message "WE SHOULD MEET."

Twenty-seven

"We're getting too close," Paul said.

Mom and Melissa were eating pizza in the kitchen for dinner. I wasn't hungry, but it seemed a safe haven, so I was sitting there with a Diet Coke and a slice on my plate that I wasn't eating.

"I love how you always make it about 'we,'" I told him. "I don't suppose I have to remind you that *I* can still be harmed by people who are mad at me." I glanced at Melissa and was sorry I'd said anything. But she chewed on her extra-garlic crust and didn't seem to notice. I knew she had registered what I'd just said, but she wasn't going to react to it now. Liss doesn't like to get me upset.

"Of course I do, but focusing on that isn't going to do us any good right now," Paul answered. He was sitting on the stove, which was on to keep the food warm, but Paul didn't have to worry about that. "The point right now is to think about who could have left that easel in the hallway."

I'd balked at the idea of calling Detective Lieutenant Anita McElone yet again. For one thing, I'd already used up about six months' worth of visits with the detective this week, and for another, I'd have to explain the whole "talking to the ghost with toy letters" concept, and I just didn't have the energy for it.

"There's the Santiago woman," my mother offered. I liked that; it sounded like a movie title: *The Santiago Woman*, starring Penelope Cruz or Carmen Miranda. "She was standing right next to the easel when Alison found it."

"Yeah," I said. "But she seemed completely fascinated by the thing, and asked me if that was the way I talked to Paul and Maxie. I also don't think Dolores is strong enough to have lugged that thing to that spot without me hearing her drag it, anyway. I mean, the door to the library was open."

"There is no door on the library," Melissa pointed out. Kids love to catch you being inaccurate. They know what you mean, but they want to have that moment where they can correct you and not be contradicted.

"But Jim did come into the room just before you found the easel in the hallway," Paul pointed out. "It's possible he positioned it there, and then just let you find it when you left the library."

"I guess." That last slice wasn't looking so bad, really. I could force down a bite or two just to keep my strength up. "I really don't think Jim or Warren is the killer. They're too nice."

Paul gave me one of those looks that indicated he might be wondering if he'd chosen the right living partner for his investigation firm.

"There's a clock running now," I said, wondering if we had any more garlic knots. "I need to answer the message on the easel."

"Do you?" Mom asked. "Can't you just leave it unanswered?"

Paul shook his head. "No, Loretta," he told Mom. "Alison can't let the murderer dictate the terms here. She needs to take the lead and start being in charge."

For once, I agreed. "The real question is what to answer," I said.

"If it were me," Melissa said, "I'd agree to a meeting, but be sure it's here in the house. That way, Paul and Maxie can be there without the murderer knowing they are, and that gives you a big advantage. And I'll bet that if you asked Mr. Avalon, he'd be sure to have a camera and a microphone you could use to record evidence."

Everyone sat there and stared at my daughter for what seemed like a half hour.

"The child is a genius," my mother said.

I had what was left of the pizza and washed it down with the soda before I went back out to the easel. "Move it somewhere else," Paul advised. "Show that you're not accepting their conditions."

So I took the easel—with some help from Mom and Melissa—to the game room, which was, as I'd anticipated, empty. Not much was going on in there until the pool table could be repaired, something Bobby had promised would only take a few days.

"Why can't we just hide in here somewhere and see who comes out to read the message?" I asked Paul.

"Anybody could wander in and read it," he answered. "Villains don't really rub their hands together in anticipation and shout, 'Bwahahahaha!' you know."

Well, if he wanted to be rational about it.

"What do you think I should put up?" I asked the gathered crowd.

"Just the place and time," Paul said.

"That's so rude," Mom suggested. "No *please* or anything?"

Melissa looked at her. "It's a meeting with a killer, Grandma," she said. "You don't have to worry about manners."

"You *always* have to worry about manners," my mother retorted.

I started to reach into the yellow plastic drawer that held the extra letters, but Maxie stuck her head through the ceiling and said, "Hold on. I've got something to show you."

It took a minute or so for Maxie to make her way down from the attic, where she'd been holed up. When she carries the laptop or something too large to conceal in her clothing, she can't go through solid objects, so she has to use doors and stairways, just like a solid person. Maxie showed up in the game room, a wicked smile on her face, carrying the laptop. If one of the other guests noticed it, by now the ways of flying objects were ingrained enough that they would barely notice.

"I've got something on that crazy necklace the old lady gave you just before she died," Maxie announced with her usual brand of sensitivity and tact. "It's something called the Key of Solomon."

I gasped. "She gave me something that ancient and priceless?" I marveled. "We'd only just met."

"Yeah, don't get too excited," Maxie answered. "You can get one for about seven bucks on eBay. The one she gave you, in silver, is worth maybe thirty."

I looked at the amulet and frowned. "Still, for someone she'd just met . . ."

"Oh, get over yourself. The thing that's interesting is that the amulet is supposed to be a way to control or contact evil spirits." Maxie grinned, no doubt picturing herself as an evil spirit. I could make the case, but the fact was, neither she nor Paul really belonged in that category.

"So that explains why Dolores was so fascinated with the amulet," I said, bringing myself back to the conversation. "She thinks she can contact 'the spirits' with it."

"Would she kill for it?" Paul asked, apparently thinking out loud.

"She had plenty of opportunities to get it from me without killing me," I said. "She could have just asked me for it. I probably wouldn't have given it away, but aside from that bizarre sleepwalking trick she tried to use, she hasn't done anything to get the amulet from me. If she is after just that, she's going about it in a really roundabout way."

"Besides," Melissa said, "she never asked Scott to get her the amulet. Whoever was sending him the messages just wanted him to scare Mrs. Crosby." I was starting to think that letting Melissa in on all these conversations might not be the best parenting strategy. But she was currently the best analyst out of the bunch of us.

I looked up at Paul. "What do you think our strategy should be now?" I asked. "Do we go ahead with the meeting and see who shows up, or do we assume it's Dolores looking for the amulet?"

"That seems like a stretch," Paul said after a moment of goatee-stroking. "If Dolores is the killer, I don't think it's for the amulet. But you still haven't questioned one suspect in the case."

I'd been anticipating this, and had an answer ready. "Well, I would have talked to H-Bomb, but the crew is out filming on the boardwalk all night tonight. Haven't had a chance."

"Oh, they're back," Maxie said happily. "It started to rain while they were out there, so they all came back. They're in the den right now. Trent was saying something about looking for you."

Damn! "Thanks for the update, Maxie," I said. "Later on, I'll show you some color chips for when I renovate the attic."

She looked as if I'd slapped her, which technically was impossible. And she snapped my laptop computer shut and carried it at top speed out of the room and toward the stairs.

"You really are mean to her sometimes," Melissa said.

"I didn't really mean it," I said.

"Why would I kill that old lady?"

H-Bomb, otherwise known as Helen DiSpasio, had been dragged, not quite kicking and screaming but certainly complaining, to be interviewed. We stood just outside my back door, where my backyard once sat so quietly and serenely. Now, it was covered with double-wide trailers, light towers, satellite vans and equipment I could not, even after having it explained to me, identify. What had been a sanctuary of peace in my sometimes hectic world had been turned into NASA mission control for the gel-and-ab-crunches set. Even in the now-light rain, it was a hub of activity.

I'd asked Trent for a few minutes of H-Bomb's time and had been rewarded with this audience, but only on two conditions, one of which was that the interview had to be filmed. I had argued, cajoled, whined and threatened to try to shake this, but Trent was used to such behavior and stood his ground.

I decided he wasn't attractive in nice guy mode *or* producer mode.

"I really don't think you would want to cause Mrs. Crosby any harm," I answered. "But I'm questioning everyone who was near to her just before she collapsed, and you were there."

"So were Mistah Motion and Rock Starr," she countered. "How come you're not *questioning* them?" She picked some imaginary thread off her bikini bottom, which was so small it could legitimately have been considered a bandage under the right circumstances. "What about Tiffney? That skank."

"Tiffney was seen passing behind Mrs. Crosby just before she fell," I agreed, a little too enthusiastically. "Mrs. Crosby turned to look, and then she collapsed. What happened?"

"How should I know? I wasn't even looking in that direction, okay? That skank Tiffney was in the key light just this side of the glass doors, and then she moved across the room to get an even better camera angle from above, where you can see cleavage. I was so migraine annoyed. I don't know what happened to the old lady."

"*Mrs. Crosby* was a very wealthy woman," I noted. "Were you aware of that?"

"I wasn't even *aware* she was there until she hit the floor," H-Bomb insisted. "I wasn't looking that way. I was totally focusing on that skank Tiffney."

Which, alas, led to the second condition Trent had imposed on the interview. I had to ask H-Bomb, "Do you have any idea where Tiffney is now?"

She rolled her eyes so broadly Melissa would truly have been envious. "Of *course* migraine not!" she shouted. "If I knew where that skank was, wouldn't I have said something by now?"

"Not if it was going to make you look bad," I asserted. "Suppose you had something to do with her disappearance— that wouldn't be so good for your image, would it?"

H-Bomb made a face that indicated complete and utter disgust with my very existence—I'd try to describe it, but there's no way I could do it justice. Suffice it to say that for a moment, her face looked like it was made of Silly Putty, a substance with which I have some history. "Oh, *seriously!*" she screamed. "First, what, I helped Tiffney kill the old lady, and now I killed *Tiffney*? Are you migraine nuts?"

"I never said anybody killed Tiffney. I just said she'd disappeared. Do you know something I don't know?"

H-Bomb said a few more colorful words, made a gesture that my mother would describe as "vulgar" and stomped away. I gave Trent, who was standing just out of earshot, my best smile as I walked back into the house.

It was going to be a great night of filming for him.

Twenty-eight

I didn't see much point in questioning the Joneses, since they certainly hadn't been in the room the night Arlice Crosby died. And Bernice Antwerp hadn't been near Arlice when she'd collapsed; in fact, Bernice had been all the way across the room, sitting down and making notes of things that were unsatisfactory, her favorite form of recreation.

But now that this long day was winding down, I did want to talk to Thomas Donovan, counselor-at-law, once again, so I called him at home. Donovan, having been properly chastened by my invisible friend with a red bandana, answered my call immediately.

"I think you need to get over here," I told him once we stopped pretending to be friendly colleagues.

"What's the problem?" Donovan asked.

I stood in the game room holding my cell phone. Mom had decided to try to teach Melissa how to play pool, having temporarily "repaired" the felt on the table with duct tape. Her theory was that Liss couldn't do much more damage to the table as she learned, and if she could play under these conditions, she'd be a regular prodigy on a proper table. The woman has such faith in her girls, it's actually a little unsettling.

"I'm not in the mood to play around anymore," I told Donovan. Now, just thinking about the lawyer dredged up memories of The Swine, and I didn't even have to try. "I'm about to arrange a meeting with your accomplice, and I think you need to be here for it."

Mom's eyebrows shot up, and Melissa, standing on an egg crate, hit the cue ball completely off the table, opening up a slight new tear in another area of the felt.

"My *accomplice*?" Donovan moaned. "Of what am I being accused?"

"I think it was you who told Arlice Crosby about the pirate ghost at the Ocean Wharf Hotel. Then you tried to cover something up by suggesting to Lieutenant McElone that I was asking about Arlice's will," I reminded him. "You wouldn't have done that if you didn't have something to hide. That something was your involvement in Arlice's murder."

Paul, pretending to sit on the low vinyl sofa next to the pool table (very nineteen fifties, red with chrome armrests), looked appalled. "You can't accuse him of something when you have no evidence," he tried, but it was too late.

"You're being absurd," Donovan answered. "I had nothing to do with Arlice's death. I had nothing to gain from it. What makes you think that I—"

"You forget I know about the e-mail you sent after you ratted me out. You told *someone* that things had gone as planned. So I'll say it again: I'm meeting your accomplice in a half hour," I told him. "Be here, or I'll be going back to McElone with a story of my own, and you won't like the way it ends."

I hung up.

Paul stood up, as if he'd really been resting on the couch to begin with. "Alison!" he said. "What did you just do?"

"It's late," Mom told Melissa. "Maybe it's time for you to go to bed."

"Are you kidding?" my daughter asked her. "It's only eight-thirty."

"You have no evidence," Paul continued. "You have no reason to think Donovan had anything to do with—"

I was already getting out letters to arrange on the easel. "When Scott was supposed to scare Arlice to death, Donovan was there," I reminded Paul. "And he really did try to make me look bad with McElone, as a diversion from *something*. And he's supposedly been looking for Arlice's missing sister, but hasn't been able to find her yet. You have to wonder how hard he's been trying."

"You think he wants all of Mrs. Crosby's money for himself?" Melissa asked.

"No, honey. Most of it will go to Arlice's charities no matter what happens." Once again, I wondered whether discussing this with her was a good idea, but there was nothing I'd hated more when I was a child than adults who'd talked to me as if I were an unintelligent being just because I was younger than they were. Most of them, I knew even then, were idiots.

"So then I don't understand," Melissa went on. "What reason would Mr. Donovan have to hurt Mrs. Crosby?"

"I don't think it's his reason that we're looking for," I said.

"You think he's working with the killer, and has been from the beginning," Paul said, completing my thought. "I concur. But who is his accomplice?"

"We'll find out in half an hour." I had completed putting out letters on the easel, spelling out the message: "ATTIC. 9 PM."

"What makes you think Donovan will come here now?" Mom asked.

"I heard the tone of his voice," I answered. "He was scared."

"Still, you can't be sure," Paul said.

"Watch him show up."

I'd set the "meeting" for the attic because I didn't want it anywhere near Trent and his TV cameras, opting against the suggestion to tape the meeting—if something happened, I didn't see how having it appear on *Down the Shore* was going to help. An added advantage was that Maxie was already up in the attic, still fuming at me but able to report if anyone tried to sneak up early and get the jump on me. She wasn't *that* mad.

I, meanwhile, was busy downstairs, fending off questions from Bernice about the lack of a religious service on Sunday morning, the lack of tea in the evening and the fact that the ghosts had not taken the Sabbath off yesterday. Apparently, she thought I had Paul and Maxie under a contract, and she wanted to act as their agent and renegotiate the terms.

Finally, I managed to break free of her grasp, just as Tom Donovan arrived at the front door. Paul, who had positioned himself just outside the entrance, walked through the wall to announce that I'd been right about Donovan and to give me a few last-minute tips on how to handle the attorney.

"The gruff approach seems to be working well," he said quickly. "Keep that up, and just keep on concentrating. Don't give him an opening. Keep right at him the whole time." I felt like he was telling me to make sure to keep jabbing away with my right and keep my left up to block punches.

There was no time to ask, however, because Donovan was walking through the door even as Paul got the last few words out. I walked over to the attorney and did not offer a hand. I also scowled. Mentally, The Swine was calling to tell me why his child support check would be late. Again.

"I assume you coming here is an admission of guilt," I began.

"It's nothing of the sort," Donovan answered. "You simply didn't give me another choice. Now, what is this absurd notion that I had anything to do with Arlice Crosby's death?"

I started walking toward the stairs, and Donovan followed me. So did Paul. I knew Mom was in Melissa's room keeping her company (and away from the attic, which was where she had lobbied to be), and the guests were winding down for the evening, or in Jim and Warren's case, still out to dinner.

"How's the search for Arlice's sister coming?" I asked Donovan, not responding to his question.

"So far, it's been difficult," he admitted. "But it's only been a few days."

"Maybe you need an investigator to look into it," I suggested with what I hoped was an edge to my voice. "Someone you trust to do a professional job."

"I'll keep your firm in mind, of course," he responded. It was probably a reflex; he was a businessman more than a lawyer, and he probably spoke to everyone that way.

"Of course," I echoed. "I'm assuming that since you tried to cast suspicion on me when you talked to the police, you won't mind when I double my fee."

We had reached the second-floor landing. Donovan was huffing a bit, and that last suggestion got him huffing even harder. "Now see here, Ms. Kerby. If you think you can shake me down for more money . . ."

Paul was just over my shoulder, standing in midair over the staircase, and grinning. "Tell him you're charging extra because you're closing in on the killer at this very moment," he said, and I passed the message on to Donovan.

He blanched, but he didn't have time to react. Instead, from behind Melissa's door I heard my mother shout her name. The door swung open fast, and my ten-year-old daughter was standing in her doorway, smiling at me and the man I suspected of being, at the very least, an accessory to murder.

"Hi, Mom!" Liss tried very hard to be perky, and it came out sort of frightening, if the truth be known. "I was just heading up to the attic!"

"You most certainly were not, young lady," Mom told her from inside her bedroom.

"I'll deal with it, Mom," I called in. I could feel my aura of intimidation fading by the second. "You know we have a meeting set up in the attic right now, Liss," I told her. "You can't come up just now. I'll come see you after."

"But I left my English homework up there," she countered.

"I'll bring it down for you when I'm through." Nice try, Liss.

"It'll just take a second," she tried, but her tone indicated she knew it was a losing effort.

"Not. Now." And I ushered Donovan toward the attic stairs, which I pulled down from the ceiling.

Mom appeared behind Melissa, smiling her public smile at Donovan. "The child is so spirited," she said, nodding faintly at Paul. Then she all but pulled Melissa back into her room and slammed the door. Now, *that* was the Loretta Kerby I remembered from growing up.

"Sorry for the interruption," I told Donovan, and saw Paul frowning at me. Don't apologize to a guy you're trying to intimidate. "I'm sure you're in a hurry to reunite with your accomplice." Not much of a stinger, I'll grant you, but it was something of a recovery.

"Just out of curiosity," I went on, not giving Donovan a chance to reply, "what happens if you don't find Arlice's sister? Who would get the portion of her estate her sister is supposed to inherit?"

"Every effort is being made to locate her," Donovan answered. I stood by the pull-down stairs and gestured for him to climb up. "After you," Donovan tried, but I shook my head.

"Please," I said. "You go first." I didn't tell him that the last thing I needed to wonder on my way up to this rendezvous was whether or not he was looking at my butt.

Donovan sighed, but he started up to the attic. I followed him up, leaving the stairs down in case our mystery guest had not yet entered the arena.

Once upstairs, where I had placed a few sheets of plywood on the crossbeams to avoid going straight through the ceiling to one of the guest bedrooms, I checked first with Maxie, who was "sitting" on a part of the floor with no plywood, arms crossed in a pose of disapproval, sneering at me.

"Nobody's shown up yet," she said, "not that you care who gets to come up here."

I refrained from getting involved in an argument with someone who was, to the other person in the room, invisible. I'd already played the ghost card in Donovan's office, and was not in the mood to pull that particular tactic out again right now. I flattened my mouth out and shook my head a tiny bit, something that I didn't think Donovan would notice.

"Is something wrong?" he asked. So he had noticed.

"Nothing you need to concern yourself with," I snarled at him, getting back into character. "I don't suppose you'd care to tell me who we're expecting up here."

He sniffed. "I'm sure I haven't the slightest idea."

"Well, I guess we'll just have to wait and find out," I told him. "Make yourself comfortable."

Donovan looked around. It was an empty room, only barely floored. There were no walls. There were windows overlooking the *Down the Shore* trailers on one side and a shuttered-up home in the distance on the other.

"How?"

"You'll think of something," I said. I don't know what it meant, either, but it was intended to annoy Donovan, and it appeared to have the desired effect. "Besides, you want to be on your feet when your accomplice arrives."

Paul must have been lurking in the space behind me, because I felt the familiar warm breeze sensation when he walked through, well, *me* to take a closer look at the attorney.

"He's not going to be easy to intimidate," he said. "He's already annoyed."

"Ms. Kerby, I don't know what you think you know, but I can assure you it's not what you think," Donovan said. Maxie rolled her eyes.

"I know enough," I said. "You've seen the will, so you know she has a sister named Jane. You and only you know what's being done to find that sister."

"That's not so. I've already spoken to the police, and they have an investigator on the case." I assumed that was a lie; the most casual of investigations would have turned up a death certificate or an obituary. Maxie had been unable to turn up either on her Web searches yet.

"Find out who," Paul suggested. But I thought he was just scoping out the competition, so I ignored him.

"That's the other thing," I said. "You hired me to investigate Arlice's death."

Donovan looked amused. "That's incriminating evidence?" he asked.

"Sure. You know perfectly well that I'm not equipped or experienced in that sort of investigation, and yet you hired me. One of your most important and wealthiest clients is murdered, and you hire *me* to investigate? Does that make sense to you?"

"I've already explained—" Donovan began.

"Yeah, Arlice was a great patron of the arts and a true believer in new businesses, and she loved to nurture young entrepreneurs. Spare me the speech, okay? You also told me Arlice didn't really recommend me the day she died. You knew I wasn't going to find Arlice's killer, and that's why you hired me. You didn't *want* her killer found." I looked over at Maxie, who seemed engrossed in the scene. I would have expected her to be in hysterics over my admission that I didn't know what I was doing.

Donovan folded his arms and scowled. "This is ridiculous. No one is coming up here. I'm leaving."

"But you're not denying it, are you?"

He had started for the attic stairs, and stopped to regard me with royal bearing. "It's a pity you never went to law school, Ms. Kerby," he said. "You would have made an excellent prosecutor."

"I never even finished college," I said—technically I had a degree from Monmouth, but this sounded tougher, more "street"—"but I know someone sweating when I see it. It's not that warm up here. Sit down, Mr. Donovan."

Donovan actually took a handkerchief out of his pocket and spread it out on the plywood before sitting. But he sat.

We stayed there for quite some time without speaking. I had somehow gotten it into my head that I held a position of advantage over Donovan if he sat and I didn't, so I stood there, aware of every muscle in my legs that wanted to rest. Maxie, without muscles to worry about, laid herself out like Cleopatra floating down the Nile on her barge, rested her head on her right tricep and smiled.

"This is cute," she said. "You're having a not-talking contest."

Paul, who seemed to think observation was the only tactic necessary in an investigation, stood inches from Donovan's face and studied it. "I'll bet his heart is racing," he said.

I kept not talking, so as not to cede the contest. I did glare at Maxie for a moment before once again occupying my mind with thoughts of the murderer about to come up the stairs.

But no one came.

"Why are we sitting here?" Donovan asked finally. "You can see there isn't anyone coming. Your whole theory is absurd. And you're wasting my time."

"You won!" Maxie laughed.

"You're right," I said to Donovan. "I shouldn't be standing here waiting. I should be getting the answers I want right now."

"How are you going to do that?" he asked.

Maxie sat up. She and I had discussed this (however briefly, considering how mad she was at me) before, and she seemed to sense her cue was coming up.

"I'm not going to do anything," I said. "I'm going to let my associate handle the rest of the interrogation."

Paul looked at me abruptly, puzzled. "What? How can I . . . ?"

Donovan looked toward the stairs. "Associate? What associate?"

I'd left a baseball bat between a couple of the uncovered crossbeams, and Maxie swooped over and picked it up, grinning an evil grin that only I got to see. What Donovan got to see was a baseball bat flying into the air under its own steam.

"*That* associate," I answered.

Maxie advanced on Donovan, hefting the baseball bat, tapping it on one hand while holding the knob in the other, no doubt as she'd seen tough guys do in the movies.

"Alison . . ." Paul said.

"Now, my associate here can't ask you the questions," I said as Donovan's eyes widened and his sweat glands went into overdrive. "But he'll ask me, I'll ask you, and you can answer him."

"Him?" Maxie asked. "Do I look like a him?"

"That's right, Vinnie," I said back. "He'd better answer them fast."

"Are you proposing to . . . Ms. Kerby, seriously!" Donovan was as white as a . . . well, what you'd think a ghost would look like if you were basing your assumption on cartoons from nineteen fifty-six. "I can file charges against you for kidnapping and assault if anything so much as—"

"You're going to file charges that say I had a ghost beat you up?" I asked him. "They'll think you're crazy; I can tell you from experience. Besides, I'm not holding you here. You're free to leave whenever you like. Good luck making it to the stairs."

"This is not admissible evidence, Alison," Paul warned me. "Anything he tells us, we'd have to prove elsewhere. This is really bad policy."

"Nothing's going to happen as long as you answer honestly, Mr. Donovan," I said, trying to make my voice sound gravelly. "Vinnie here isn't really a mean guy. Don't let the fact that he was executed by the state of Texas worry you; they execute everybody down there."

Maxie seemed to enjoy that part quite a bit. She smiled broadly and took a large "step" toward Donovan, which made him flinch.

"I don't have anything to tell you," he said.

"That's too bad for you," I answered. "Vinnie?"

I stepped aside, and Donovan's eyes sort of flitted around in their sockets as he tried to decide—I'm guessing—whether to stay still on the floor or make himself a larger target by attempting to bolt for the stairs. Maxie cocked the bat back like Mickey Mantle aiming for the fences.

"Ms. Kerby . . ." Donovan began.

"Vinnie wants to know who contacted you about Arlice Crosby's will—*before* she died," I started. It was a guess, but an educated one. The only motive in the case seemed to be the will, and a killer would have to know about the contents of the will, or why would they bother?

"Not a living soul," Donovan wheezed. "I swear that's the truth."

Maxie took a couple of practice swings. She probably would have made a decent women's softball player.

"Vinnie doesn't think it is," I said. "So I'm going to ask you again, and this time, I want you to think *really hard* about your answer, okay? Now. Who contacted you about Arlice Crosby's will, and what did you tell them?"

"That information is confidential," Donovan said, his voice a hoarse squeak now. "I wouldn't tell anyone—"

"Bad answer, Donovan," I broke in. "One last time: Who contacted you?"

"Not a living soul," he repeated. "I can't tell you anything else, because that's the truth."

"Go to it, Vinnie," I said, and Maxie raised the bat over her head.

"Please!" Donovan pleaded.

Now, in the interest of full disclosure, Maxie would never have touched Donovan with that bat. We'd talked about that in advance. Her job was to intimidate, never to do any injury. It was the way I'd conceived the plan, and the only way Maxie would agree to participate. So there never was any physical danger to Tom Donovan.

But it still chilled my blood to get that far, and then to hear a creak on the attic stairs.

Maxie froze. Donovan froze. I'm relatively sure I did, too. But the one thing we definitely had in common was that we were all looking at the opening to the attic to see whose head would appear in that opening. And the last possible head I could have imagined was the one I saw.

Melissa's.

"Did you find that English homework?" she asked, pretending the suggestion she'd made previously had been real. "I'd really like to give that a look tonight, and . . . What's Maxie doing with that bat?"

Maxie looked sheepish and put the bat down.

"Maxie?" Donovan asked. "Who's Maxie? What happened to Vinnie?"

"Who's Vinnie?" Melissa asked.

"This is why you don't plan a gambit like this, Alison," Paul began. This, clearly, was the best time to lecture me on investigative techniques.

From the bottom of the stairs, I heard my mother's voice. "Melissa! Did you go up there? Didn't I tell you not to?"

I looked at Donovan. "Oh, just go," I said. "Nobody was ever really going to hurt you." He got to his feet and started down the attic steps in what was, for him, a hurry.

Making a mental note to admonish my daughter for disobeying both her mother and her grandmother, I threw up my hands in a gesture of futility, and looked to my two dead friends.

"That's it," I said. "I'm beaten. We'll get no more done tonight."

I climbed down the stairs behind Melissa, who kept asking questions I wasn't in the mood to answer. I didn't say anything even as Mom, Paul and Maxie joined behind me, offering suggestions, criticisms (in Paul's case) and other chatter.

They followed me all the way down the stairs to the front room, where Jim and Warren had returned, and were actually drinking red wine instead of beer. They must have brought some from their excursion into town.

"Can I have some of that?" I asked Warren. "I've had a day."

"Get a glass," he said.

But something caught the corner of my eye, and I walked toward the game room instead of the kitchen. The plastic easel was back in the hallway outside the library, but the letters had been rearranged again.

"MAYBE NEXT TIME," they read now.

And for some reason, that did it. I turned toward Mom, who was of course directly behind me. "Get Jeannie and Tony on the phone," I said. "I'm going to call Lieutenant

McElone. Again. And get the TV crew into the den. I've had enough."

"What's going on?" Mom asked.

"We're having another séance," I said. "Right now. We're going to get in touch with the spirit of Arlice Crosby."

"But I haven't heard a word from Arlice," Paul, who had dropped in from the ceiling, noted.

"I know that, and you know that," I told him. "But the murderer doesn't know that."

Twenty-nine

I asked Paul to put out an alert on the Ghosternet that we were looking for as many otherworldly visitors as we could get. I wanted the house to be filled with spirits, just in case Dolores's gizmo really could take some measurements. Paul also sent out the word to Scott McFarlane, who showed up in very little time. I'm sure he looked determined, but I would have no way of knowing for sure.

I got Donovan on his cell phone as he drove home. Given our previous encounter, it took a good deal of persuasion, but I assured him he would be in no danger whatsoever, and he agreed to come back to the house. I think when I told him Lieutenant McElone was coming and was expecting him, it might have made the difference.

Melissa, already in the doghouse with me for her attic stunt, still had the gall to ask if she could stay up late to watch the séance. I was, if you'll pardon the expression, dead set against it.

Naturally, she prevailed anyway. I'll spare you the negotiations. Just suffice it to say that rooms would be cleaned, dishes would be washed and homework would be done with no complaints for a long period afterward. I might not always stand my ground, but I always drive a hard bargain.

Word of the new séance spread around the house like wildfire, and within twenty minutes the den was once again packed (with the predictable exceptions of the rumored Mr. and Mrs. Jones). This time, Trent made sure to keep his cameramen hovering about the room, not trained only on the three remaining members of his photogenic cast. I had every window in the den open, and it was still pretty warm from the crush of humanity.

It was odd to notice that, like in classrooms from childhood, people tended to go to the same spots in the room, as if they had been assigned.

They even left a space where Arlice Crosby should have been.

Bernice, of course, positioned herself back on the sofa, and made many of the same complaints about not being able to see. But they were even shallower than the last time, because mere minutes after I'd announced the event, Trent had managed to hang a TV monitor high on the wall (all the while assuring me he would pay for any necessary repairs) to help Ed the director with his task while I conjured the spirits available to me.

I was surprised at how many of them had answered Paul's Ghosternet broadcast. For the first time, I could see ghosts who weren't Paul or Maxie, mostly older people dressed as if they were going to a mid-priced restaurant in Boca Raton. White belts and shoes abounded. Other spirits were invisible to me, but were clearly in contact with the specters I could see. It had never occurred to me that my ability to see ghosts might develop in time. I wasn't sure how I felt about it, but there was no time for self-therapy with this crowd in the house. I'd have to remember to be freaked out later.

There was one, a man in his late fifties, I'd say, decked out in biker regalia and an actual German Army helmet, trying very hard to get Maxie's attention near the ceiling. She was attempting with equal force to look bored, but it was lost on the guy. He kept jabbering on, and she kept not making eye contact.

Near the side table, slightly higher than the living humans' heads, there hovered a red bandana. I wanted to make sure I knew where Scott McFarlane was the whole time we were in this room. The last thing we needed was for him to be too close to anything else he might be blamed for later.

I waited until Tony and Jeannie showed up, told Tony my plan (Jeannie would not have acknowledged it) and asked him to watch the areas of the room I couldn't, and especially to keep an eye on Melissa and Mom, who were inching their way in from the far door, where I had begged them to stay. Tony said he would make sure they didn't get too close if something started to happen.

When Lieutenant McElone showed up at the back door, I made a beeline for her before she got too close to the freaky crowd in the den. McElone is not a fan of deceased spirits and doesn't like coming to my house.

"The only reason I came here at all was that you said you knew who killed Arlice Crosby," she reminded me. That was, after all, what I'd told her on the phone. "Now, who did it exactly, how do you know and why couldn't you just tell me on the phone?"

"Well, saying I *know* might be overstating it just a little," I admitted.

McElone's eyes got angry. "So you got me down here by lying to me?"

"Look, Lieutenant, I really do think we can find the murderer in this room tonight if you just go along with what I want to do." I didn't have the whole plan worked out yet, but I had the beginnings of it. What had seemed like a great idea when I was steaming mad after seeing the new message on the easel was starting to fade as anxiety took over from determination. It is not, I'm sorry to say, an unusual pattern for me. "I'm going to announce that I'm in touch with the spirit of Arlice Crosby and that she knows who injected her with insulin Thursday night."

The detective's expression went from exasperation to mock pity. "Oh, that's a pip of a plan," she said. "I'm so glad I was here for its inception. It's like a little piece of history just unfolded right in front of me." Then her mouth curled on the right side, and she added, "Are you out of your mind?" And that's the moment when her eyes betrayed her—McElone glanced nervously into the den.

"Quite possibly," I said. "But I'm not the one who's afraid to walk into this house."

"This place is freaky," she said.

"You don't know the half of it."

I spun on my heel and walked purposefully into the den before McElone could come up with one of the seven thousand logical arguments against what I was about to do. Once again, the stepstool from one of the upstairs bathrooms served as my platform, and I stood up on it. But this time I had left the bathrobe in my bedroom, convinced it had not enhanced my "conduit to the supernatural" presence at all.

Donovan walked in just as I rose above the crowd, and I nodded in his direction so that McElone could see. She sneered at me, indicating she had seen him and needed no additional help.

"Thank you all for coming on such short notice," I began.

"I didn't have a choice," Bernice groused. "The noise would have kept me awake."

"This evening will be much different than our last séance," I plowed on, not responding to her. "This time, we are here to solve a murder."

Linda Jane Smith, standing in the same spot she had been Thursday night (about three people to my right, next to Rock Starr), looked amused. "Really, Inspector," she said. "How will we do that?"

"We will expose the killer of Arlice Crosby," I said, having lapsed into a contraction-free speech pattern for my role as medium, "by contacting the spirit of the victim."

I had instructed Mom, Jeannie, Paul, Tony and Melissa to pay careful attention to the faces of our suspects when I said that. McElone would be doing that without my prompting, I figured. They'd give me their reports later when we could talk, if there was still a need. I could only look in one direction, and I can report without any reservation that Linda Jane lost her amused look when I made that pronouncement.

"Like, how are we going to do that?" H-Bomb asked.

"I will make contact with her spirit the same way I communicate with the two spirits who occupy this house," I said.

"Paul and Hortense," Rock Starr remembered.

Maxie made an exasperated face. "Hortense?" she said.

"Yes. But for this séance, there are many more spirits in the room," I announced, a little too fervently, in retrospect.

From my other side, I heard Dolores Santiago say, "Yes. There are twenty-six spirits in this room." I turned to face her, and saw she was placing the converted surge suppressor on the side table and, to my eye anyway, it was flashing its lights just as often as it had the last time, so I had no idea how she could make such a statement.

But, of course, she was off by quite a number of ghosts. There had to be fifty present, according to the count Mom and Paul had given me before I'd walked in. I looked for Scott's bandana, and it had not moved. Good.

"Thank you," I answered. "Now, I will request complete silence from each of you, as I must concentrate very deeply to contact the wandering, possibly traumatized, spirit of Mrs. Crosby."

"How do we know you're telling the truth?" H-Bomb immediately piped up. "You could say, like, Biggie and Tupac were here, and there's no way we could prove you were lying."

I had to rearrange my expression, as I'd just started working on "serene and searching" and now had to work on "authoritative and believable."

"I understand your skepticism," I told the bikinied reality star, who looked like she needed someone to define "skepticism" for her. "But I think I can allay your fears." (Now, H-Bomb looked positively baffled, but I chose not to speculate on why.) "Arlice has been in contact before, but very briefly. She is only now getting acclimated to her new level of consciousness."

"You didn't answer her question," Rock Starr noted, his abdominal muscles practically puckered in their irritation. I could tell because Rock had decided to go shirtless tonight. "How do we know it's the old lady?"

"You will know because she will make herself visible to you when she becomes strong enough," I said.

I thought Dolores's eyes were going to actually leave their sockets. "She'll be *visible*?" she said. "That's astonishing!"

"Apparently, the ability to materialize is connected to the vigor of the emotion the spirit is feeling," I said. "Arlice has communicated to me, in the short times we have had to discuss the matter, that she is very angry. I believe that will work to our advantage."

"That's fascinating," Dolores said. "Does your talisman help you communicate with the spirits?" She pointed to the amulet hanging from my necklace.

"Yes," I told her. "It is not essential, but it acts as a kind of amplifier."

She absolutely giggled. "Ooh!" she oozed. "How marvelous!"

H-Bomb put her hand to her ear. "What?" she screamed. "We can't hear you!"

"Now, please let us have no more interruptions," I said more loudly. "I will attempt to make contact with the spirit of Arlice Crosby."

I closed my eyes very deliberately and tilted my head back a little. And then I heard Scott's voice whisper in my ear, "I think I know who did it."

My eyes sprung open, but I managed not to say anything. The crowd clearly thought this was a sign that I had achieved my goal, or was pretending to, and gasped just a little. And to my left, barely past the ear where I'd heard the voice, I saw a floating red bandana.

"Is that you, Arlice?" I asked loudly. "Have you crossed over from the other side to communicate with us at this moment?"

Trent, not wanting to talk because it would ruin his camera crew's taping, put his hand over his mouth in what appeared to be amusement.

Some of the guests, especially Jim and Warren, started to look around the room for a sign of an extra presence. Mistah Motion pointed at the bandana, but didn't say anything. Speaking was his second language.

Little did they know, they were surrounded. I could see more than four dozen ghosts of all sizes and shapes, and . . .

Wait a second. I could see *all* of them. How the hell did *that* happen? Could it just have been the increased ghost energy in the house, or was I developing my talent by hanging around with Paul and Maxie? There was no way to know, but I could surely see more ghosts than at the Haunted Mansion in Disney World. And that included the one wearing the red bandana standing next to me. He looked to be in his mid-sixties, with a slight growth of gray beard, powerfully built but not very tall. And there was some deep scar tissue all around his eyes. Just the way he'd been described to me. I wanted to say, "Scott?" But I had to go on with the show.

"Arlice," I said, "you were taken from us here, in this room, only three nights ago. And we know now that someone who was here that night did something to hurt you. What did they do? What did you feel?"

I waited, as if listening for an answer.

"Somebody stuck her with a needle," H-Bomb said. "Everybody knows that. Duh."

If my looks could kill, there would have been one more ghost in the room.

"Arlice says that someone here did something unspeakable, something evil," I said, starting to relish the role a little more. Between this and my Method acting with Donovan, I was starting to think I'd missed my true calling. "She says that person was someone she once loved, but someone she hadn't seen in many years." Okay, it was a stretch, but I was back into my Method acting and went where the scene took me.

"Alison, do you know what you're doing?" Paul asked. But he was smiling just a little. And Scott, now that he was at least a little visible to me, was nodding; yes, that was what he'd discovered. How he'd come across the information I didn't yet know.

I had to assume that Jane Smith wasn't really dead, or I'd have no suspects. So I looked from one woman in the room to the next—Linda Jane, who seemed so friendly and straightforward, was considerably younger than Arlice Crosby had been, but it was possible she could have been the killer. And we knew the sister's name really was Jane Smith, but Linda Jane's birth name was Weatherby. I looked to see if Lieutenant McElone was observing Linda Jane. She wasn't.

Bernice, sitting on the couch looking as she always did,

was a sleeper candidate. She was the right age to be a close sibling to Arlice, but had no connection Maxie had been able to uncover online. McElone wasn't looking at Bernice, either.

She was looking at me. That was no help.

H-Bomb clearly was not Arlice Crosby's sister. I really didn't think she'd killed Arlice, but I didn't like her and was a little afraid of her. I also was pretty sure she'd done something to get rid of Tiffney one way or another, but I had no proof of that, either.

If I was wrong and Arlice's sister *wasn't* the killer, that left Jim and Warren as suspects, although that seemed a stretch. Tom Donovan was a considerably more likely candidate, as he had something to gain, at least in theory, if Arlice died and her sister couldn't be found. The years of legal fees alone could bring millions to his firm. And he was the whole firm.

All that flashed through my mind in a second, but I didn't have time to finish. I had to playact a little more. "Arlice, why would someone do such a terrible thing? Arlice? Are you still there?" I waited a few seconds, pretending to get an answer. "Arlice, I'm having trouble hearing you. Can you tell me more? Can you still hear me?"

"Oh, for goodness' sake," Maxie yawned. "Cut to the chase. Even *I'm* getting bored."

Out of the corner of my eye, I saw Dolores Santiago chuckle.

For some reason, that's when it all came together. Dolores, who had put herself on the Senior Plus tour the day before it was to begin, right after Scott McFarlane had failed to scare Arlice Crosby to death. Dolores, who had been standing right next to Arlice when she collapsed and, now that I thought of it, was unusually tall, like Arlice. Dolores, who had been closest to the easel with a message from the killer, just as I discovered it. And it was Dolores who had shown such a rabid interest in the amulet Arlice had given me—the one Arlice said had been in her family "for generations."

I couldn't figure it all out in a flash, but it was worth exploring. "Dolores," I said, "have you been able to make contact with any spirits since you've been here?"

She seemed confused. "Contact?" she asked.

Jim and Warren glanced oddly at each other. The cast of *Down the Shore* looked even more vacant than usual.

"Yes. Have you been able, let's say, to see any spirits here in the house?"

Dolores worked hard to keep her same expression, but she couldn't manage it entirely—her eyes narrowed just a bit. "I've been able to get some very interesting readings on my instruments," she dodged.

"Who are you talking to?" Jim called to me. But I was intent on Dolores.

"You haven't actually seen or heard any ghosts here, have you?" I asked. Paul, stroking his goatee, started to nod slowly.

Trent made sure a camera was watching me closely. Ed also had a camera pointed in Dolores's direction. Both video images were visible on the overhead monitors he'd mounted on the wall, but I didn't have the time to look up. Linda Jane walked a little closer. Had I been wrong?

"No," Dolores said, looking at her shoes. "I've never actually seen a spirit myself."

"Who the migraine are you talking to?" H-Bomb wanted to know.

"Then why did you just laugh at what Maxie said?" I asked Dolores.

Suddenly, there was no sound in the room. Dolores's head snapped up to glare darts at me. The camera operators stopped moving. Mom put her arms around Melissa's shoulders to prevent her from getting any nearer to the action. I'm not sure I was breathing.

I looked at the monitors. One showed a picture of me.

The other was pointed at empty space.

"Okay," Warren said. "I'll play. Who's Maxie?"

Even Maxie didn't answer him. Instead, Dolores tried to break into a smile and said, "I'm sure I have no idea what you're talking about."

"That's funny, because I have an idea you do," I answered. I nodded at Paul and Maxie, and they swooped directly at Dolores. The biker guy who'd been trying to impress Maxie followed her.

"What's going on?" Trent hissed at me. "There's nobody there!"

The ghosts' sudden movement startled Dolores, and she put up her hands. Then the ghosts went directly through her to the other side of the room, and she stood there, hands up defensively. For a moment.

"So, you can't see them?" I asked. I stepped down off the stool, just in case I had to make a sudden move in another direction. And to make me a more difficult target.

"All right, so I can," Dolores answered. Her voice had dropped half an octave, and she no longer seemed the flighty ghost hunter she'd been her whole stay here. "So what? That doesn't mean I did anything to Arlice. I wasn't even looking at her when she fell; I was asking you a question."

"But you're ambidextrous," I reminded Dolores. "You could have been injecting Arlice with the insulin that killed her even while you were looking at me. We were packed in close that night, just like now."

By now, the crowd was staring at what was to them empty space. But they stopped asking for an explanation, apparently convinced there was someone there, even if they were unable to see anyone.

The room seemed to be closing in around Dolores and me. "This is silly," she said, trying to regain her original demeanor. "You're just trying to find a killer to make yourself feel better. I understand, dear. But you shouldn't blame yourself for what happened to poor Arlice."

"I don't," I said. "Not anymore. When it first happened, I thought she'd still be alive if I'd only kept my mouth shut about our séance that night. But you were going to kill her no matter what, weren't you?"

McElone, still in the kitchen doorway to avoid any spookiness she couldn't see, took a step inside, hand on her gun, but she didn't make any effort to stop me. If I turned out to be wrong, I guessed, she could say she'd had nothing to do with it. If I was right, McElone could make an arrest and come off looking heroic. She's not a stupid cop.

"I don't know what you're talking about," Dolores said. "I barely even knew Arlice Crosby."

"I'm thinking you knew her better than you'll admit," I countered. "I think you knew her very well indeed."

"Does anybody know what the migraine she's talking about?" Mistah Motion wanted to know. It was probably past time for him to be in the tanning booth. Besides, he hadn't done an ab crunch in close to half an hour, and the blood tended to pool in his midsection when that was the case.

"Arlice Crosby had a sister who stood to inherit a very generous sum when she died," I said. "But no matter how much searching was done, nobody could find her. Isn't that right, Mr. Donovan?"

Donovan, who'd been eyeing McElone while inching toward the front door, stopped in his tracks and assumed the look of a raccoon caught in an SUV's headlights—terrified and annoyed at the same time.

"We haven't found Jane Smith, no," he answered.

Linda Jane's eyes widened, and she shook her head, but it didn't look like she was denying anything—she was just startled to hear two-thirds of her name involved in the case.

"I stumbled across a tombstone in the High Valley

Cemetery marked for Jane Smith," I said, "but I suppose that's a very common name. I think maybe I was wrong, and Jane Smith is right there with her ghost-finder stick on the table."

But Scott broke in. "No, you were right, Alison," it said. "That's what I was trying to tell you before. Jane Smith did die a few years ago, but she's here right now." Scott McFarlane, now almost as visible as Paul and Maxie, pointed at Dolores, or in her general direction. I could see him, but Scott still couldn't see me, or anyone else.

"She's a ghost." I said. "She's not on the TV monitors."

He nodded. "I could tell when she walked by me before," he said. "I didn't know who it was at the time, but I could feel her soul, the way I feel when I meet other people like me. And she's got a cold one." He looked positively unnerved.

I turned toward Dolores. "That explains a lot," I said. *Not a living soul*, Donovan had said when I asked who he'd been working with.

"You're not serious," Linda Jane said. "There's someone there?"

"Oh, it's insane," Dolores protested. "She's acting on pure speculation."

But she didn't deny it.

"You mean you never saw her?" I asked Linda Jane. "She's been rooming with you all week."

Linda Jane paled and tried to speak but came up short. She eventually shook her head; no, she had never seen Dolores Santiago.

"But you saw her, Detective," I said to McElone. "She said she talked to you after Arlice died. Dolores Santiago."

McElone's face flattened out, and she shook her head. "I don't know any Dolores Santiago," she said. "I saw her name on the tour list, but everyone I asked said she never showed up."

What?

My mind reeled. If McElone had never heard of Dolores, and everyone was asking whom I was talking to . . . was it possible?

"Paul," I asked quietly. "Do they not see her?"

"It's possible," he said. "Think back. Has she ever interacted with anyone who doesn't see us?"

I didn't have time to think, but he was probably right—Dolores has been visible only to me, the ghosts, my mother and Melissa. But wait—what about . . .

"Mr. Donovan," I said loud enough for it to be audible throughout the room, "have you ever seen your client?"

"Oh, don't be absurd," Dolores tried, but her voice was shaking. "I don't know what you're talking about."

"Answer the question, Donovan," McElone insisted.

"We communicated strictly through e-mail," the lawyer said.

Bernice was snoring on the couch, too, but she'd probably wake up and comment on the way the lumpy cushion made her neck ache.

The snoring made me remember something. "So that sleepwalking bit was bogus, wasn't it?" I asked Dolores. "Were you just trying to get the amulet?"

"It was *mine!*" she hissed. "It was from my family. When that old witch died, I should have gotten it." The fact that she was already dead seemed somehow immaterial to Dolores.

"I don't understand," I said to her. If I could get her to admit to the crime through questioning her methods, it might be enough. "Why did you want Arlice dead so badly?"

Dolores's expression hardened, and her nostrils seemed to flare. "She was so superior, with her money and her noble causes," she hissed. "She couldn't be bothered with her relations anymore after she married *him*."

"What's she saying?" Trent demanded. "We can't hear or see anything there."

"I'll tell you later," I answered.

I looked at McElone, who was fingering the handcuffs on her belt. But she had proven many times to be something of a skeptic, and I could only imagine she was wondering if any of this was real.

"So you didn't approve of Jermaine Crosby?" I asked Dolores, just to keep her talking. "Is that why you and Arlice hadn't spoken in such a long time?"

"After she married him, I never spoke to her again," Dolores answered. Her body seemed just a little less substantial, as if the stress of the moment was distracting her from staying as solid as she'd been up to now.

"Are you getting this?" Trent asked Ed the director. Ed nodded.

"Half of it, anyway," he said.

"Will we be able to use it?" Trent followed up. Ed shrugged.

Trent moved over from his perch on the windowsill where he had been watching his cast to speak directly to the area around which he'd seen me addressing Dolores (without getting himself into camera range, of course). "You're saying you killed your sister after you were already dead? You injected her with insulin? How did you do that? Where did you get it?"

"Don't push me, sonny," she replied. "I'm not about to confess just to boost your ratings." Trent looked confused, and he actually walked right past Dolores and through four more ghosts.

"Is there anybody there?" he asked.

"I know how you got the insulin," I said to Dolores. "There was enough in the house to do the job, once you heard Arlice was here. But where did you get all the extra vials we found later, that you left out as clues?"

Paul raised his index finger. "There's a hospital not three miles from here," he said. "And their security procedures don't take into account people who can't be seen and can move through walls."

"Enough!" Dolores said. "You have nothing that proves I did any of what you're saying! You've failed completely!"

I needed to regain control of the situation. "But you can't be worried about the legal system at this point," I said to Dolores, trying to avoid McElone's eyes. "They can't do anything to you. Why didn't you just kill Arlice when you had the chance? Why send poor Scott after her? Did you think he'd scare her to death?"

"Who the migraine is Scott?" Rock Starr wanted to know. Even H-Bomb didn't look at him.

Dolores shook her head sadly. "That was the plan," she said. "A blind ghost—can you imagine the luck? I could tell him anything. Never spoke to him, so he couldn't identify my voice. Couldn't see me come and go to leave messages. Talked via a child's toy. Told him I could get him to the next level of existence when the fact was, I was using him to get there myself."

Scott's eyebrows merged in the middle of his forehead.

"What does that mean?" I asked Dolores, trying desperately to motion McElone toward us, but she wouldn't budge. "You were trying to ascend to some other type of afterlife?"

"Exactly. I knew I'd never get there if I killed my own sister, but if someone else did it, I figured I would be freed from the burden of her, the weight of her. I could leave this place and move on. But he just couldn't do it himself. Swung the sword right over her head, the fool. I was livid when Donovan reported back to me."

McElone walked over to Donovan, fingering her handcuffs. The attorney looked positively nauseated.

Scott's mouth tightened. He put out a hand to balance himself, or to get a read on what was near him. And he moved gracefully, for a blind man who didn't know his surroundings well, toward Dolores.

"Who's the fool, lady?" he growled. "I did something I shouldn't have done, but I did no harm. You murdered your own sister, so you're never moving on!"

"It's worth it," Dolores told him with defiance in her eyes.

"I don't get it," I said, trying to defuse the situation. "You couldn't inherit anything from Arlice. Why were you in the will if you were dead?"

"That witch never knew I'd died," Dolores answered. "Always busy flitting around, giving to charity, helping the *op-er-a*, showing off her money. We hadn't heard from her in thirty years. She didn't take the time to visit our parents' graves. She didn't know I was lying there next to them because she never bothered to find out, and there wasn't anyone to tell her."

I looked at Donovan. "There was her lawyer," I reminded Dolores.

Donovan moved very slowly toward the door, but McElone was already on her way there. "Don't move, Mr. Donovan," she called out from across the room. Swell. She was going to protect us from the lawyer and not from the killer.

Donovan froze.

"That's right," Dolores laughed. "Stop him. He was the one who was going to make money from Arlice's estate. Looking for a sister who wasn't alive. He knew it; I'd contacted him. Told him about the plan at that hotel. He agreed to take her to see pirate boy here." She gestured toward Scott, who bit his bottom lip in anger. "E-mailed me after you found the evidence, and then he set you up with the cops. That was awfully nice of you, Alison, truly, making yourself seem so suspicious."

I growled a little. "But that wouldn't make money for you, Donovan. What was your cut?"

"He would 'spend' all sorts of money on an investigation, and bill it to the estate," Dolores answered for him. "There were millions in it for him, weren't there, Tommy?"

"It was all legal!" Donovan tried to shout as McElone loomed up behind him. "I didn't do anything outside estate law. A woman e-mails me and says she's Arlice Crosby's dead sister. I'm supposed to believe that?"

"Oh, you believed it well enough," Dolores said. She seemed to be enjoying herself now.

"Is there somebody there, or not?" H-Bomb demanded, probably just to get the attention of the cameraman assigned to her, whose lens had strayed toward me.

"What is she saying, Alison?" Linda Jane asked me.

I didn't answer. "Where'd you get the insulin, Dolores?" I asked the ghost.

"I was rooming with the nurse, thanks to you," she answered. "No reason to let *her* know I was there, so I could watch and listen. I knew there was another diabetic in the house. I could have planned ahead if I'd known Arlice was coming to the séance. I was just hoping to track her down when I came for the tour. I'd heard there were ghosts here, and maybe there was one who was more . . . efficient than pirate boy here. But this was even better—Arlice, right in the room with me, and not even realizing it after all those years! But there was no time—I had to get it fast. So I went to my room, where the nurse had a stock of insulin and a small rubber plunger."

"An aspirator," I clarified, for some reason.

"Yes, there was one missing from my kit," Linda Jane said. "How did you know?"

"Then I went into the other room and took some insulin from the woman in the bed. She didn't seem to notice," Dolores said. Her smile was getting more disturbing by the second.

"Mrs. Jones was the other diabetic," I thought aloud.

"How did you know that?" Linda Jane asked.

"Dolores just told me." I looked back toward the ghost. "How'd you get to be Dolores, anyway?"

She waved a hand. "Who'd want to be Jane Smith when

you could be"—she pulled herself to full height and raised her head to an aristocratic pose—"Dolores Santiago?"

I decided not to pass that on to Linda Jane Smith. "And what about—" I started to ask.

"Enough!" Dolores shouted. "I don't have to answer your questions!"

"Lieutenant McElone," I called. "We have a confessed murderer here. Wouldn't you like to arrest her?"

"You got any suggestions of how?" McElone answered. "I can't cuff air."

"You see?" Dolores gloated. "I'm beyond all reproach. I gave that witch what she deserved, and there's nothing you can do about it." She actually laughed, just like in the movies, but a little scarier.

"Maybe *I* can't," I told her. "But you killed someone. You killed someone I liked. I'm not the kind of person who stands by and lets that happen." I looked at Melissa. She was watching me closely, like she always does when there's a problem. She talks a good game, but at ten, she's still watching her mom to figure out how to act.

"She got justice. And like I said, there's nothing you can do about it."

I glanced at Paul, then Maxie. "And like *I* said, maybe I'm not able to do something, but I know people who can." I nodded at Paul, and he reciprocated. He gestured toward Maxie.

And they started closing in on Dolores.

Her expression of triumph and defiance quickly evaporated as the two house ghosts reached for her. And when she saw the biker guy following Maxie, and a few of the other spirits joining in, she gasped.

Then she vanished.

"Damn!" Maxie yelled. "I was all set to break her nose."

"What just happened?" McElone called. She hadn't put handcuffs on Donovan, but was holding his arm, and it looked like she was holding it tightly.

"She got away," I explained. "What should I do?"

"How the hell should I know?"

Paul was looking contemplative, and he closed his eyes. "I don't think she's gone far," he said in an unusual, dreamy voice. He seemed to be taking the room's spectral temperature.

"Maybe she's gone for good," Mom attempted.

"Will someone *please* tell me what happened?" Jim shouted from the other side of the room. "I'm stone cold sober, and it's scaring me!"

But of all the people in the room, the least likely one said the most crucial thing. "How come that black thing is floating around in the air?" H-Bomb asked.

Sure enough, Dolores's black "ghost finder," the revamped surge suppressor, was still suspended by itself, as if held up by invisible wires. Trent gestured to Ed, who said something into his headset, and one of the camera operators spun to capture it.

The black box, red lights still flashing randomly, held its position for a moment, just long enough for Paul, who was about ten feet from it, to turn and head in its direction. Then it moved.

The back-end panel opened, and a small, very effective-looking knife appeared from within. A hideous disembodied cackle of laughter began and started to grow louder. Then the box dropped to the floor, and the knife stayed in the air and started to move very quickly.

Toward me.

Melissa gasped behind me. The scene seemed to go into slow motion. But it didn't give me more time to react, and before I could do anything, I realized the knife was going to make it to my chest. I couldn't move fast enough to stop it.

But somehow, Scott did. I don't know how he got there, but he stood in front of me faster than I could blink. And he raised his arm, approximating from sound or movement where Dolores might be, and he swung with all he had. This time, his aim was accurate.

There was a crack in the air. The knife fell to the floor. I recalled, vaguely, how to breathe.

"Did I get her?" Scott asked. "I hit *something*."

"I think you did," I answered. "You saved my life."

I almost jumped when I felt something encircling my waist, but that turned out to be Melissa's arms, and I never have a problem with a hug from my daughter. She wasn't crying, but she was working very hard at not crying, I could tell.

"Look," Maxie said. She pointed at the floor.

Dolores, motionless, had reappeared on the floor of the den, and was starting to moan. She moved a little, just as she regained what passed for consciousness, and her hand went to her jaw. She looked up and saw a gang of at least twenty ghosts standing around her.

Her first impulse was to reach for the knife, but a high-heeled, black-booted foot was already on the blade. "I don't think so," Maxie said.

Biker guy reached down and pulled Dolores to her feet. He held her blouse by the back of the neck. "What can we do with her?" he asked.

Before this had a chance to get ugly, I called out again. "Lieutenant!"

McElone looked over. No doubt she couldn't see what all the fuss was about. "Now what?" she asked.

"Is there a jail for ghosts?"

There's a reason I live in New Jersey—the national language here is Sarcasm. "Yeah," McElone responded. "It's right next to the one where we keep vampires."

"There is a state of being," one very distinguished-looking deceased gentleman offered. "We can't always interact with physical objects, but we can create a state of mind. A prison that exists on our plane, if you will. You probably wouldn't be able to see it, but it would certainly contain our captive here. In all likelihood, forever. It simply requires the group of us here to donate some of our own ectoplasm, which we can do through concentration. I've seen it done, although not for this purpose. I think it would work."

Dolores's eyes had widened as he spoke. "It's not possible."

"Actually, it is," one female spirit said. "I saw them do it to a ghost dog that had gone mean, once. There really wasn't anything else they could do, the poor thing. He got over it in a couple of hundred years."

Now, Dolores's voice was a croak at best. "You wouldn't," she said.

"Why wouldn't we?" Paul asked. "Crime is crime, even if you're dead when you commit one."

He reached out toward Dolores, but her eyes were already rolled back into her head, and she was chanting something very faintly, unintelligibly, at a rapid pace. She almost seemed to be hyperventilating. And she made the sign of a triangle in the air, again and again.

"Oh my," Paul said.

Before he could grab her, Dolores had vanished. Well, no. She had dissolved. There's no other word for it—she seemed to disappear into a mist, and then a fine white powder, a tangible, physical, visible one, which hit the floor and lay there in a small pile.

"What the migraine is *that*?" H-Bomb asked.

Linda Jane dropped to her knees to examine what was left of the murderous ghost. "I have no idea," she said.

Paul was motionless, staring at the powder. "I'd heard it was possible, but I've never seen it before," he said.

"What just happened here?" Trent asked.

"We made white powder," I told him. "Explain that to your viewers."

Melissa hadn't let go, and I hadn't wanted her to. I hugged her good and hard and then told her she needed to go to bed. Which is a parent's way to cheat a kid—she'd never sleep now, but I needed the time to decompress.

McElone dragged Donovan over from the door. "The Dolores . . . person . . . is gone?" she asked.

"That's right. Thanks for the help."

She raised an eyebrow. "There wasn't any way I could arrest her. What did you want me to do, fire my weapon into a crowd when there wasn't anybody there to shoot?"

"You have a point," I sighed. "I just felt very alone there for a few minutes."

McElone looked warily around the ceiling. "I can't imagine you *ever* feel alone in this house," she said. "This place is freaky."

Thirty

In the end, McElone took Donovan in and booked him on charges of conspiracy (although it would be a rough job explaining with whom he'd been conspiring), attempting to defraud the estate of Arlice Crosby and various other violations of laws that, frankly, I didn't understand. He said he'd fight the charges, and I thought he had a good chance to beat the rap, given that the chief witness against him no longer existed and had been dead when the crime was committed. But a cadre of municipal and county accountants, trained to find the money that lawyers siphon off estates, could prove more difficult to evade.

The case file on Arlice Crosby's murder was left open.

It's always interesting around Harbor Haven.

Since she was no longer a suspect, Linda Janc could leave whenever she liked, and she told me she'd probably go the next morning, assuming she could arrange travel. I said, honestly, that I would be sorry to see her go.

"It's been an experience" was all she said. "But it was certainly not boring, no matter how you look at it."

"Maybe you'll come back someday," I said.

She smirked with the left side of her mouth. "Uh-huh," she said.

We woke Bernice Antwerp up again to get her to bed, and she did, grousing all the while that the couch was more comfortable than the bed I'd given her and that she didn't see why she had to go up to the bedroom when she could sleep so well in the den.

The *Down the Shore* cast and crew retreated to their trailers and hotel rooms, respectively. Rock Starr looked a little pale, and his abs were considerably less pronounced than they'd been earlier in the evening. I'm told stress can do that.

H-Bomb, thong bikini unruffled, yawned the whole thing off and said she was going to head back to the boardwalk. It was only midnight, and she was getting ready for a night of serious partying.

After the guests had retreated, I sat with a bottle of red wine and exhaled for a long time with Jeannie and Tony. Mom took off pretty much as the guests were going up to bed and probably needed some alone time herself.

Tony had been astounded by all that had gone on, of course, as any sane person would be. But I was on my third glass of wine before Jeannie spoke at all.

"I'll tell you one thing," she said to me. "You sure do put on a hell of a show."

They left soon after. Tony and I exchanged many looks, all of which said the same thing: "There's no point in arguing with her."

That left just me and the three deceased people. They weren't drinking wine, but I could easily take up the slack. "I knew Dolores was weird, but I was miles off on how weird," I told Paul.

"I can't believe I didn't know she was a ghost," he answered. "I'm not sure how she looked so . . . solid. It must have taken tons of concentration. She had me fooled—clearly she knew when I was around, because she put on that show about worshipping the amulet. She'd planted clues all over the place to throw us off."

"So the amulet didn't mean anything?" I asked.

He shrugged. "As far as I can tell, all it meant was that Arlice liked you and wanted you to have something to remember her by."

I smiled at that. I fingered the amulet hanging from my neck.

"You have to feel better, Scott," I said. "Not only did we prove that you did no one any harm, but you actually saved my life when Dolores came at me with the knife."

Scott had been talking very little so far, and he now seemed distracted. "Yes, I suppose so," he said. "I'm glad you didn't get hurt, Alison."

Paul looked at him strangely. "Scott," he said, "is something wrong?"

He took a long time to respond. "No. I don't think so."

He was looking a little glassy-eyed, but I figured there wasn't much that could happen to him, so I decided to return to the subject at hand. "I don't understand why Dolores didn't just vanish after Arlice was gone," I said. "She'd done what she set out to do. Why not leave? She could have done it whenever she wanted."

"She seemed to enjoy watching everyone scramble," Paul said. "She left us clues. She made sure to be around whenever anything happened. I think she was reveling in it."

"That was one crazy old broad," Maxie offered. She was heavily into deep philosophy. "She got her lawyer to book her into this tour just to see if she could get a chance to off her sister. I mean, is that random or what?"

We all sat there (well, I sat—the ghosts sort of hovered) and stared off for a moment. I wasn't sure whether this was good wine or not, but I wanted more.

"Seems like I can see all the ghosts now," I said,

wondering if my speech was slurred at all. "There must have been fifty in the room tonight."

Paul and Maxie looked at each other and smiled.

"What?" I asked.

"There were at least a hundred and twenty-five spirits here tonight, Alison," Paul informed me. "I think your increased ability is, at best, limited."

"Oh." I wasn't sure whether I was glad or disappointed.

"Something is happening," Scott said suddenly. He stood straight up in the air, stiff as a board.

Paul moved in his direction, but when he got near, Scott put up a hand. "Don't do anything," he said. "I think this might be a good thing."

Scott's eyes opened wide as his form became more and more difficult to see. It was as if he'd swallowed a klieg light, and it shone from within him. I had to shield my eyes from the glare. Then the light went out just as Scott said something I couldn't make out.

When I could look again, he was gone.

Paul and Maxie, openmouthed and wide-eyed, circled the spot where Scott had stood. Neither of them spoke for at least a full minute, which doesn't sound like a long time, but try it and see.

Finally, Paul cleared his throat. "I guess we just saw Scott move on to the next level," he said.

"How'd he do it?" Maxie wanted to know. "He didn't seem to try or anything."

"I guess it had to do with his saving Alison and helping to unmask Arlice's killer," Paul said. "But who knows? I haven't understood a thing that's happened since you and I . . . ended up like this."

"*Died*," Maxie said. "We died. Say it. We're dead now."

"Yes," Paul nodded. "We are."

"Say it."

"We're dead." Paul was still examining the area where Scott had been standing. "But we're not necessarily done."

* * *

We sat there, none of us really speaking very much, for a while, and then I decided I'd had enough for one day. I couldn't remember the last time I'd slept. So I bade my two housemates a good night—I have no idea what they do in place of sleeping—and headed toward the staircase.

In the front room, just before the stairs, I saw something standing in the shadows now that most of the lights in the house were out. I didn't remember putting anything there, and as I drew closer, I realized it was the large plastic easel.

I shook my head. I hadn't put that there, and neither had anyone else. Could Dolores Santiago have tricked us all? Was she still around? Would there be some threatening, taunting message spelled out on the board when I reached it?

"Paul," I said quietly. No one appeared.

I was afraid to look, but there was nothing else to do. So I approached the easel very slowly—I wasn't sure, after all, that it wouldn't blow up or that some hideous weapon wouldn't leap out of it. And then I saw that there *was* a message spelled out in the black plastic letters. Right next to the red bandana, which was hanging out of the drawer where the letters were kept.

The message read:

I
CAN
SEE

Thirty-one

On Tuesday, Linda Jane and I spent some time on the porch, me with a headache from too much wine the night before, talking about what had taken place over the previous few days. By the time she left, she was actually open to the idea of returning with another tour if Senior Plus were to ask sometime in the future.

That afternoon, after we'd had a chance to clean up, Melissa and I welcomed two new guests, a married couple, to the room *Down the Shore* had occupied. They seemed a very nice couple, although they got a glimpse of the four o'clock Ghost-o-rama when I wasn't quick enough to get them out of the house, and they seemed . . . amazed, in a good way. The remaining guests from the previous week barely looked up.

The Senior Plus guests were all gone by Wednesday (the day before Bobby was to come and repair the pool table, much to Warren's chagrin), after having filled out their evaluation sheets. But there was only one I couldn't resist reading, and her answers were shocking. According to the scores Bernice Antwerp had given my guesthouse, she'd never stayed in such a wonderful place in her life—she specifically cited "that lovely H-Bomb girl"—and would be thrilled to come back again.

I wasn't sure if that made me happy or scared.

The Joneses had left early Wednesday morning for points unknown. Two months later, I'd see photos of them on every front page in the country and strain to remember what they looked like when they checked in and out, the only times I'd seen their faces. It turned out that the gentleman was actually Senator Not-Jones and the lady was *not* Mrs. Senator Not-Jones. Luckily, they'd been spotted in a vacation spot other than my guesthouse, so no reporters came stomping by. Except Phyllis, who found the whole thing hilarious.

She ran a number of articles on Arlice Crosby's murder but never printed a definitive piece on the solution to the mystery. After interviewing me, Melissa, Mom, Jeannie, Tony, Linda Jane and the entire *Down the Shore* cast, Phyllis pronounced the story "too confused" and ended up writing that Arlice had died of an overdose of medication for her diabetes, which was technically true.

By Wednesday evening, Myrna and Phil were the only official guests left until the weekend, and they had gone out for dinner, saying they wouldn't be back until quite late, as they were going to a restaurant somewhere on Long Beach Island. The TV crew was scuttling about somewhere on the beach filming "pickups," Trent had said. I didn't ask what that meant.

He was still smarting because Detective McElone had confiscated his footage from the night of the second séance, saying it was "pertinent to an ongoing investigation," one which, Trent knew, was unlikely ever to be closed, so his footage was unlikely ever to get returned.

We had ordered a pizza for dinner that night and sat around the kitchen table—Mom, Melissa and me—waiting for our two resident spirits, due by invitation. Maxie had grumbled all day, in one of her moods, and had balked at being asked to join us, but I'd insisted, and told her it was a matter of life and afterlife.

Paul, meanwhile, had shown up as requested, on time and eager to hear what might be of concern. I think he believed I was about to undertake another investigation and could barely contain his excitement.

"So what is this all about?" he asked as soon as he popped through the wall. "Something you need to ask me about?"

"Wait until Maxie shows up," I said. "I don't want to have to say everything twice." Melissa hid a smile. Ten-year-olds are terrible at hiding their feelings, except when you wish they wouldn't.

"Maxie?" Paul seemed confused. "Maxie doesn't usually have much to do with . . . Oh. Research." Even if he weren't transparent, I'd have been able to see the wheels in his head spinning: Maxie's role in investigations was research, so I must want to talk to her about research. Paul, like many men, can be extremely singular in his thought process.

Speak of the ghostess, Maxie stuck her head through the ceiling right at that moment. "Do I really *have* to show up for this?" she asked. "I was doing something."

"Yeah? What?"

She frowned. "Fine," she moaned and dropped down through the ceiling, settling on the stove. "What's the emergency?"

The three of us breathing people grinned, reached under our chairs, and pulled out paper hats and noisemakers. "Happy birthday, Maxie!" Melissa shouted as we put on our garish headgear and blew out ridiculous noises.

Maxie's mouth opened and closed a few times. She sputtered. She flapped her hands a bit. She looked completely flabbergasted.

It was terrific.

"Why didn't anybody tell me?" Paul immediately demanded. "I could have put on a silly hat, too."

Melissa handed him an extra we had for exactly that purpose. "You know what a bad liar you are, Paul," she told him. "You never could have kept the secret."

Paul put on the hat and looked sheepish even before it rested in a point on his head. "It's true," he said. "Happy birthday, Maxie."

Maxie had taken the opportunity to regain her composure. "Do I look any older?" she asked, posing like a very bad model.

"Not a day," Mom answered.

"Let's get this party started!" the guest of honor shouted. "Where are my presents?"

I tried to resist her demand for a minute, knowing I had an ace up my sleeve. "Wait," I told her. "I have something for you in the other room." I got up to walk to the door, then turned and looked at Maxie, who had an impish grin on her face. "And no fair peeking."

I pushed the kitchen door open just a bit and said, "Okay." Maxie's mother, Kitty Malone, walked in, and her daughter's face, already radiant, lit up a little more. "Mom," she said quietly.

Kitty had been coming by periodically since I'd informed her that her deceased daughter was available for visiting, and the two now seemed to enjoy a warm relationship, as far as I could tell. Kitty walked in carrying a small box wrapped with pink paper.

"Hi, sweetie," she said, looking in Paul's direction because she could see the party hat. She can't see or hear Maxie; they communicate through written notes. Paul took off his party hat and handed it to Maxie, so Kitty could look in the right direction. "I brought you a little something. You're thirty years old today." Her eyes teared up a little.

Maxie swooped down from the ceiling and gently took

the box from Kitty. "Tell her I say thanks," she said, wiping something from her eye. Melissa relayed the message.

It's not easy shopping for a ghost, I'd discovered. They don't need anything, really, physical objects in the real world are hard for them to carry around. So I was interested to see what Kitty had brought her daughter.

Maxie, of course, tore through the paper like a buzz saw through fat-free margarine. Inside was a tiny jewelry box, which she opened. Her face went absolutely white (not a huge change, but noticeable), and her eyes barely managed to stay inside their sockets. "Oh my god," she said quietly.

She turned the box for all of us to see. Inside was a ring in the pattern of a skull and crossbones. "Look," she said. "Isn't it awesome?"

"I remembered how much you loved it," Kitty told her daughter. "I found it in your bed stand, and I figured you'd want it."

Maxie swooped back down and hugged her mother. Kitty seemed to feel the embrace, and she smiled broadly. Maxie hovered down and stood next to her mother. "Nobody's beating *that*," she said. "But I can't wait to see you try!"

"I was just about to get to that," I said. "Melissa and I—"

There was a knock on the back door, and through the glass I could see a teenager holding two pizza boxes. I grabbed my wallet out of my tote bag, hanging on the back of my chair, and opened the door.

"Harbor Pizza," the kid said. No kidding. I thought he was delivering very flat bowling balls in white boxes. "You the garlic or the pepperoni?"

"Garlic," I said. "And by the way, it doesn't do anything to ward off vampires." I looked at Paul. "Does it?" He shrugged.

The kid handed me our pizza and I gave him enough money to cover the food, the tip and a little extra for putting

up with that joke. Then I came back inside as he walked
away with the second box.

"What about my present?" Maxie shouted.

"Oh, just a second," I said, and then halfway from the
back door to the table I stopped. "Just a . . ."

"What's the matter?" My mother.

"Why'd he bring two pizzas?" I asked. "We only ordered
one. Why'd he bring two?"

"He had a garlic and a pepperoni, and he didn't know
which one was ours," Melissa said. "Can we have some
now? I'm hungry."

"He shouldn't have had two," I insisted. "Unless . . ." I
put the pizza down on the table, and Melissa immediately
dove on it before someone could tell her not to. I walked
back to the door and looked.

The pizza delivery boy's car was still there.

"Of course," I said.

"Of course what?" Mom asked.

"Stay here," I told her, opening the door. "Paul, want to
come along?"

"What about my present?" Maxie demanded.

I walked out without answering. Sure enough, about a
hundred yards away, I saw the kid from Harbor Pizza exiting one of the *Down the Shore* trailers. He walked back to
his car and drove away.

"What's going on?" Paul asked.

"The whole crew and the cast are on the beach," I said.
"But somebody ordered a pizza from—"

"Tiffney's trailer," Paul said, completing my sentence
for me.

"Exactly." There was no need to hurry, but I started
to run toward the trailer, feeling like I'd better get there
before Tiffney vanished. Again.

Once there, I knocked on the door. And sure enough,
there was no answer. Tiffney was following her instructions to the letter. Well, almost.

"Come on, Tiffney, I know you're in there," I said loudly. "Let's talk."

"I'm not here," Tiffney shouted from inside. "We can't talk."

That thing about not being the sharpest tool in the shed? Tiffney would need considerable honing to reach that status.

"You are there," I said. "You just told me you're not there. That means you're there."

The door opened, and there stood Tiffney, a little tomato sauce on her cheek, dressed in a pair of cutoff shorts and a *Down the Shore* T-shirt that had been washed many, many times.

"What does that mean?" she asked.

"Good question," Paul said, but of course she couldn't hear him.

We went inside, where I also found the female camera operator sitting at the "kitchen" table, eating pizza. Tiffney offered me a slice, but I declined. I wanted to keep this brief, what with a birthday party for a ghost going on in my kitchen.

"Let me see if I can guess," I said. "Once H-Bomb started complaining about you getting too big a role on the show, Trent decided to give her what she wanted, but to do it in a way that would make you a bigger star. Or that's what he told you, right?"

"Yeah." Tiffney chewed on her pizza ("I'm *really* hungry; do you mind?"). "He said if I disappeared, everybody would be looking for me, and the fans would go crazy wanting me back. But since the show doesn't air for another couple months, we had to keep it real quiet. So Trent didn't tell the police."

"And he tried to hire me to find you, because he figured there'd be no danger you'd get found before he wanted to bring you back. Who else knows about this?"

Tiffney's eyes looked up and to the right; this indicated

she was thinking. "Everybody else in the cast except H-Bomb," she said, meaning just the two guys. "Trent figured it would be better if she really thought I was gone."

"I came along to film Tiff when she wasn't in the trailer," the camerawoman, whose name turned out to be Sandy, added. "I got her out on the beach, walking around, looking lost."

"Was that where you were when the CSI team was searching the trailers?" I asked.

"I guess so," Sandy answered. "I never saw them doing that, so we must have been out filming."

"But not when she gave a homeless guy named Darryl her credit card as a humanitarian gesture."

Sandy giggled. "Actually, that was me. Trent didn't want Tiff out there with those guys, so I put on a blonde wig and worked a little magic with my figure. Those makeup people can do *anything*."

"With the fan protests getting louder online, the pressure was on H-Bomb," I thought out loud.

"Yeah," Tiffney confirmed. "Trent wanted her not to know where I was."

"Even more fun if Tiffney were a suspect," I said so Paul could hear. "Because then the search for you, Tiffney, would be more intense, and the audience would know you were innocent. It builds drama. So Trent helped you put together that"—(inwardly, I shuddered a bit)—"mannequin to make it look like H-Bomb was threatening you just as you disappeared. Wasn't that it?" I asked Tiffney.

"I guess," Tiffney said. We were reaching her limits in the area of human interaction.

"So what was that side trip to Sea Bright all about?" I asked. "How come Trent decided to make me drive all the way down there when he knew you were here in your trailer—you *have* been all this time, haven't you?"

Tiffney nodded. "I slept and ate here most of the time. Nobody would look for me here once you found Bonnie."

She pointed at the mannequin, which was in a corner near the bathroom. "That's what we call it."

"And the trip to Sea Bright?" I reminded her.

"Trent figured we could throw everybody off, so he made Sandy give my credit card to this disgusting drunk on the beach, and then Trent got me a new black AmEx card for me." Tiffney actually pulled out the card and showed it to me. I pretended to be impressed.

"So, in the middle of all that was going on, I drove to Sea Bright and back and talked to that guy for no reason," I said to Paul.

"Welcome to the detective business," he said. "You have to assume everybody's lying to you."

"How long is he keeping you cooped up in here?" I asked Tiffney.

"Oh, it's not that bad. I get to go out for filming with Sandy, and at night sometimes when nobody's around, as long as I stay in disguise and don't get, like, migraine-faced and make a lot of noise. And Trent says I'll be back on the show in a couple of days."

"Don't tell me, let me guess. He's going to find you himself."

Tiffney looked at me like I'd said she had just gotten accepted to Yale. "Of course not! Trent's not on the show. He's deciding now whether Mistah Motion or Rock Starr gets to find me."

Reality television.

I promised a number of times not to give away Tiffney's secret and then begged off, saying I had to get back to my daughter (who had probably by now eaten both our shares of pizza).

When I left the trailer through the door—as Paul took the less conventional route through the wall—Trent was standing just outside, his car parked next to one of the other trailers. The rest of the crew was still off somewhere shooting more dramatic footage of drinking and flirting.

"So," he said, grinning. "You figured it out."

"Yeah." I glanced at Paul, standing by with his arms folded, daring me to stand up for myself and my "profession." "You said yourself you could talk that girl into anything. I should have picked up on that. But I still guess I wasn't as bad an investigator as you expected."

"On the contrary, you were exactly what I expected," Trent answered. "I knew you'd find Tiff if you looked for her. But I also figured you wouldn't ever take the case, because you were involved with the murder and because we put that scary mannequin in the trailer for you to find. So I felt pretty safe."

I sneered at him. Well, I *think* I sneered. If you haven't practiced it in the mirror—and I hadn't—you can never be sure. "And our little excursion to Sea Bright?" I asked Trent.

"I couldn't look like I wasn't doing *anything* to find her," he explained.

"And the cops never showed up there because you never called them, right?"

Trent didn't make eye contact. "Something like that. Lieutenant McElone heard about it through you, I guess, so I told her I thought Tiff had gone home in a huff."

"Uh-huh. Here's the deal, Trent." I was making this up as I went along, but it felt like the right direction. "I want to be paid for finding Tiffney."

He raised an eyebrow mockingly. "But you never took the case," he said.

"I went with you to Sea Bright. So I was part of the investigative team. And I found her. So you can pay me a fee, or you can let me call my friend Phyllis, who writes for some Internet news sites, and tell her everything I know about your stunt. Her story would probably get picked up nationally long before your show gets to air." Why not? I could always use the money, and my alternative in dealing with this situation was to punch Trent hard in the stomach, which probably wouldn't have done me much good overall.

Trent looked surprised, but we negotiated a price that seemed outlandishly high to me and probably a bargain to him. I walked away without punching him, which was also mutually beneficial.

Though it would have felt great.

Back inside, Paul was telling Mom and Melissa he'd finally heard from the spirit of Arlice Crosby, who was just getting used to her new state of being. "She had no idea what happened when she died," Paul said. "She wouldn't have been any help in the investigation at all. But she seems very much at peace."

I regaled the gathering with the Tale of Tiffney until Maxie could contain herself no more. "Where's my *present*?" she demanded.

Melissa and I exchanged a glance. "Okay. Here's what we're thinking. I still need the extra bedroom for guests."

"You're taking the attic from me? That's my present?" Maxie looked appalled. Which was part of the plan.

"Well, yes. But in a way I think you'll like. Like I said, we need the extra income from more guests. So I am going to be renovating the attic as living space."

"You really suck at giving presents," Maxie said, then quickly added: "Sorry, Mom."

Kitty waved a hand when Melissa told her what Maxie had said; it was irrelevant to her.

"If you'll let me finish," I said. "See, Melissa is getting bigger, and if I learned anything from the past week or so, it's that I'm not crazy about having her living right among all the guests all the time. So I'm thinking we'll move her into the new attic bedroom and have her current room for guests. It's a little bigger and has its own bathroom, so I can charge more, and you'll have company up in the . . ."

But Maxie had stopped listening after *move her into the new attic bedroom.* "Melissa's going to be my roommate?" she almost whispered.

Oops. I thought she'd like the idea. "Well, I wouldn't put it that way, but . . ."

"That's *great!*" Maxie swooped down and gave Liss a hug. "I can't think of *anybody* I'd rather share a room with," she said.

Melissa grinned. I wondered how she'd feel when she was fifteen and Maxie still thought of her as a roommate, but for now, it was the perfect solution for all parties concerned. I'd talk to Tony about construction plans tomorrow.

We talked and laughed for quite a while. I managed to snag one slice of pizza away from my mother and my daughter, and then I pulled an ice-cream cake out of the freezer, and we lit a candle and sang "Happy Birthday" a couple of times.

Maxie even managed to blow out the candle. And she was clearly delighted by the entire night.

"What do you think, Maxie?" I asked her. "Can ghosts eat ice-cream cake?"

She floated down from the ceiling and landed on the unoccupied kitchen chair. "I have no idea," she said. "Let's find out."

SIXTH IN THE PEPPER MARTIN
MYSTERIES FROM

CASEY DANIELS

TOMB WITH A VIEW

**Cemeteries come alive for amateur sleuth
and reluctant medium Pepper Martin.**

Cleveland's Garden View Cemetery is hosting a James
A. Garfield commemoration. For Pepper Martin, this
means that she'll surely be hearing from the dead president himself. And when she's assigned to help plan the
event with know-it-all volunteer and Garfield fanatic
Marjorie Klinker, she'll wish Marjorie were dead . . .
too bad someone beats Pepper to it.

penguin.com